Friends and Infidels

By the same author:

SUCKING SHERBET LEMONS

Friends and Infidels

MICHAEL CARSON

LONDON
VICTOR GOLLANCZ LTD
1989

03590523

First published in Great Britain 1989
by Victor Gollancz Ltd,
14 Henrietta Street, London WC2E 8QJ

© Michael Carson 1989

British Library Cataloguing in Publication Data
Carson, Michael
   Friends and infidels.
   I. Title
   823'.914[F]

ISBN 0–575–04156–0

Typeset at The Spartan Press Ltd,
Lymington, Hants
and printed in Great Britain by
St Edmundsbury Press Ltd, Bury St Edmunds, Suffolk

For Ken and Lilian Fayers

1

The Eastern Region of Ras Al Surra is still remote. Remote too, obscure passages in a book seldom opened, are its towns and villages.

Saffina, the largest town in the Region, was until recently the remotest of all. Saffina's contact with the outside world lay solely seaward. It seemed to have turned its back on the desert, mountains and scrub to the landward, all its houses hugging the shoreline in a three mile strip of shacks and the porous mud-brick mansions of the more prosperous traders.

If in the old days you had wished to approach Saffina from the land, you and your four-legged transport would have had to negotiate a formidable array of natural and man-made obstacles: watchtowers and customs posts built to protect all the entrance routes to the town from the incursions of the wild, commerce-trampling bedouin. Then, finally, when you were within sight of the town, a tidal lagoon, avoided only by negotiating a coastal plain checkered with quicksands, would bar your way; these barriers serving to keep Saffina strong and rich to the seaward, from whence came its wealth of fish, slaves and spices. The people of Saffina looked out and guarded in.

It is said that long ago some of the men of Saffina sailed away from their town on the Eastern shores of Arabia and, after many years of travel in their dhows, found the eastern shores of the Mediterranean Sea. There they settled and from a new city and a new sea, looked out.

Ask those who remain the name of their country and they will answer "Saffina". Pretend to misunderstand. Ask: "No, not your town, your country." They will still reply "Saffina".

But the forward-looking king of Ras Al Surra is trying to

change that age-old answer. He seeks to make the present-day inhabitants look around them and see that they are part of a larger whole than before.

Schools have been opened to teach the children of Saffina the Koran, the Three Rs and their place in the new thrusting Ras Al Surra. Foreigners have arrived — to perform the jobs that Ras Al Surrans are deemed incapable of doing — in the form of overweight Egyptian teachers; Pakistani plumbers; dour Palestinian consultants. They have little in common except for heads full of oil-revenue salaries and what those salaries will achieve for families far away. There is a British Head of "Research" called Nicholson; an American missionary, Mary-Anne Sissons, in the asbestos hospital that hugs the creek; a British soldier, Hepworth, in charge of the Desert Regiment. All but a few of these newcomers, when they are considered at all by the people of Saffina, are seen as new slaves to replace the Africans, who have now sighed into the richly patterned fabric of life in the town, darkening it, bringing the memory of African gods to the very threshold of the mosques, enlivening the town's nights with drum rhythms and providing new strength to its dhow crews.

Latterly, the foreign contingent has been swelled by occasional sightings of lean Frenchmen in denim shorts who have begun their elegant three-hundred-and-fifty kilometre strip of black road from the Capital. When the road is finished it will carry the Power Station to lighten Saffina's nights and frighten away its stars. It will bring the tourists who slave in that different world: the Capital area, where oil-revenues have permitted to be laid down, like a magic carpet, the Twentieth Century; where bedouin and passing dhow crews from places like Saffina rubber-neck and avoid harm — from passing cars, from the curious glances of the Capital sophisticates, from the Japanese goods they cannot resist but cannot understand — only with the greatest difficulty. When the Frenchmen's road is finished it will cut a swathe through the heart of the Eastern Region of Ras Al Surra and place infection or a blessing there, depending on your point of view.

Most would say a blessing. The American missionary will.

She craves medicines and trained helpers for her war on diseases. The shopkeepers will; the cut-off Egyptian teachers will. Perhaps only some British Embassy man of the old school of Arabists, with his love for pasts beyond recall, will bemoan the loss of proud camels loping off over dunes to nothingness; will tut at the arrival of electricity and Japanese wizardry, pointing out that he, somehow to his everlasting credit, was there "before all that". He saw the beautifully carved doors, the dhow-building, the last gasp of the slave trade, the Call to Prayer heard against the backdrop of a night sky, a sieve of stars.

This dissenter, however, will be chided: "But one couldn't live like that, could one?"

Unabashed, the Arabist will reply: "I quite envied them their traditional life actually. The freedom."

Ah, yes. The freedom. One can quite envy people their freedom and exalt in their lack of light and medicine when one has a refurbished merchant's house, papered with rugs and blessed with duty free spirits to return to in the Capital area. But, had the American missionary lady been present, she would have pursed her lips. Then, if asked, she would have gone on to litanise the freedom that disease has in such a place as Saffina. She would have said that, across the tidal inlet, there is a place called Zarut. There, only last week, she had discovered three cases of smallpox. The drinking water, if it can be so called, is alive with death. Freedom? Certainly the women and children are free to weep; the men to lament. A kind of freedom, perhaps . . .

So at present Saffina aches for change. If you survey the market place you will see the ache; feel it too. Enterprising cigarette salesmen have given bright electric signs to shop-keepers which hang over shop-fronts, wires dangling, waiting to be connected to the promised power station. A large picture of the young king presides over the market place from a vantage point above the door of the mud-brick post office. A bouquet of coloured bulbs fashioned into a patriotic motto likewise waits to be charged. In the storerooms of the shopkeepers the electric rice cookers and miniature television sets drain their anti-damp crystals. The entrepreneurs work out complicated calculations of deterioration versus prosperity on their hurrying worry beads and will the French roadbuilders to extra efforts.

The fishermen, drinking sweet, evaporated-milked tea, ache also. Beside them stands a large refrigerated truck that they own in common. It will take plump Saffina fish to the Capital and make them a handsome profit — once the road arrives. The road to them is an animate creature, a wild, uncoiling black snake, whose home is in the Capital from whence comes all good. When fully uncoiled, the black snake will lift all to a paradise of prosperity and ease. Their truck will sail away on the road. At present it can get to the Capital on the rough track only with the greatest difficulty.

Take one last look at Saffina. Go out in a dhow on a moonless night and drop anchor. You will be able to discern the extent of the town from the pin-pricks of light of a thousand oil lamps. These small lights do not put the stars to flight. It is not quiet out there on the calm sea. The waves lap the sides of the boat. Fish jump, creating a split-second flash of phosphorescence. The water sends you the sounds of the town. Drum-rhythms echo across the sound-box sea from Zarut. A mother shouts to a child too late out in the dark. Mahogany voices reach you from circles of men seated around an oil-lamp of Rembrandt light. You want to dive into the water and watch the phosphorescence do to you what it has just done to the fish. You crave thereby to be a part of the magic.

But then Nicholson returns late to his compound near the centre of the town. He is angry to find his compound in darkness and shouts to his servants to start the generator. After a few attempts the generator churns into life. Lights go on around the perimeter fence and in the rooms of Nicholson's house and the servants' quarters. Nicholson can settle down to another evening in cool and comfort. But for you the spell is broken. The white light from his compound has emphasised the darkness of Saffina. The generator's sound has drowned out the cries of humanity. The many layers of stars above your head now seem less dense. The heavens themselves have lost much of their mystery.

A swim no longer seems such a good idea. Idly, you wonder, as you make your way back to the shore, what Nicholson does with himself at night.

2

Nicholson was the first and greatest beneficiary of the change that was coming to Saffina. He lived in a fenced compound next to the sea — a neat little place composed of white offices, cells, accommodation for his Ras Al Surran, mainly bedouin, men — the men who guarded and did Nicholson's bidding. The compound had constant electricity supplied by two Lister generators and Nicholson had caused his whole compound area to bloom with an array of palms, grasses and flowers. His detached bungalow looked out over barbed wire to the eastern ocean.

He had made himself very much at home in Saffina. He had a responsible job and it was thought, by those few who knew what it entailed, that he did it well. He did himself well too, all his supplies flown in from the Capital area on the weekly government flight that landed at the Desert Regiment airstrip five miles behind Saffina. He boasted the only telex in the Eastern Region.

So perhaps it would be sensible, indeed obvious, to assume that Nicholson backed progress in Saffina. Was he not the advance guard of that progress, the foreigner with his comforts who signalled the coming of those comforts for all? But the obvious and the sensible do not always coincide with the way people think. And, in fact, Nicholson did not welcome change. He was happy to be a bright beacon in the dark of Saffina's nights, but did not want to look out on a plethora of bright lights. The possibility of lights for every-man disturbed him. Light would have robbed Saffina of the mystery that provided him with his "Research", made the area accessible to outsiders, slowly but inexorably eroded his privilege, coaxed questions about his function.

On a night not so long ago, such considerations were not

uppermost in Nicholson's mind. Rather, he was concerned about John De Lobo, his Goan houseboy.

As he told his only compatriate in Saffina, Hepworth, the head of the Desert Regiment, while sitting on the verandah under the night sky, after an excellent dinner prepared and served by John De Lobo:

"He wants to leave! The bugger reckons he's gathered together enough filthy lucre to start a hamburger joint in Delhi. I've offered to up his pittance but it's no good. He's quite determined. Makes no secret of the fact that he can't stand Saffina."

"Surely you can find another Hindi, Simon. They seem to be two a penny round Saffina," Hepworth said.

"They are. They are. Ever since Fadl came to the throne they've been landing off the dhows in droves. But Hindis who can cook and iron like John are rare birds, I tell you."

And Nicholson sipped his brandy.

Hepworth leaned forward and said, "What you need is a wife, old boy."

"Good brandy," observed Nicholson, ignoring the remark and pettily peeved that Hepworth had not had the decency to comment on the quality of the brandy. "What I need is a Ras Al Surran houseboy who won't piss off and leave me high and dry."

Hepworth, happy to have irked Nicholson by once again mentioning matrimony, shook his head knowingly as he lit a cigarette, and decided to irritate him a little more. Resurrecting old arguments — the bayoneting of long-dead corpses — served to pass the time with Nicholson and made up for the fact that neither had anything further to say to the other.

"You can't rely on the locals. They haven't the least idea what's required," Hepworth said.

Nicholson took the bait, though he knew he was taking it, and took pleasure in his certainty that Hepworth did not know that he knew.

"They can be trained," he snapped. "Look at what the Yank woman has done with her nursing orderlies at the clinic. They're really quite good."

13

Hepworth gazed intently at the filter of his cigarette and smirked.

"They most certainly can be trained," continued Nicholson. "And I've heard that lads from Jaheel make good houseboys."

"Jaheel? Can't say I've heard of it? Where is it? The interior?" asked Hepworth.

"It's the next village up the coast from here. Thought you might know it, seeing as chaps from your regiment are supposed to patrol it twice a month."

Hepworth nodded and gestured to Nicholson, as if signalling, "Ah, yes! *That* Jaheel."

But Nicholson, refusing to acknowledge that Hepworth might know the place after all, continued, "There isn't much to it. A few fishermen in adobe shacks where the Wadi Kabir meets the sea. You can't drive there from here. Not even by Landrover. Have to go by boat or hike over the mountains."

Suddenly Hepworth yelped and started rubbing his ankle. "Bloody mosquito! Bit me right through the sock! You need to get yourself some mosquito coils, old man."

Nicholson turned away from the sight of Hepworth rubbing his ankle and gazed instead at the stars above his head. He found that he was suddenly thinking of God. He looked away, smirked at Hepworth — but more at himself — and said quietly, "You know, I just might do that and see if I can find a likely lad. I should do it sharpish so that John can train him up before he goes. Wish I could go by boat, but it's out of commission. I'll get the motorbike out . . . That's what I'll do. Did I tell you about the boat, by the way?"

Hepworth shook his head and Nicholson told him about how his launch, a converted Arab dhow, had come to grief.

The men's conversation continued as the full-moon rose out of the sea directly in front of Nicholson's verandah. A glistening pathway led from the verandah across the sea to several moored dark dhows.

As he half-listened to Hepworth talking about a saucy night out in Hong Kong during a stint there with the British Army, a tale Nicholson knew by heart, Nicholson thought of Saffina and of the darkness all about him. "Not a bad place to measure out a life," he repeated to himself again and again, a litany to block out Hepworth's dreary ribaldry.

He resolved to look in Jaheel for a servant.

Early the following Friday morning Nicholson set off for Jaheel on his Honda Track motorcycle. The air-conditioned Rangerover had been left in the garage so that he could indulge himself on the motorbike, a treat he was seldom able to allow himself, so demanding did he consider his work to be, so important the correct front.

The armed guard at the gate of the compound opened the gate wide and allowed himself the hint of a smile at Nicholson as he passed and saluted. Everyone in Saffina was pleased to see Nicholson on his motorbike. It showed that he was off duty. Nobody needed to fear this Government Man when he was on his motorbike. He would not take anyone away. He would not "research" that day.

Riding along the track that led out of Saffina, Nicholson enjoyed hearing the cries of the children that followed his wake. He always felt that he appeared to be earthy and of the people on the motorbike.

From the start of his trip to Jaheel, Nicholson could see where he had to leave the bike. The mountains fell steeply into the sea in the distance. He had to make many inland detours to avoid the wheel-swallowing mud and the lethal quicksands of the coastal plain, and it was more than an hour before he reached the mountains, though they were only five miles north of Saffina as the crow flies.

There, the motorbike roared over the foot-high scree where mountain met sea in a crumbling heap of pebbled cliffs. From here he had to follow the path along the cliffs made by donkey trains and sandalled feet.

Nicholson parked and locked the bike. He looked round, then, taking a canteen of water from the pannier, set off towards Jaheel.

He walked at a leisurely pace, taking time to stop and pick up stones and shells along the way. The shells on the cliff path were dry and flaked away when rubbed because of their thousands of years stranded above the sea. White horn shells, like dry icing fallen from a wedding cake, were so aged that the memory of sea had gone out of them. Nicholson held one up to his ear and was not able to hear a thing.

He knew next to nothing about geology but was suddenly keen on the subject. Had he been in Hatchards at that moment he would have bought a book. He fancied that it would have been nice to find something interesting to put on his Kuwaiti chest at home.

The thought of home made him look over his shoulder. Behind him, through the heat haze, he could see the shoreline stretching back to Saffina on its thin peninsula. The white hospital stood out against the blue of the creek that crept behind the town. The sun had climbed high into the sky and he took some comfort from the blur in the distance that marked his compound. He stopped and turned completely, taking time to imbibe the sight. Inland from Saffina, he could make out the eroding, flat-topped outcrops of upland, moonlike against the dead, flat land all around. Then, further inland still, he could see the date-palms of Bilad Saffina, the airstrip and the buildings of the Desert Regiment close by.

Nicholson turned back to the lonely track and walked on for five minutes or so. When he next looked behind him, Saffina and its environs had disappeared from view.

Perhaps it was the heat of the sun beating down on his bare head, but Nicholson suddenly found his thoughts crowding in upon him in haphazard piles which he was not able to sort out before they collapsed, like the scree he was walking upon, into an untidy heap. It occurred to him that he had seldom been alone so far from Saffina before. Warning lectures, designed to frighten stray tourists, came back to haunt him. He had told them never to leave the main tracks, never to walk alone. If they protested, he told them "They got a UNESCO man in the Interior last year. This isn't bloody Disneyland, you know!"

He looked anxiously to right and left then — like the wretched tourists, pampered expatriates from the Capital, who were increasingly braving the two hundred mile unpaved track to Saffina, trying to convince themselves that they were intrepid travellers and not merely hired hands — half believing his own propaganda.

He told himself that he deserved his job in Saffina after the loyal service he had put in during the Civil War and the mopping-up operations that followed. Then Nicholson would disappear from the Askar Base for months at a time, sharing the same life as his tough bedouin troops, proving himself to be as tough as any of them, able to survive the torture of long desert marches, put up with brackish water, eat their food, kill without compunction.

In the early days he had been an officer seconded from an Intelligence unit of the British Army. His time in Ras Al Surra should have come to an end with the king's victory in the Civil War but he was asked to stay on. At a time when his colleagues were looking for new, lucrative battle-fields elsewhere, Nicholson had found himself being recruited as Head of Research for the Eastern Region.

He had never regretted his decision for a moment. What, after all, would he have had to look forward to had he returned to the British Army? A dirty little war in Northern Ireland where women with prams were the enemy? A cold pointless trip to the South Atlantic, a war to help win an election? No, he did not regret what he had done. His job was, as Hepworth often told him, "A cushy number". It also had a few thrills to keep him from getting bored. The point now was to make sure he could keep his comfortable sinecure at a time of rapid change.

Nicholson passed the ruins of the old city of Jaheel, built on a promontory above the sea. Though little substantial re-mained, he could see that it must at one time have been quite an impressive town. A long dry-stone wall stretched steeply from the mountain side to the eroding seashore; beyond that the dome of a mosque survived, and some half-demolished walls.

After a further fifteen minutes, Nicholson reached the steep sides of the Wadi Kabir. A hundred feet below him lay the valley floor, as flat as a football pitch. On the far side of it, on a table of land twenty feet above the valley floor, stood Jaheel. Out of sight of the old, ruined town it was; tiny, barely noticeable, among the spectacular mountains behind it. The cathedral walls of the Wadi Kabir stretched inland towards the fastness home of the Beni Omar tribe. Where the valley ended a carpet of sea stretched all the way to India.

Like a sailor too long becalmed in the rum-drunk doldrums, the village of Jaheel had forgotten its former swaggering pride. No longer bustling as the streets of its predecessor had been, the village that Nicholson saw was dark in the dark, hot in heat, a mere shadow of its former self. Built near the earth, humility was Jaheel, humility Jaheel's people.

"Look at my works, ye mighty, and despair!" sighed Nicholson as he rested and looked down on the village across the valley. A donkey brayed mournfully from within the maze of mud-brick houses. He tried to remember the name of the man he had to see, the owner of Jaheel's only shop. Then he stumbled down the steep sides of the valley and asked a group of old men, sitting in the lean shadow afforded by a wall, where Hameed Nasr could be found. They told him and he left them with their compliments on his Arabic flattering his ears.

Two hours later Nicholson was tramping his way back to his parked motorbike, well satisfied with the promises of Hameed Nasr that he would find him a houseboy who would serve him well.

While in the man's shop, Nicholson heard some gossip which might prove useful. He also found, among the sacks of spices and dusty packets of Tide, a beautiful old silver dagger. He bought it. He did not even bargain, for it cost him a fraction of the price he would have had to pay in the Capital.

3

The lizard darted diagonally across the white wall and as it moved it seemed to change colour and lose itself to the watcher's eye.

The boy never ceased to marvel at the beautiful creatures, though they were as familiar to him as the Islamic texts which hung on the four walls of the room in their heavy, wooden frames. It was the only room of the house. A room that served for all the events of the family: the great events like a birth or a death and the everyday ones of eating, sleeping and praying — the room played host to them all.

The boy lay on the flowery mattress, the room's only furniture, and watched the lizard closely. In common with all his people, he had little sentiment for animals. There simply wasn't time for such things. But house lizards were different. They were clean creatures and not to be harmed. Little boys were chastised when caught molesting them.

Dawn's rising light entered the room through its open door and the boy waited for the first sound of the day. Every morning he would lie thus and wait to see what that sound would be. Either the muezzin would sound the Call to Prayer, thereby waking the cocks, who would respond to his litany of praise for God; or the cocks would crow first and awaken the muezzin who had a habit of oversleeping. But this morning the muezzin was heard first. Perhaps the new Chinese alarm clock brought for him from Saffina by one of the faithful was doing its job.

A cock crowed and was answered by others all around the drowsy village of Jaheel. Somewhere a donkey brayed. The lizard darted through a hole in the woven palm-frond ceiling and was gone. The boy knew that it was time to get up. He remembered that this was no ordinary day. His best dish-dash hung on a nail above his head waiting for this day of days.

The boy's father had risen early and gone out to tend his goats. He would be expecting his son at the mosque in a few minutes but the boy did not move. He was not certain he wanted this day to begin and lay still looking for the lizard.

It was his father who had told him when he was very small that the lizard is a blessing to any home and that if there are no lizards in a home there is no love there either. When his mother, that Well of Love, as his father called her now, had died, he had not seen a single lizard for a full month. True, they had returned now, but his father said that their numbers had diminished and drew obvious conclusions.

The old man, his father, still wept openly when he talked of his wife. It embarrassed the boy to see his father so weak. Yet, alone with the goats where the perpendicular sides of the Wadi Kabir afforded privacy, he too had given himself over to sorrow.

His father had embarrassed the boy in other ways also. He had caused something of a scandal in Jaheel by visiting the unmarked grave where his dead wife lay to pray and leave something green upon the sand there. The other men of Jaheel had been heard to remark that such ministrations as his father practised were an offence to Islam and the custom of those who say there is no God. But the boy knew that his father loved God more than the gossips did. His father did not sit by the sea at night and drink the date liquor bought from the tribes of the interior. His father had never been known to turn away a needy man from his door, be that man Muslim, Nazarene or a misguided worshipper of cows.

So sometimes the boy would accompany his father to the grave of his mother. While there the old man forgot the presence of his only son and stared at the mound of sand, his lips moving silently and an expression of the greatest pain and, yes, anger, on his face. At such times the boy could only watch the strange communion his father experienced.

For the boy, life was full of mystery.

He dozed and was awoken by the sound of his father's voice.

"Ibrahim! Ibrahim! Get up at once! On your last morning at home you miss the mosque! How could you, my son! We were going to pray together for your safety. I hope this is not the way you will behave in the Englishman's house."

Immediately Ibrahim got up and begged pardon of his father. He knew why he had allowed himself to sleep on. He was not sure he wanted the day to begin and half wished that Hameed Nasr the shopkeeper would forget that he must take him away from Jaheel along the difficult track to Saffina, to work in the house of the Englishman. But he dared not show his father the fear he felt and briskly went outside to a corner of the yard where three porous pots of water hung, a man's height above the ground. Ibrahim tipped some of the water over himself and washed with it. The wasted water drained into the thirsty sand.

Returning to his room he put on his dish-dash. Then he sat down while his aunt, his father's sister, brought him breakfast of pressed dates and weak coffee flavoured with cardamom. This she poured from a large brass coffee pot with a graceful spout, the shape of the prow of an ocean-going dhow. The pot had been in the family since his mother had brought it to the house as part of her dowry long years ago.

Ibrahim and his father sat opposite one another but they ate the simple meal in silence until at the very end the old man said to Ibrahim, "By God, I shall miss you, my son!"

"And I shall miss you, father."

Then, out of the corner of his eye, Ibrahim saw a house-lizard dart across the wall.

Hameed Nasr said barely a word to Ibrahim during the long journey from Jaheel to Saffina. As the only shopkeeper in the village, and by far its most widely travelled inhabitant, having worked as a servant in Bahrain and Kuwait for many years, Hameed Nasr felt he was entitled to respect. This manifested itself in a reticence and an arrogance of manner that set him apart from the talkative humble people of Jaheel. They nevertheless accepted the shopkeeper's stance as a product of his wide experience of the world.

While sitting in his shop surrounded by a cacophony of items — Indian cloth, Korean fishing nets, Chinese pots and pans, cigarettes, sacks of sugar and salt, rice and tea — Hameed Nasr resembled a Sufi in his cave, and a Sufi moreover in league with jinn. How did Hameed Nasr manage to collect together such exotic goods from the four corners of the world if he did not have help from the spirit world? And the shopkeeper was always careful to foster the aura of mystery and, yes, fear that surrounded him. He seemed to resent customers as an intrusion, as if selling any of his goods somehow impoverished him. Children sent to him with messages became uncharacteristically swift and business-like — found, paid for and took the items as fast as they could in order to get out of his sight. Hameed Nasr possessed neither wit nor charm nor generosity. But he did possess a shop. God had blessed him with prosperity. If this went with a sour countenance it was not for the people of Jaheel to question the workings of God through Hameed Nasr. Anyway, he was fair and did not overcharge.

Hameed Nasr owned six lithe donkeys that he had brought from the village of Sabab, deep in the interior. They were the best donkeys in Ras Al Surra and he and Ibrahim walked behind five of them along the treacherous path past the old city of Jaheel, then down to the coastal plain that led to Saffina.

Once on level ground Hameed Nasr swung himself up on to the back of one of the animals. He did not suggest that Ibrahim should climb up too. So the boy walked behind and watched the dainty steps of the donkey on whose back Hameed Nasr sat straight and still. An aroma of fish wafted over Ibrahim from the sacks slung over the beasts. Hameed Nasr was taking a consignment of dried fish from Jaheel to Saffina Market where it would be sold to the bedouin for camel fodder. The sacks of fish needed to be carried by donkey. Ibrahim could walk.

Halfway to Saffina a hot wind, the Shamal, began to blow. That meant it must be about two in the afternoon. The Shamal was a better indicator of time than any watch. It blew throughout the whole month of March and when it blew the thermometer outside Nicholson's front door rose ten degrees in as many minutes. The wind originated in the Empty Quarter of Arabia. It turned easy spring days into a dusty hell. Now it blew Ibrahim's dish-dash against his body and heated the garment as if it had been left in front of a fire. His sweat glued the wind-blown dust to him, blanched his face and stung him.

But neither the Shamal nor the silence of Hameed Nasr worried Ibrahim. His spirits had risen once the dreaded leavetaking with his father and the villagers was over. Now his head was full of future and it was a strange new feeling for him to "look forward to" something. Never before had he been this far away from Jaheel, nor had in prospect a new bed in a new room in a new place. Every day mysteries were suddenly dwarfed by this one great mystery: an unfamiliar future.

He faced it with joy. The evening Call to Prayer would not find him in Jaheel. Even the Shamal and the straight sullen back of Hameed Nasr could do nothing to dampen his enthusiasm. All fear was blocked out by the wonder of novelty.

At about four in the afternoon Hameed Nasr left Ibrahim outside the gate of Nicholson's compound, telling him he must make his own way from now on. Ibrahim could not understand why the man left him so abruptly but then he realised that the market would be open and Hameed Nasr would want to go there directly in order to complete his business.

Ibrahim turned and gazed through the barbed wire into the compound. It might have been another planet. And, if it were not another planet, Ibrahim was about to enter another country where the customs of home did not apply. The Ras Al Surra that Ibrahim knew stopped abruptly at the gate of the compound, and, in the form of an impaled piece of wandering desert brush or a poor bedouin family, could only watch, caught by the sight of a green and concrete village placed in the middle of the sand of Saffina, as beautiful and verdant as the most fanciful mirage and just as unattainable.

Every day people could be seen gazing into Nicholson's compound as Ibrahim now gazed. Their eyes gave not a thought away. They did not seem to be awed by the sight, maybe not even envious. But their curiosity about the strange, square, un-Arab place, was unabated after several years of its presence among them. Perhaps one of the Arab wives from the stricter Wahabi interior would lift her veil, forgetting a tradition of centuries, in order to better imbibe the sight. Nicholson knew of the interest his compound held for people. He liked to think that it in some way gave them something to work towards. With industry and obedience to the king and his representatives this, one day, might be their town also.

Ibrahim told the guard at the gate who he was and was taken inside the compound and introduced to Nicholson who was at work in a large office. The air of the room was cold and made Ibrahim shiver.

"So you're my new boy," said Nicholson in the Arabic that Ibrahim had only ever heard on his friends' radios. "I hope you will be happy here."

"Thank you, sir," replied Ibrahim.

Nicholson smiled at him and told the guard to take him to his room in the main house.

"I'll see you later in the day. Wash and rest after your journey. You must be tired."

Ibrahim thanked Nicholson and followed the guard.

In the weeks that followed Ibrahim was taught his duties by Nicholson and John De Lobo. He learned how to clean a linoleum floor, use electric gadgets, even how to serve an acceptable gin and tonic.

His new knowledge came easily to him after that first day. He marvelled so much at everything he saw that the day became a landmark in his life that he knew he would never forget. He saw so much that the impressions exhausted him. From the first night on a soft, high bed, a bed with the structure of a fishing net made out of slim metal wire which gave him a night's sleep full of odd dreams, to his second night in Nicholson's house, the boy had been stuffed full of new experiences.

Nicholson had seemed to enjoy taking time to give Ibrahim a conducted tour of the strange electric country that was his home. In twenty-four hours Ibrahim experienced an electric oven, a stereo system, a video player, hot and cold running water, a harmonium, a walkie-talkie, a food mixer, a vacuum cleaner, a three piece suite, binoculars, lavatory and wallpaper, rows of books, air conditioning . . .

Before falling asleep on his second night away from home, the jumble of impressions so enveloped him, flooded his brain, that he felt as he did each year at the end of the Ramadan feast. He was replete. A jinn had taken him to a strange land and shown him all the wonders of the world. There could be nothing else to see after what he had seen. He had seen everything.

But the greatest miracle happened as time passed. Slowly but surely everything began to take on an easy familiarity until the things in Nicholson's house became as real and ordinary as any water pot at home. Sometimes he would stop himself in the act of using, say, the vacuum cleaner and wonder, "Who made this? Who thought of it?" One day he went so far as to ask John De Lobo. John, who had adopted a big brother role towards Ibrahim, stopped the vacuum cleaner and, in the buzzing silence that followed the cessation of the motor, said, "The Ingleezis. They think of these things. Then they make them and sell them."

"Do they make them in the Capital?"

"No, of course not!" John replied. "They send them from England to Ras Al Surra. Everything in this house comes from England. You Ras Al Surrans send the Ingleezis your oil to pay for it."

Ibrahim nodded.

"The huge generators for making electricity that are coming here are from England too. Of course," John added with pride, "we are making these things in India too."

"So why don't we buy them from you? India is closer than England. It is just over the sea."

John looked to right and left before replying. "England has got you here." And he put his hand in his pocket. "Ras Al Surra is in the pocket of the English."

Ibrahim wondered for a moment, then said, puzzled, "But we are Arab. We have our king. We are free."

"So if you're free, why is Mr Nicholson here? He is like a special policeman. He can order all the bedouin who work for him to do his bidding. It's his job to report to the government if you are bad and say bad things about the government. He's English."

"It's strange. But maybe there are Ras Al Surrans in England who are special policemen and report to the English government about bad Ingleezis," stated Ibrahim, he thought quite sensibly.

John De Lobo began to roll around the sittingroom, however. "You must be joking! That isn't the way things work! Don't you know anything about the world?"

"I don't understand your laughter!" countered Ibrahim, kicking the vacuum cleaner, embarrassed.

John, seeing that he had upset Ibrahim, took hold of his shoulders, and looking hard into his eyes, said, "I'm sorry, Ibrahim. It's not your fault you don't know how things work. Well, let me put it this way. England used to do the things in India it is now doing in Ras Al Surra. We told them to bugger off and after a lot of fuss they did. The English used to control lots of countries — in Africa, Asia and America. But if you look at a map of England you will see that it is a very small country — much smaller than Ras Al Surra."

"Show me!" commanded Ibrahim.

John went over to Nicholson's bookshelf and took down an atlas. He put it down on the coffee table and opened it at a map of the world. Then he pointed to a little red triangle. "That's England there," he said. But before he could go on with his political science lesson, John had to answer a barrage of questions from Ibrahim about maps. He did not understand the concept of picturing the world. John helped him by drawing a plan of the living room on a piece of paper. He drew the armchairs, the sofa, even the vacuum cleaner. Then he told Ibrahim that a map of the world was like that only much bigger.

"So where is Ras Al Surra?" Ibrahim asked.

John pointed to it.

"We're much bigger than England. Where's India?"

John pointed to India with pride.

"And India is much bigger than Ras Al Surra and it makes England look like an ant next to an elephant."

John smiled, pleased with his teaching.

Ibrahim returned to his vacuuming, new thoughts whirring through his head sufficient to drown out the noise of the English gadget.

In the weeks that remained before John De Lobo left, Ibrahim learned a lot, both about his job as a houseboy and about the wider world and the way it worked. He was miserable when it came time for John to leave Ras Al Surra. He tried almost every day to get John to change his mind, but to no avail.

"My wife and babies are in Delhi while I, at the peak of my strength, am a eunuch in Ras Al Surra! Don't ask me to stay, Ibrahim. But, before I go, let me give you a piece of advice. In the short time we have worked together I have come to see that you are clever and can learn quickly. I, alas, am an ignorant sort of fellow. I do not have very much to teach you. I would advise you to find yourself a teacher. That's what you need more than anything else. Learn English if you can. For, just as the English have a great deal of knowledge and power though they come from a small island, so their language carries that knowledge and power. Learn their language and their power will be within your grasp. My Arabic is not good enough to tell you everything I know. Learn English, Ibrahim."

Then, a few days later, John De Lobo, his "Long March" suitcase beside him, was leaving for India on board an ocean-going dhow and Ibrahim was left alone to cope with the running of Nicholson's house.

Ibrahim wept on his bed on the night his friend left, but determined not to forget John De Lobo's advice.

4

Ibrahim had been working at Nicholson's for nine months when the day came for Saffina's generator to be switched on.

Electricity poles had been erected all over the town and stood like lightning-struck trees. The whole aspect of Saffina changed with the arrival of the poles. Saffina, a white town when viewed from a distance, now seemed to exist as if behind bars.

Originally, it had been planned to bring the road to Saffina and transport the heavy equipment for the power station along its smooth length. However, through his contacts, Ibrahim had heard the muttered complaints of the merchants and Sheikhs about the slowness of electrification. Was not the Eastern Region the very last area of Ras Al Surra to receive the blessings of electricity? Was that not a gauge of what the government thought of the Region? Nicholson, somewhat alarmed, had flown up to the Capital and persuaded the government to bring the whole power station to the town by sea.

The power station arrived in modules on a purpose-built Japanese module-carrier called "Jumbo". The ship made three journeys between Japan and Saffina in order to carry the power station, which looked like a great crown heading toward Saffina, silver pipes, ruby-red towers, gold-yellow catwalks, all ready to be trundled into place by the special vehicle with its man-tall wheels across scrubland to the power station site at the back of the town.

Saffina's people turned out to a man when the first consignment was spotted. Nothing like it had ever been seen before. News of the sight spread like wildfire to the interior and all that day ragged people kept arriving at the shoreline to view the miracle and the sight of tens of Japanese technicians wearing white coats with an elephant printed on the front and sporting blue hardhats. The people stood in large groups some distance away from where the ship had beached. They had been largely silent. The height of state-of-the-art technology had silently drifted on to their shores. Whispered ejaculations of wonder passed their lips as the module was wheeled over the sand at a snail's pace. When it had gone past its weight had formed a hard-packed track. Sizeable pieces of rock had been broken to dust, fragile desert plants stared up out of the hard-packed earth looking like fossils.

Ibrahim had watched from Nicholson's kitchen the arrival of that first section of the power station. In common with everyone else he was struck dumb by the sight. But when, five weeks later, the next module arrived, he merely nodded to himself, went out on to the verandah to look for a moment. By the time the third and final module arrived the Japanese were left to unload it alone.

A week before the opening of the power station, Nicholson was informed that the government was laying on a special plane to conduct the Minister of Power and Telecommunications and other VIPs to Saffina to conduct the opening ceremonies. They would arrive late in the afternoon and leave the same night.

He laughed when he got the news. "Too bloody scared to spend the night!" he thought. But he was relieved too. There had been talk that the king might choose this occasion to grace the Eastern Region with his first visit. Nicholson was pleased that he had decided against this, both because of the extent of the security operation he and Hepworth would have had to mount for such a visit, and because a royal visit would somehow put a stamp of normality on the Region. It was well known that the king was terrified of this area, the part of Ras Al Surra that had put up most resistance to his authority. It was peculiarly reassuring to Nicholson to know that his terror lived on.

Then, in the course of that last week, he got a succession of memos, which added to his mirth. The minister, one memo said, had "other commitments" and was sending a minion to throw the switch and cut the ribbon. A second memo then asked for Nicholson's help in filling the plane. Many of the invited guests, their memories of civil war atrocities suddenly jogged as they held their invitations, had backed out. Nicholson, now definitely feeling in a party mood, sent back a list of people who might be prepared to brave a day trip to Saffina. Then he set about making preparations.

The day itself had been a busy one for both Nicholson and Hepworth. The men of the Desert Regiment were drafted into the town in a policing capacity and Nicholson added many of his own staff to help in this. Both men had spent most of the day touring the town to make sure that everything was being taken care of.

At sunset, he and his guests from the Capital stood on the verandah of the bungalow and looked out over the town as it faded into the dusk. The Call to Prayer rang out from the pepper-pot minarets, while his guests talked and drank champagne in the dying dusk, waiting for the coming of the light.

The switch was thrown ten minutes later and the darkness retreated from Saffina for once and for all. People cheered as they had cheered the end of Ramadan. The Desert Regiment's band struck up and Saffina's musicians competed with it in the market place. But above all this could be heard the strange, wild ululations of the women, a glottal shriek frightening to all not familiar with the sound and its merry intent.

The guests at Nicholson's house discussed the proceedings, refilled their glasses and accepted the snacks that Ibrahim offered them from a heavy wooden tray.

The conversation moved over the narrow range of expatriate topics: what a minister had done to his children's Sri Lankan nanny; the price of Newcastle Brown in the liquor stores; the English navvies who drove the latest Mercedes; the cost and ostentation of the king's new palace; the queers at the British Council; and, of course, the events of the day and their impact on Saffina.

Nicholson became more and more depressed as the evening

wore on. He did not like the sight of Saffina at night which lay before him. He wished that, like a firework, it would burn brightly for a while, be a joy to his guests, then fade and die. As a fleeting novelty, a back-drop for his drunken party, it was fine. But as a permanent fixture, a daily reality, the light disgusted him.

He felt like a man who has smoked opium for many years and sees his own amazing private visions. Suddenly, one day, all the people around him turn to opium and his precious, private visions become the clichés of the market place. He did not totally take the position of the British Embassy man at the party that all change was bad. Rather he felt that the final defeat of Saffina's nights was a threat to his own privilege, a diminution of his power and uniqueness as a foreigner alone with great sway and even greater prestige.

His depression deepened, his worries heightened, when the British Council representative came over to him towards the end of the party and said, somewhat drunkenly, "I'm off to London day after tomorrow. We've had a request to supply Saffina with an Inspector of Schools who will go round and help improve the performance of all those lazy English teachers. I wonder, can you suggest any housing that would do for a Brit inspector?"

Nicholson, with barely concealed dislike, replied, "No. And in my view it would be a gross error to send anyone here just now."

The Council man did not seem to notice Nicholson's mood and continued, "Well, we've got chaps everywhere else, but not here. London thinks it's time to open it up. We've had quite a number of applications for the job of inspector. Good to see there are still some Brits around with the spirit of adventure, eh? In a few months we may have some Brit teachers out here too. By the way, did you know that Save the Children are sending a nurse to help out at the clinic? Change in the air, Simon. Change in the air."

"Yes," said Nicholson curtly.

"Yes," the Council man said. "And, talking about change in the air, I noticed on the flight down here that the Frog road from the Capital has reached Abna. A few more months and Saffina will be an easy day-trip from us."

Nicholson frowned. "Maybe, but it wouldn't be a trip I'd fancy."

"Why not?"

"Insurgents, of course!" hissed Nicholson impatiently. "Just because they've been quiet doesn't mean they've gone away, you know."

"Oh, come *on*, Simon! We all know that the insurgents have tired of the struggle and are being good little boys waiting for oil money to fall from the Capital all over them. We had one on the television the other week saying how much he regretted his wicked past life and how King Fadl had bought him a Toyota pick-up and a herd of goats."

Nicholson scowled but said nothing.

Either oblivious, or determined to ignore Nicholson's mood, the Council man turned the knife. "The insurgents are like the rest of the expats here — present company excepted, of course — out for the main chance. The Capital is booming. Never seen anything like it, and the road will spread the wealth to Saffina in no time at all. Give it a year and things will look very different. By that time the British Council might even be in process of opening a branch office here — if Maggie will dip into her purse, of course. Perhaps you should think of joining us. With the breaking out of peace you might find more security if you turn your "research" into an analysis of the requirements of English language learners."

Nicholson shuddered. He turned away from the Council man without another word, hoping to get away from the party. But instead he found himself facing an Embassy wife dressed in a Qashqai shepherdess's dress and weighed down by bedouin silver jewellery.

"Mr Nicholson," said the Embassy wife, "I just wanted to compliment you on your houseboy. Such a treasure! I spilled some of your excellent dip on my dress earlier and he knew exactly what to do. One can't get servants like him in the Capital for love nor money. Where *did* you find him? *Do* tell!"

"Ibrahim? He comes from a village near here. Jaheel."

The woman rattled her jewellery, startled: "You mean he's Ras Al Surran?"

"Yes, 'fraid so."

"Well I never!" she gasped.

Nicholson excused himself, thinking dark thoughts about the Embassy wife. Sometimes, he felt, he hated the English. There was something so damned emasculated about them. He'd prefer a bedouin any day of the week. Something there. Not like the English — dry, brittle shells marooned from the ocean of life, full of dusty myth, mouthing clichés and arch empty banter. The bedouin were alive. Not for one moment did Nicholson include himself in his drunken assessment of his kith and kin as he weaved his way through his guests, making for fresh air and a quiet moment. He walked down the steps of his verandah and around his bungalow to a place by the wire which faced the ocean. He had expected to find the spot deserted but he was disappointed in this.

A woman was standing, her back to him, looking out at the ocean. Nicholson could not make out who it was at first, but as he approached the woman turned, momentarily startled by the sound of his footsteps. Nicholson saw that it was Mary-Anne Sissons, the matron of the clinic. He also saw that she had been crying.

"Well, so you wanted to get away from my party too, Matron," said Nicholson, staring hard at the ocean to allow Mary-Anne to dry her tears. In fact Nicholson could not recall having seen Mary-Anne all evening. He had invited her out of good form but had not expected her to come.

"Yes, you may be right, Mr Nicholson. I'm a bit of a party-pooper, I'm afraid. I've been in Saffina too long, I guess. But it is a fabulous party and I am happy you invited me." Then Mary-Anne returned her gaze to the ocean: "It's a big day for Saffina, isn't it, Mr Nicholson?"

"It certainly is, Matron! I'm not altogether sure I'm happy about it," and Nicholson gestured towards the bright lights outside the compound. "Spoils the view!"

"Why, shame on you!" smiled Mary-Anne. "But I know

what you mean. When you've been here as long as I have you kind of regret any changes."

"How long have you been here now, Matron?"

"Now, let me see, fifteen years — sixteen come Thanksgiving."

"A long time," conceded Nicholson.

"Yes, a long time. Perhaps too long," replied Mary-Anne, still gazing out to sea.

The pair did not say anything else. They stood together in silence, each mourning the passing of old Saffina from their own perspectives. Mary-Anne was praying that the coming of electricity and the road would bring with it the hospital facilities she had always dreamed of having, would lower infant mortality rates and prolong lives. If the truth were told, her attack of melancholy had only come on since arriving at the party. There she had felt completely swamped by the mass of people. They all spoke her native language, but, so used to Arabic had Mary-Anne become, that she could no longer make polite conversation in English. Also, her interests were a million miles from theirs. Her hopes anchored in the sky. In their company she had felt like a freak. Sometimes she felt even now a freak in Saffina. Even now Arabs would ask her what she was doing here, why she was not at home minding her children — or, more and more these days, her grandchildren. Would she be a freak wherever she went? Had she lost her home forever? When finally she returned to Fort Morgan, Colorado, she felt she would be as uncomfortable there as she was now at Nicholson's party. Her love of the Lord and her work in His missions had painted her forever into the last corner of Arabia. These thoughts she could not communicate to Nicholson. She did not know him. She wondered if there was a person on earth with whom she could have a heart to heart. There was only the hoped for Him behind the sky. And sometimes even He . . .

"I think I had better get back to the clinic, Mr Nicholson."

Nicholson had forgotten Mary-Anne Sissons. He had been repeating, "What a pity! What a pity!" over and over to himself.

"Right you are, Matron. Not to worry, eh. Tomorrow is another day."

"God willing!" said Mary-Anne Sissons, in Arabic. She smiled and left Nicholson there, walking towards the gate of his compound looking very lonely and somehow poor in her overwashed cotton print dress with the too-long hemline.

"She really ought to do something about her wardrobe," thought Nicholson. He returned with a sigh to his house.

When he had watched Hepworth drive the last of the guests off to their plane, Nicholson sat drinking in his living room, looking from the window at the hundreds of bare bulbs lighting Saffina. He pursed his lips and lifted his glass towards the lights. Conjecture about what might be taking place in the shadows away from the narrow beams of oil lamps was dead. Now boring lives could be enacted under the unflattering light of a bare light bulb.

He thought about what the British Council representative had said, but then decided that to think about all that just now would be too depressing. The lights in the night were enough to be going on with.

Ibrahim was clearing up. Nicholson, very drunk, poured himself a Scotch and offered Ibrahim one, while congratulating him on a job well done. At first Ibrahim refused the offer politely but Nicholson went on and poured him a glass, saying that plenty of Muslims drank. Ibrahim was curious and intimidated by Nicholson's insistence. He accepted a glass and raised it to his lips, then swallowed the contents in one gulp. Nicholson at once refilled his glass and he drank it down. It burned his throat but he felt no different and wondered why his father always spoke so angrily against alcohol.

"Sit down, Ibrahim. You've earned a rest," said Nicholson, gesturing to a place beside him on the sofa.

Ibrahim did so. Nicholson looked at him hard. The lad had fine features. There was African there somewhere but overlaid with paler genes which had given his nose height and elongated the face. "You have beautiful eyes, Ibrahim. Real limpid pools. A fellow could dive into those eyes and never surface again," Nicholson said in English.

35

The lad nodded, a gesture he always made when he did not understand, and wondered what to do.

"Have you a girlfriend?" Nicholson asked him.

Ibrahim shook his head. He understood the words but not the concept. Either one was single and women were shadows of temptation or one was married and one woman was yours to do with as prescribed.

Then Nicholson touched him. Ibrahim did not move. He watched, detached somehow, as Nicholson, his greased hair glinting in the light, his thin lips slightly parted, tried to pull up his dish-dash.

He fumbled around, mouthing endearments, until Ibrahim placed his hand over himself and said, "No!" though he did not know why the word had suddenly come out in English.

Nicholson removed his hand and picked up a magazine from the coffee table. He leafed through it, ignoring Ibrahim, who sat on, wondering if he could go, but not daring to.

There was a sound from the wall. A house lizard darted from behind the television set and started slowly climbing the wall. The sight at once transported Ibrahim back to another room in another world.

He watched the creature for a long moment. Then he exclaimed, "Good! Good! This is the first time I have seen a lizard here, sir!"

In a flash Nicholson stood up, rushed across the room and banged his magazine against the wall.

Ibrahim watched, stunned, as Nicholson stepped back and fell on to the sofa. There was a patch of blood on the wall where the lizard had been.

"You'd better give that a clean in the morning," stated Nicholson, returning to the magazine.

"He has killed the lizard for no reason!" thought Ibrahim.

He stood up and left the room without a word to Nicholson.

The next morning, after a night without sleep, Ibrahim got up and left Nicholson's house. He took everything with him. He would go home.

When Nicholson heard from the guard at the gate that the boy had gone he wondered about it for a while. Then he shrugged and chalked it up to experience. After that he let it be known in the market place of Saffina that he was in need of an experienced Indian servant.

Ibrahim walked through the gate of Nicholson's compound, back to Arabia. The approaching spectre of grey, sun-killed sand and rock alarmed him strangely. It was odd and disorienting to be away from Nicholson's air-conditioned world. Bars of fear clouded his vision and he saw his father, arms outstretched in a semitic gesture of questioning at his abrupt return. And, in his mind, he saw behind his father a moving mass of curious neighbours laughing at his failure to make good. The job with Nicholson had not been easy to obtain, he knew. There would be many questions to answer. And Ibrahim did not know the answers.

He tried to put aside his fears and concentrated on the immediate problem of how to get home. He could walk of course but it was approaching high summer and he did not relish the prospect. No, he would have to find a boat. It might not be too difficult. Dhows were all the time plying their way up and down the coast to Jaheel and then on to the Capital. He would find one of them. But it must not be a vessel bound for Jaheel. He must find one that continued on past the village. He did not feel ready to confront anyone from home. It would have to be done. But not yet.

To get to the jetty Ibrahim walked through the market place. Although it was full daylight every light bulb was lit up. Nobody had thought to turn them off after the celebrations of the night before. Perhaps it had not occurred to anyone that lights should be turned off during the day. Perhaps it reassured the people of Saffina that their new source of power was not a dream. Of course, nobody in Saffina had yet received their first bill.

The fish market was closing up. Heaps of scattered fins and entrails were all that remained of the mass of fish that could be seen in the early morning. Through the offal crept a gang of

37

shabby cats, while a couple of men raked up the debris before shovelling it into the converted Landrover that served as rubbish cart. Ibrahim noticed that one of the men was from Jaheel, the father of a friend. He pulled his headcloth tightly over his face as he passed by.

Walking through the maze of streets that led to the jetty, Ibrahim tried to form an answer to the question he knew everyone would ask.

"Why?"

"He killed a lizard."

The boy spoke the answer out loud and was hit by the absurdity of it.

"He killed it for no reason! *No reason!*" An Indian labourer, his face turned ghost-grey by the cement he was toting, turned to stare at Ibrahim. Ibrahim stared back with despair in his eyes and thought of John De Lobo.

Two boats loaded with sacks of cement lay at anchor a little way from the shore. There was no sign of any boatman and Ibrahim sat down on the sand in the shadow of the Customs House. He kicked his sandals from his feet and wiped his sweating face with the end of his headcloth.

The jetty was situated at the entrance to a shallow creek which crept round the town of Saffina, filling and emptying with the tides. Across the narrow channel that connected the creek to the ocean stood Zarut, the area where the great trading families had lived and, in the old days, had presided over the importation of slaves and exotic spices. A small motor launch crossed and recrossed the channel many times each day, always struggling against the strong current.

Ibrahim watched the ferry. Black-veiled women carried plastic water-containers over to Zarut, which did not have any fresh water of its own, while sleeping babies hung from them like extra breasts. He did not pity the women their daily grind. In a way he felt they were fortunate. They did not have his problems. *"Because he killed a lizard."*

Suddenly Ibrahim's mood brightened. He remembered that Nicholson had tried to make him drunk and then sought to make love to him. Perhaps he could tell home that! But all but the most pious would laugh at that. They had a matter-of-fact attitude to such things. Access to women was out of the question — so one found satisfaction where it could be found. They would ask him what had stopped him. That was no good. He became morose again.

A tall, gaunt, middle-aged man wearing only a loin cloth padded down the steep beach into the water and waded out to one of the boats. Ibrahim got up quickly and shuffled into his sandals. He ran towards the boat and shouted to the man:

"Where are you going?"

"Askara," answered the man as he swung himself up into the boat.

"I want to go to Jaheel. It's on your way. Will you take me with you? I'll pay!"

"How much will you pay?"

"Five hundred gursch."

"One rial."

"Seven hundred and fifty."

Those Askara people were all the same: pirates and rogues, thought Ibrahim.

"All right. Get on board!" said the man.

Lifting his dish-dash to the thigh Ibrahim waded out to the boat and pulled himself into it. He helped the man cast off. After some trouble with the outboard motor the boat started off down the creek and out into the open ocean.

It was exhilarating to be out on the sea after all this time. Ibrahim's body swayed with the boat as it ploughed through the swell. The sweat on his body vaporised in the sea breeze and cooled him delightfully.

Once clear of the creek the boat turned northwards and followed the coast. Ibrahim watched the white low-slung town of Saffina passing by. Over there was Nicholson's compound. There, on the back verandah, hung the washing he had put out to dry the previous afternoon. It made him feel strange to see it waving at him. Depression, so briefly dissipated by the sea and the breeze, settled upon him once more. He moved to the back of the boat, nearer to the boatman, sitting down on a sack of cement. He gazed out to sea, towards India.

A turtle popped its head out of the water a few yards away from the boat. It disappeared only to reappear a moment later on the other side of the boat. It was approaching that time of year when the turtles sought a quiet stretch of sand on which they could dig their nests. Ibrahim wished he could direct the turtle away from Saffina, to the quieter beaches near Jaheel where she could lay her eggs undisturbed.

The turtle too was good luck for the people of Ibrahim's village. For where there were turtles there was plankton and plankton meant shoals of fish. But today the sight of the turtle did not bode a good catch to Ibrahim. It put him in mind of the varnished shells of huge turtles that decorated Nicholson's verandah. And he thought, "He kills all the things I love."

"What were you doing in Saffina, Jaheeli? It is a long way from home," the boatman asked.

"Working," replied Ibrahim.

"Where?"

Ibrahim told him.

"But you are not working now . . ."

"No, I am not working now. I . . ." And he thought: Why not? Why not tell this stranger everything and discover what he thinks?

Ibrahim told the boatman everything that had happened.

"By God! You are the Father of all Fools!" the boatman exclaimed.

Ibrahim had nothing to say in reply. He knew then that the reaction of the boatman would be mirrored by his father's. He hardly heard the man as he railed against him. The boatman devoutly hoped, by the prophet's beard, that none of the six sons he had sired upon the daughter of a good Muslim would grow up so girlish as to run away from God-given prosperity over the death of a lizard, some whisky and a little lust! Did he not know that such a job was the dream of all the poor young men of Askara! The boatman finished his harangue by shouting: "Jaheeli! Jaheeli!" at Ibrahim, as if it explained everything.

Then Ibrahim knew that he had made yet another mistake. The boatman would tell the story to all and sundry the whole length of the coast. And, as he told it, it would grow hugely. He would become as notorious as the boy from Um Hoot who had dressed as a woman and pleaded with his father to let him marry a man.

Ibrahim replied not a word to the boatman. He could not and looked away — back, behind the wake of the boat, to where the white town of Saffina shimmered in the blazing afternoon. A perverse, back-to-front mirage of painful memory.

His hands lay, idle, on his lap.

What would his father say?

The sun was approaching Mecca and the west when the boat reached Jaheel. Along the shore Ibrahim could make out the narrow dug-out boats of his people drawn up along the beach in an orderly line. Beside them worked the men mending their nets to be ready for the next morning's fishing.

The boatman brought the boat into the shallows about thirty yards from the beach and Ibrahim jumped into the water and waded ashore without saying a word to the man.

Rabiah and Salem, his cousins, were working at their nets and they ran over to greet him as he came out of the water. They were full of questions about Saffina and the life he had been leading there. But Ibrahim answered them curtly by telling them he would talk with them later. The other fishermen he greeted politely, while making it clear that he wished to go home and see his father at once.

Soon he was following the path away from the sea that led to the well of Jaheel and thence to the mosque, the Koranic school and the jumble of dwellings of the village. He looked up at the village. Nothing had changed. Nothing at all. It gave him a fright to find everything as it had been when so much for him had changed. Jaheel was like a piece of meat that had been put into Nicholson's freezer. For months it would glisten, cold, hard and unchanging. Then, when needed, it lay on the plate and became flesh and blood again, unchanged by all the time that had passed. Home was like that and he sighed as he passed the women gathered round the well. He felt no appetite for home after his time away. Home was no longer an integrated place where everything fitted together; where questions had well-tried answers. Now all was out of joint and there were no easy answers.

As always, the door of his house lay open. Ibrahim removed his wet sandals and entered. His thawing mind saw that nothing had changed there either: walls, ceiling, rugs, were all as remembered. He lay down and looked at the ceiling. How could it be? His home, so much a part of him, so dear to him, unchanged and as innocent as ever when he had seen and experienced so much that would make home gasp.

A cockroach crawled across the floor near the mattress where he lay. Deliberately Ibrahim made a fist and brought it down heavily on to the insect's back. The impact of the blow left the creature a red-brown stain on the floor and Ibrahim watched fascinated as one of the cockroach's legs moved pathetically. He began to cry then and was angered by his tears.

"The Ingleezi has made you a girl!" he told his soft self. And he brought his fist down again and again on to the wreck of the cockroach, ignoring the pain which each blow sent through his hand and arm.

Then, once more, he lay back and gazed at the ceiling.

He was sleeping when his father came in. The old man had not heard about his son's return and exclaimed, "Ibrahim, my son! Praise be to God! You have come home to us!"

Ibrahim did not know what to say to his father, so said nothing. His father continued a torrent of greeting and kissed his son over and over again. Ibrahim smiled but his heart drilled deeper and deeper into a solitary well of hopelessness. He wondered briefly if he could spit out the ache but it lay too deep for that. He might as well try to spit out his soul.

At last his father finished his greetings and was about to go and tell the other villagers, debating whether he had a sheep suitable for slaughter, enough rice and eggs for a feast. He playfully reprimanded his son for not giving him notice of his return.

In the midst of his excited chatter he lit a piece of charcoal, placed it in a chalice-shaped crucible, and heaped incense on top. A bright blue plume of smoke rose towards the ceiling of the house as straight as a stick in the still air. Then he turned to Ibrahim, and, gazing at him solemnly, said, "If only your mother were here. She would have known how to go about things. As it is I am an old man who does not know how best to greet his only son. Have many wives, Ibrahim! Do not be as you find me, lonely and helpless in old age!"

Then Ibrahim wept. And his weeping took hold of his whole body and shook it so that his father mistook it for laughter. And Ibrahim thought, This then is how I rid myself of my pain. But not that way either. The pain grew when his father took him in his arms and crooned the question, "Why?" into his ear. It was the question he most feared and renewed his grief for no words came to answer his father and he saw the boatman once again and the words he had spat at him earlier in the day: "Jaheeli! Jaheeli!"

At last Ibrahim recovered enough to say, "Mr Nicholson killed a lizard for no reason. I have left my work with him."

Still lying against his father's breast the boy watched the old man's breathing, waiting for the angry inhalation prior to the inevitable explosion of wrath. He felt like a little boy again, there, so close to his father's body. But now Ibrahim wished it could have been his mother's body to which he clung. She would surely have been able to put the hurt to rest.

He waited and then felt his father's arms around his shoulders. He drew him gently away to a position where he could look into his son's face. He said, "Ibrahim, perhaps the foreigner does not like to have such creatures about him. Different people have different customs. Surely that is not the only reason?"

"That is the reason, father."

The old man shrugged and raised his right arm towards heaven. "You are young, my son, and not wise in the ways of the world. But you have taken this step and perhaps God did not wish you to be away from your home. I must confess that your letters gave me much cause for concern. It some-times seemed to me that you were forgetting the ways you have been taught. Perhaps it is no bad thing that this has happened. Lizards are not to be killed, at least not in Jaheel. It is a strange house that does such things."

Ibrahim's father stood and with a smile made to leave the house to find his aunt and ask her to prepare a meal for them. Then, almost as an afterthought, he said, "Yes, perhaps it is God's will. I need somebody to tend the goats and look after the boats. Catches have shrunk almost to nothing without you. There is too much work for one old man."

And he left Ibrahim to himself.

5

Some weeks after Ibrahim's return to Jaheel, a plane landed at the International Airport in the Capital area. Among the passengers was a too-thin, too-tall, bespectacled young Englishman, who was to have a considerable part to play in Ibrahim's life — and, indeed, in the life of Nicholson.

The young man's name was Peter Drury and he was to take up his post as the first English Language Inspector of the fledgling schools of Ras Al Surra's Eastern Region.

He had been recruited in London by the Council man who attended Nicholson's party and had been promised an adventurous two years, a bungalow in the desert and a Landrover for getting about. He had also been warned that his job would be a demanding one, perhaps not too rewarding professionally, but definitely "an experience".

At his interview in Davies Street the Council man was pleased to note that Peter Drury had survived two years as a school teacher in a wild and woolly portion of Western Sudan.

"Does your Arabic pass muster?" the Council man had asked Peter Drury in the course of the interview.

"Aiwa."

"Jolly good! No health problems?"

"La."

"Fine. An eminently suitable candidate. When will you be free to take up your appointment?"

"Immediately."

"Excellent."

After three strange days in the Capital area during which he had mostly sat in a small office at the Ministry of Education pleading for transport, Peter Drury loaded his suitcases into the back of his very own Landrover and set off for Saffina.

He had had to drive North for twenty miles along a six-lane

freeway before turning off on to a single carriageway, but still very smooth road. Only when he turned south did the tarmac become intermittent. He passed gangs of roadbuilders operating vast pieces of machinery as they pushed the tarmac ribbon towards Saffina. Then, after an hour of on and off road driving, he found himself on a rough crenellated track which would continue the whole way to his destination.

"Now I'm really on my way!" he thought, and he beeped his horn happily.

It was a good feeling to leave the concrete behind, to be heading for an adventure. He had accepted the post on that condition. It hadn't promised to be anything else. Everything was chaotic at work by all accounts. He would not be able to do much for the English language, only what could be done "in the difficult circumstances", as the Council hand-out had put it. But, to be honest, work was not the main thing for Peter Drury. The main thing was to be in the last corner of Arabia with all that that meant.

The sun was rising towards its zenith as he passed by a long series of conical hills, the odd village surrounded by blank mud-brick walls and watchtowers, huge palm plantations in the distance, all symmetrically laid out, as mathematically accurate as graph paper or a piece of Forestry Commission land in Wales.

Not Welsh himself, Wales had nevertheless become his country by adoption. Happy chance had put him into a Welsh university. He took his B.A. in Education and passed with Honours, but for most of the three years it was the Welsh mountains, rather than Welsh educational prowess, that had consumed his youthful energy. In Snowdonia there was hardly a track or a climb of the hazardous or very hazardous variety that had not seen his thin frame by the time he ascended the steps to receive his degree. He had stayed on at university another year, a teaching diploma his excuse, but the mountains his reason. Then, after that, he had gone to teach in Bangor. He hadn't been sure he wanted to teach but was sure he wanted to be near his mountains.

As a teacher he had been able to take the children out to his mountains and had managed to shed a part of his teaching load in History in order to become the school's "Outward Bound" teacher, a job he mainly enjoyed. True, he had not been too keen on carting the soft city children up the mountains with their school lunches and thermos flasks which slipped out of their satchels and broke — but it was better than the stuffy classroom alternative.

But he kept seeing jobs advertised in the newspapers. Jobs in teaching, true, but jobs in tempting places: Peru, Nepal, Burma. He started to apply for them. He applied for everything everywhere but inevitably the answer came back: "We have carefully considered your application but unfortunately . . ." At last he applied to Voluntary Service Overseas. They seemed glad to receive his application, interviewed him and said he might be suitable for the Sudan and would that be all right? They named the village he would be teaching in. He rushed to find an atlas, and, seeing the amount of brown shading in the area to which he would be sent, at once said yes — only to discover that the brown shading denoted desert and not mountain.

That was a pity, but he stayed in the Sudanese village for three years instead of two and wept inconsolably as he bumped away from it in the beat-up lorry, the cries of his kids, "Goodbye Sir!" echoing in his ears and pricking his tear ducts with a hole that would not heal.

He had loved those children in the Sudan. They had made him a teacher. In three years he had taught more than a hundred of them basic English. When he left them, waving in their wilderness home, he felt that he had, with great effort, climbed to the summit of the most difficult mountain in the world; had stood on the pinnacle of his life's achievement weeping with joy and sorrow and gratitude before the kingdoms of the Third World.

There he had been challenged. It had been a challenge to make one Bic pen last long enough to draw a picture on his bedsheet that would show Wales to these children of desert and scrub. A challenge to have his class sing "The Numbers Song" or "Ten Green Bottles" when they had not eaten that morning. It was a challenge to overcome the indifference of the powers-that-be; to distinguish between "The People" and "The People's Representatives". He left his children able to write simple English sentences in the sand — for the sand was their copybook. He left them able to say, "Waste not! Want not!", knowing they did not waste, but wanted.

In return the children gave him an abiding love for forsaken places. They had taught him that flat desert sands could contain high mountains and spectacular views. They had also, as has been said, drilled a permanent hole in his tear ducts. Only to recall them set him off. The three years in Sudan had hardened his body but softened his soul.

On his return to Bangor he blubbered into many a pint pot. Back at the Comprehensive he shouted, "Ungrateful wretches!" at his kids and parents came in to complain. He stood it a year then enrolled on a course which would teach him how to teach English as a Foreign Language.

How he had resented the time back in Britain! He could not adapt. He felt sick when he saw W. H. Smith and all the opportunities such a shop contained for learning and excitement. If one could take that one shop out to his village, what a difference it would make! But here the kids pulled on their mothers' coats and wanted to be taken to some place more stimulating. They soon tired of the thousands of wonderful things, only one of which would have kept his kids in the Sudan marvelling and involved for a year.

After his Sudan experience, consumerism could no longer consume him. Peter Drury felt that he had eaten the dry desert fruit that brings real knowledge of Good and Evil. His experience of sharing the majority's poverty had shown him a truth which he knew all politicians in Britain and elsewhere in the rich world recognised but would not face: that their grandiose striving towards development and self-enrichment was impoverishing the world, making its future dark, its ribs show, its belly distend.

Peter Drury knew he had to leave Britain or go mad.

Now on the track to Saffina, Peter Drury sang songs. He was

elated. He could have been driving across the moon's surface but the moon was where he wanted to be. The moon and his memories and the thrill of anticipation were more than enough.

After four hours' driving he turned left and headed east, back towards the coast and Saffina. The track became, if anything, much worse than before. But to make up for this the scenery was much more spectacular. The track followed the sides of a steep valley and he saw to his delight that water glinted below him. Around the water a belt of palm trees grew. The swathes of green, tiny patches on the brown carpet of rock and dust, were a joy to behold, were poignant because of the dead desert all around. He sang louder and looked for a place to stop and have a swim.

Finding a place where he could pull the Landrover off the track without having to negotiate too many rocks, Peter parked, leaving the vehicle sighing and ticking, and walked down the valley sides towards the water. Then, past a clump of palm trees, he came upon what he had hoped to find: a deep cleft of rock and a pool of limpid water as clear as glass and perhaps twenty feet deep. He sighed and thanked God and the British Council.

Off came his clothes and into the water he dived. He let out a mock protestation at the cold of it. He splashed about. He gargled and fountained water from his mouth into the air, trying to soak the darting fireflies. Tiny colourless fish nibbled at his flesh giving him bites which felt like kisses. He swam wildly and as he swam he shouted his elation and the rocks sent back the echo of their agreement. This was heaven.

Then he lay beside the pool as the sun sank and lost some of its power. He dozed and dreamed of his children there with him by this pool, their black, scarecrow bodies shining from the water, their mouths stuffed with Mars Bars.

When he awoke the sun's rays were filtering down to him through the palm fronds behind him. It was time to be getting on. It could not be much further but he must make haste.

49

He spotted the Education Office on the outskirts of Saffina straight away. A painted "flame of education" was emblazoned on its front wall.

Everyone had gone home for the day, but one man had stayed, aware that the new Inspector of English was coming.

Peter drove back with the man along the track he had come only minutes before. He drove through a pass in the mountains and emerged on to an area of flat scrubland. In the distance was a palm-tree plantation, in the middle of which was a small village, Bilad Saffina, which he had passed on his way in.

And there in the dead centre of the flat scrubland stood a strange-looking asbestos bungalow.

"That's not it, is it?" Peter said. The man smiled and rattled a bunch of keys.

"What did they build a bungalow out here in the middle of nowhere for?" Peter asked.

"They maybe build a school here for Bilad Saffina," replied the man.

Peter nodded and swallowed hard. The man from the Education Office opened the door of what Peter had already christened The Prefab and politely gestured the new English Inspector to step inside.

The sun was setting now but it was still hot and even hotter in the house. A strange house to be brought to, he thought, after a day of mud-brick biblical real-estate, palm trees and a track unchanged for centuries. All plastic and asbestos it was and appallingly hot. Stifling in fact. The windows were made of aluminium, but, badly constructed, slid open only with a lot of effort. The paint job was a blinding white. It was obvious that the place had not been lived in up to now. But could it be lived in?

The heat. The house seemed to take all the heat of Ras Al Surra and focus it like a magnifying glass. The gods were laughing at him prior to adjusting the glass and frazzling him up in a trice. He thought of the summit of Cader Idris and the cold wind which could be chilling him at this moment.

The front door led into a large, very square room with a

window in two of the walls looking out on to the desert and the nearby flat-topped upland. Across the room he came to a complicated intersection. Right lay the kitchen, straight on a bedroom and a W.C., then, on the left, two more bedrooms and the bathroom. The packing paper of the lavatory had not been taken off. It announced "Fordham's Seamless Flush" rather reassuringly, he thought. In one of the bedrooms he found the furniture, the only items he had encountered so far, a table, a chair, a bed and flowery mattress. He sat down on the mattress.

Sweat was pouring off him and he gazed at the grey linoleum on the floor with distaste. An army of huge ants marched across it. His sweat dropped on to it and turned the beach-like rivulets of accumulated fine sand to mud. There was an air-conditioner in the wall. That was something anyway. He went over to it and turned it on. Nothing happened. Maybe the chap's gone off to turn on the electricity, he thought.

Then he heard a strange noise. It sounded as if a large lorry had pulled up outside the house and was revving its engines. At last the volume decreased and seemed more like a bus idling at a stop. A bare bulb went on over his head, an ugly bare bulb set into a cheap aluminium fitting, a sad mockery of Danish design. The air-conditioner rolled into life and a blast of dirty, but cool, air swept across the room. Ah, he thought. Then he thought: Oh!

The man returned, smiling, proud to have started the generator. He went around the prefab switching on all the lights. He said in English, "After eight hour sail generator sleep."

"Why?" asked Peter, still fuming that he had not been told he would be on a generator.

"Generator not good. After eight hours tired. Hindi generator no good. Lister good. Lister English. Number 1. I sea captain. Bombay, Zanzibar — all over. No good Hindi generator."

Peter ignored the personal details: "How long generator sleep?" he asked, sticking to English to allow the man to show off his prowess.

"Much sleep. Eight hour in day she sail. Sixteen hour sleep."

"Only eight hours! Why?" He felt stupid asking all these questions but he asked them anyway.

"Hindi," replied the man. "Hindi generator very bad. Sleep much. Hindi men. No good Hindi. Hindi man speak 'God is great' to zib . . ." and he pointed towards his groin to clarify matters further.

"They don't, do they?" Peter managed.

Then the sea captain asked him for a beer. Peter frowned but reached into his cold box and gave him one. He did not drink it but kissed Peter's hand and left, refusing Peter's offer of a ride back to the Education Office.

In the encircling gloom Peter Drury considered the implications of only eight hours of electricity a day in these temperatures. He would have to ration it out carefully. Cooling was the main thing. Still, he told himself, he'd be out at work for part of the day, and in the afternoons he'd be in the sea or at the pool back up the valley. Maybe he could get a boat . . . So, if he turned on the generator in the early evening he could get the place nice and cool and be able to use electric light until bedtime. That would be all right.

He studied the place, trying to look on the bright side. He wondered to himself about the generator. Hadn't the affable British Council man said that Saffina had recently been electrified? Indeed, he fancied he had passed a spanking-new power station on his way out of the town. "Out of town." Yes, he was out of town. Lummy, but it was hot! Not the best environment to come down with a severe case of culture shock. But then he stopped himself; it was no good being negative. Think of that pool down the road and the kissing fish! Also, compared to his thatched hut in the Sudan this was a palace. Things could be worse. Much worse.

There was the memory of sun, a gash of red across the sky seen through his window. He walked into the kitchen and saw the fridge. Bugger! He hadn't thought of that. If he had only eight hours of electricity how would he keep food cool? He would be without ice for great chunks of the day! That was not a pleasant prospect. And what about his tape-recorder?

Gloom was beginning to descend again with the setting of the sun. The heat boiled his brain and let off a steam of visions of home. Britain, after all, was not so bad.

He turned on the taps and the water came out yellow. Hadn't better drink it, he thought. He let it run. It continued to come out yellow. Then he remembered his Boots water-purifying tablets. He found the cup of his thermos and poured some water into it, added a tablet and waited impatiently for it to dissolve. He drank it down. It was like swallowing a swimming pool but he savoured it nonetheless. He supposed that Wilfred Thesiger had used water-purifying tablets in the Empty Quarter. And the Empty Quarter was just down the road! He felt that the draught put him in communion with fellow-travellers.

Back in the room with the mattress, the air-conditioner had cooled the air nicely. Slowly he unpacked. He laid everything out on the table.

At eleven he got ready for bed and went out to switch off the generator. He watched the light slowly fade with the sound of the motor then walked back to the prefab, using the light of the moon as his guide.

Lying down on the mattress to sleep he soon found that he was intolerably hot. At last he got up and stood under the shower in his underclothes. The unwholesome water was wonderful. Then he padded back to bed dripping wet in his soaking vest and shorts. He lay down wet on the mattress, put the uncomfortable present moment out of his mind, and fastened on to the future . . . as a drowning man fastens his grip on a lifebuoy . . .

Two weeks after Peter's arrival in Saffina, Nicholson said to Hepworth, "It's getting out of hand."

"What is, old boy?"

Nicholson lay back in his wicker lounger and contemplated the stars above Saffina. He had dined well and drunk hugely. His Goanese cook had really excelled himself. The moon rose obligingly out of the sea to his left, throwing the moored dhows, his own modernised Sambuk among them, into stark relief. The bottle of Armagnac sat, still reassuringly half-full, at his elbow. A beautiful sight.

"What is, old boy?" repeated Hepworth.

"Oh, everything!" sighed Nicholson. "It's just not like the good old days during the Civil War. Nothing's happening — well nothing *good* anyway."

"No. True," replied Hepworth. "It's not like the good old days. Still, the fact that it's so peaceful must in great measure be due to your work here, Simon."

Fawning bastard, thought Nicholson, employing an epithet he thought on each and every occasion he met his only English-speaking companion in Saffina. "No doubt! No doubt!" he said absently.

"So what's getting out of hand?"

Yes, what was? He must have had too much to drink. He shrugged and looked hard at the candle spluttering in the glass holder on the table in front of him. Its light caught the Armagnac and made it glow like a fire from a town invisible behind a mountain.

"Forget it," Nicholson said, suddenly wanting to be alone with his bottle — but more than that, wanting to be away from the ravaged and florid face opposite him.

But then Nicholson remembered. "Yes, I do know what's getting out of hand. Bloody civilians! There are too many bloody civilians around for my liking."

"Only that inspector fellow and the Save the Children nurse," Hepworth observed with tranquillity.

"It's the start of the rot I tell you! An inspector of English! If it goes on like this we'll be surrounded by Wimpy Bars and plumbers' wives walking the pram to the Suk in curlers."

"Not a pretty prospect, old boy," conceded Hepworth.

"Not pretty at all. And you know where that leaves us, don't you? Out on our ears, that's where."

"Come now, I think you're being a bit alarmist, Simon."

"Am I? You don't think the King is keeping two foreigners here because he wants to, do you? Do you really think that he pays our salary and perks for the pleasure it gives him?"

"Well, no . . . but . . ."

Nicholson leaned forward in his lounger. "Too bloody right, no! As soon as the King is convinced there are no insurgents around the Eastern Region, and none in Saffina itself, then it's goodbye to us. 'Thanks for all the help, kids!' and a cocoa in our place. It's already happened in other areas. And if you ask me we're only hanging on by the skin of our teeth."

"I suppose you're right. But remember, Simon, the Eastern Region is the most sensitive. The King's never even visited here in all the time he's been on the throne. Still a long way to go before it's safe, I reckon."

"Do you?" interrupted Nicholson impatiently.

God, Hepworth was dense. Nicholson wondered for a moment whether he actually hated him. Still, he mustn't start drinking alone. There was no one else to talk to in Saffina. He could go to one of Mary-Anne Sissons's prayer meetings at the hospital but that wouldn't be the same. And there was the new nurse and the inspector of course. But, no, they wouldn't do either. He needed someone of his own kind and Hepworth would have to serve.

"Tell me what has happened to justify your opinion? Bugger all, that's what!" he said to Hepworth, without hope of getting a sensible reply.

Hepworth bent his glass towards Nicholson in a gesture of protest, but his companion went on, "Oh, I know, you take your troops on endless patrols; you search vehicles and you even bring in people for questioning — but what have you found of a really serious nature in the last year?"

"Well . . . er . . ."

"I mean, apart from the odd case of whisky?"

"Now, Simon, that's not exactly fair."

"Isn't it?"

"How were we to know?"

"OK. But what do we have to show for our rather expensive presence in the Eastern Region of Ras Al Surra?"

55

Hepworth did not reply. He was smarting from the remark about the whisky. It had been a blunder all right but there wasn't any need for Nicholson to rub it in like that.

Hepworth and his men had been out on patrol, setting up road-blocks and searching for guns and contraband. They had stopped a smart white Landcruiser and found a box of Johnnie Walker Black Label. Hepworth had confiscated the whisky and put the driver of the vehicle under arrest — for alcohol was forbidden to Muslims — only to learn later that the whisky belonged to the Ras Al Surran ambassador at the UN who came from Saffina. It could have happened to anybody.

"I repeat," insisted Nicholson in his quiet, authoritarian voice, "how have you and I shown ourselves to be good value for money in Saffina? The government must be feeling pretty confident about the security situation if they're sending unaccompanied females and effete English inspectors here. I mean, that British Council bod isn't even on a compound. Have you seen him, by the way? A real weed. You wait, all we need now is for the King to make a visit and find the area all shipshape and Bristol fashion. No explosive charges in the Turkish Delight. Not the hint of a dark look on any swarthy Saffina faces — and it'll be twenty kilos' worth of baggage for you and me and a second class ride to Gatwick. Then where would we be?"

Nicholson was silent after that. He let the words sink into Hepworth's plodding brain.

Hepworth used the silence to repeat to himself, "Where would I be? Bloody hell!"

Hepworth had been in Ras Al Surra for four years. Like Nicholson, though not in such an exalted position, he had seen active service during the Civil War and was now enjoying the pickings of peace. He'd had it rough then and reckoned that he deserved his present sinecure. Surely it couldn't be taken away, could it? And what about Dorothy? And the kids' education? It was costing him dear to keep the two girls away from the terrors of the Comprehensive. The Convent took a sizeable chunk of his salary — money he would never be able to earn in England. And if only that were the end of it! But it

56

wasn't! Not by a long chalk it wasn't. Nicholson might be able to find himself something else to do. He was only in his thirties and came out of the top drawer. Probably knew a Lord or a couple of Captains of Industry who would see him all right. But him? Who wanted a tobacconist's son of forty-six with a violent past?

Hepworth gazed out at nothing in particular, and the pension advertisement came into his mind — the advertisement he had seen in his twenties. Five line drawings on the page. A man changing from a smiling youth with the whole world at his feet in the first picture, becoming greyer and more anxious as the face made its way down the page. And under each picture an appropriate comment: "They say this job doesn't have a pension." Well, the man did not care at twenty-five or thirty-five, but at forty-five it got much darker and he cared but it was too late. The drawing of the man at sixty-five was totally desperate, as desperate as the face in The Scream. "What am I going to do now? I should have —"

For Hepworth the Pension advertisement had been his memento mori but the terrible thing was that he had never acted on the advice. Having married Dorothy — who only felt alive in a shop — there had never been enough, never anything spare, to obey the old, but still true — and becoming truer — pension advertisement.

Nicholson looked at Hepworth and noticed the sweat breaking out on his furrowed brow. "You see what I mean?" he told his uncomfortable companion, "It's getting out of hand."

"Yes, Simon. I see what you mean."

"Do you know," sighed Nicholson, "I haven't uncovered anything since that arms cache in Zarut fifteen months ago. Fifteen months! The buggers are as good as gold."

"So what can we do?" said Hepworth in a whine. "We've worked ourselves out of a job."

"Now, hold on!" countered Nicholson, holding up a thumb between himself and the moon. It was fascinating to see how easily the moon could be blotted out. "We're not finished yet. What can we do? Good question, Hepworth, good question. What can we do? What *must* we do?"

"Must? I'm afraid I don't follow."

"Well, I think *must* is appropriate, don't you? I mean it's quite a bad show for us if we have to leave. On that I think we are agreed. Not much in the way of prospects for either of us. Not everywhere they want English types to lord it over the wogs these days. Few years too late for that sort of thing. You and I are a dying breed. We've been painted into a corner, shunted into a siding, kicked up a gum tree. You get my drift? Yes, I think 'must' is the word here. What must we do?"

Nicholson took a sip of his Armagnac and rolled the word "must" around his mouth with the liquid.

Hepworth waited.

"What must we do?" Nicholson found that he could even blot out the moon with the very tip of his little finger. "Let me present you with a possible scenario. No, don't interrupt. Here we are . . ." He looked around the compound for effect, then to the ribbon of light that spread over the sea, past the shadow of his Sambuk and out to the moon, a heavy gold medallion above the ocean. "Here we are, lords of all we survey. We say to one man 'Come!' and he comes. We say to another 'Go!' and he goes. We say to yet another 'Bend over!' and he bends over. We're kings here, you and I. Especially I. This small sandpit and the humble homes of the poor and needy are our domain . . . and the mountains behind and the deserts and the Great Rub Al Khali. All ours. We are kings. Agreed?"

"Well, I suppose so," conceded Hepworth, not really seeing what Nicholson was driving at.

"Ah," continued Nicholson theatrically, "but our kingdom is besieged. The barbarians are at the gates. The Beat the Baby Nurse and the English Language Enhancer have already entered our domain. They'll shout back over the ramparts, 'It's lovely here! Come on in!' What must we do? What must the kings do? We must repel the invasion ruthlessly. We must defend what is ours and convince the Great King to the North by so doing that all is *not* well in his vassal Eastern Region. Not well at all."

"Good idea!" enthused Hepworth, at once at home in the spirit of the thing. It was just like a War Game. "But how?" he asked.

"Ah, how? How indeed! THE question. As usual, dear Hepworth, you have gone straight to the kernel of the problem. How? To answer that question let me take you back to the topic we discussed earlier in this conversation: namely, What is the harm of all these amateur expats coming to Saffina and getting on very nicely thank you?"

Hepworth leaned forward and wrinkled his florid forehead thoughtfully. "Well, for one it would — it will show the government that foreigners can survive here and not get killed by insurgents and a hostile population. So it will erode our power until we seem to be superfluous."

"Right on both counts. You put it very succinctly," said Nicholson patronisingly.

"So what must the kings do?" asked Hepworth, completely swept along by Nicholson's train of thought.

"We must stop the invasion by showing the Great King to the North that it is not safe for the advanced guard."

"But how do you do that?"

"By *making* it not safe for them, of course!" replied Nicholson, his voice rising an octave and momentarily startling the dozing guard at the gate of his compound.

It was well past midnight when Hepworth left Nicholson's compound and aimed his Landrover towards the Desert Regiment camp, where lay his lonely single bed. The camp was situated on the far side of Bilad Saffina, about six miles from the centre of Saffina itself.

Hepworth's head pounded from his huge alcohol intake, but more from what Nicholson had said. He could not be serious, surely. It was just drunken expat chat, wasn't it? But with Nicholson one could never tell. Hepworth had thought that the game of Russian Roulette they had played last year had been one of Simon's jokes. He had fired the Browning revolver three times into his mouth, matching Nicholson in coolness. It was only when Nicholson had pronounced

"Draw" that he had shown Hepworth it had not been a joke by discharging a live bullet into the Kuwaiti chest. Hepworth had shown his appreciation of that joke by vomiting over Nicholson's favourite Bakhtiari rug. No, you could never tell with Simon.

Hepworth was one of a common breed of men. From childhood on there had been something lacking. He was not aware of the lack; felt, indeed, that he was complete and rounded. He knew where he stood. He was for God and Queen and Country and Family Life and Tax-exempt Jersey bank accounts. He would have laughed at you if you had pointed out his fondness for being led; his need to be "one of the boys"; his morality culled from *Boys' Own Paper*. And, indeed, he might have threatened to biff you if you had attempted to debate his lack of independence of thought; might well have done so, had you dared hint that he was hopelessly addicted to alcohol.

He had a singular early childhood, having been born in Sumatra where his father had been a rubber planter. His parents had thought they were well out of the firing line — doing their bit for King and country by producing the raw materials that enabled the war to run smoothly — but they had been mistaken. Within a few weeks of Hepworth's birth, the Japanese had invaded Sumatra and mother and child were incarcerated in a P.O.W. camp for the duration of hostilities.

Hepworth said he did not remember those two years of captivity and asserted that his earliest memory was of standing on the steps of Raffles Hotel in Singapore prior to being shipped back to Blighty. Back in Britain his father had never been able to adapt, lost all his savings and ended up standing unsmilingly behind a till in a tobacconist's guarding the open counters from marauding secondary modern kids as he had once guarded thousands of acres of rubber trees against marauding insects. This sad, disappointed man had taught Hepworth about the world, had pushed his son towards the manly virtues and an army career.

Mankind, according to Hepworth, was arranged on a scale from 0 to 10. Those whom he reckoned come out between 0 and 5, he would dominate without mercy. He stood at 5. He was happy to admit himself to be "an average sort of cove". Above that, towards people who rated from 6 to 10, Hepworth was, whether he knew it or not, as malleable as any Jaheeli servant to the wishes of any person so endowed. Nicholson, for Hepworth, was high up on the scale. Perhaps he was even a 10.

The Landrover jogged past the graveyard and the boys' school, then it slowed down as it passed the hospital.

He strained to see if a light was burning in the bungalow occupied by the new Save the Children nurse, Joanna. There was. He wondered if he should drop in on her for a nightcap. He decided against it but then the prospect of his lonely room changed his mind. Who knows? Tonight might be *the* night! Perhaps tonight Joanna would unbend and accept his amorous advances. He U-turned the Landrover and headed back towards the hospital.

He had been trying to seduce Joanna since the night he had first met her, a fortnight before. Then he had presented himself at her door with a bottle of British Embassy champagne, pilfered from their last Queen's Birthday bash. He had thought that it, along with his uniform, might do the trick but Joanna had drunk her share and then icily rejected his advances. And when Joanna turned icy, he had learned then, there was nothing for a chap to do but shiver and retreat.

But tonight he felt he could fight a lion; more than a match for beautiful, cold Joanna.

He drove into the hospital compound and braked hard at her door.

It took three hefty knocks to bring Joanna to the door. She was wearing her housecoat and an incongruous pair of fluffy slippers.

"Not now, Bob," she said.

Hepworth refused to be cast down. "But every pussy-cat needs a little love and companionship" he said as he swayed on the threshold.

Joanna made to close the door and Hepworth added, "Oh, come on, Joanna! Aren't you going to ask a poor lonely mercenary who's ever such a long way from home in for a little dwinkie?"

"It's late!" replied Joanna coldly. "And I'm doing a drug inventory. I'm off on the helicopter to the Interior tomorrow."

"Lucky old Interior! Well I won't stop you working. Let me watch and shove a cup of coffee into my fist and I'll promise to be a good boy."

"Oh, all right." Joanna bowed to the inevitable and opened the door.

"Knew you would," said Hepworth, pleased as Punch to have made it so far.

Joanna went into the kitchen and put the kettle on, then she returned to her tidy piles of bottles, bandages and syringes all spread around a large carton on the floor.

"Where are you off to in the Interior?" Hepworth asked.

"Askara, Jaheel and some tiny place in the desert where we've heard there's an outbreak of polio. I've got to check that. If there are any cases we'll bring them here to the clinic or maybe fly them up to the Capital. We'll be leaving a couple of orderlies there to give shots."

"How's Nurse Ratchet?" asked Hepworth, swaying on the spot.

"How's who?" snapped Joanna.

"Nurse Ratchet — that's Simon Nicholson's name for Mary-Anne. Got it off the video of some Yank film. Good, what!"

"One Flew over the Cuckoo's Nest. I don't think the name is very good. Nurse Ratchet was wicked. Mary-Anne is close to being a saint."

"Just a little joke, Joanna," said Hepworth.

"Well, jokes are supposed to be funny and that isn't. That's just cruel."

"You've got a lovely bum, Joanna."

"Yes, I know," said Joanna. "How's your wife?"

"She's three thousand miles away getting a daily supply of double glazing estimates and lots of lovingly delivered bottles of Gold Top."

"Good for her!"

"I love you," said Hepworth.

"Yes, so you've said. Not interested. Sorry."

The kettle boiled and Joanna went out to see to it.

"Don't fight it," purred Hepworth as he followed her into the tiny kitchen.

Joanna laughed loud and mirthlessly. "Fight what? Nothing to fight round here 'cept polio, smallpox and malaria. Now go and sit down like a good boy and I'll bring you your coffee."

Hepworth did as he was told. He thought, "She's probably having it off gutless with that big black driver of hers." He hated her when she got all nursey with him and the way he came back for more. He'd more or less let it be known in the Capital mess hall that he had his legs under the table in Saffina with the new Beat the Baby nurse. The officers believed him too. "Typical of old Hepworth. Never long without a pretty little filly! Certainly has got a way with the ladies! Randy bugger, old Hepworth!"

He thought himself a bit of a ladykiller and, truth to tell, he had not been rejected that many times in his life. He usually won his battles. His war with Joanna taunted him like a mirage and, along with all the other uncertainties in his life at the moment, made him doubt himself and wonder if he was getting past it. He saw the man at sixty-five in the pension advertisement.

"It's because I'm married, isn't it?"

"Is what because you're married?" asked Joanna, down on her knees beside the piles of drugs.

"You know damned well what."

"Maybe it is a little bit because you're married, but mostly it's because I'm not attracted to you in the least."

"Not the tiniest weeniest tintsy wintsy bit attracted to me?" wheedled Hepworth.

"Don't be pathetic, Bob!" she snapped.

"I see! So you think I'm pathetic, do you?" said Hepworth, mock-petulant.

"If you could only see yourself!"

"If I could only see myself, is it?" said Hepworth like a small child.

Joanna pursed her lips and continued to count out the drugs.

"I see," said Hepworth after a long moment.

Joanna said nothing.

"I see!"

"If you've finished your coffee, please go," said Joanna flatly, suddenly very tired of Hepworth, and strangely depressed to be having to fight him off when she had enough that was real to fight each day. And tomorrow was another of those days.

"All right I shall!" He put down his coffee cup on the edge of the table. It slipped off and broke on the floor, splashing coffee over some of Joanna's bandages.

"Oh God, I'm sorry, Joanna! Sorry!" he said as she looked at him, her eyes narrow.

"Just go!" she shouted.

"All right! All right! I'm going! Goodbye!"

He opened the door, lurched through it and slammed it loudly behind him.

He drove out of the hospital compound at breakneck speed and gunned his vehicle down the track to his camp, throwing up pebbles and a low cloud of dust behind him. A desert fox darted across the road and Hepworth swerved, trying to hit it. He could not be sure he had, but the attempt was something. He cursed Joanna. Who the hell did she think she was? A nurse! Nurses? Famous for it.

He seethed to the gate of the camp. A weary sentry came out to open the gate for him. Hepworth took note of the man's number. "Bloody sleeping! He could see me coming a mile off but couldn't be bothered getting off his arse to open the bloody gate! Don't know what the place is coming to!"

He skidded to a halt outside his quarters, walked inside, took off his shirt, lay on the bed, checked that his gun was under the pillow and loaded. Then passed out.

6

Back in Jaheel days turned to weeks and weeks to months in ever-repeated circles of work, prayer, talk and sleep. The sun continued to edge towards the Tropic of Cancer as if it wanted to find out how much pain it could inflict upon Arabia. Then, just as people thought that relief would never come, back the sun spun towards Capricorn and life became bearable again. People started living their days instead of escaping them by tricking the heat by rising before sunrise and sneaking away to the shadows towards noon, while the sun played the hooligan high in the sky.

The turtles laid their eggs in thousands upon the beaches and then departed or died while the summer sun, which turned stranded parents to dust, incubated eggs. The baby turtles made for the sea and were devoured by birds, crabs and, finally, fish. Multi-coloured birds from Africa summered in the area, looking as garish and out of place as mad tourists; then, like the mad tourists they were, they flew away just as the weather became cooler.

Life went on in Jaheel much as before. If any changes could be discerned they were, perhaps, typified in their slowness by the slight glow that haloed the hills to the south of the village, emanating from the street lights in Saffina. Ah, and, of course, people came back with stories . . .

Another school had opened in Saffina and the Suk was full of strange machines that washed clothes. One wag had even suggested that they now had a machine in Saffina that kept wives happy in bed and allowed husbands to stay with their male friends and chatter. But the wag was tutted to silence. The same emissaries brought back tales of the foreigners who were coming to work in Saffina. A harbour was being built; a factory for making model dhows and sambuks had been set up and the models were fetching astronomical sums in the Capital and were being exported too. So and So had been photographed on his walk back from Saffina by a woman with yellow hair who was wearing only two tiny triangles of cloth. And the woman had offered him money for posing for the photographs. So and So had refused of course. But wasn't life becoming strange?

For Ibrahim life resumed in Jaheel as if he had never been away. He worked hard in the boat and pleased his father with his catches. Then, when the weather was calm and the wind blew off-shore, he took out his circular handnet and cast it expertly into the shallows. On a good day the net would be filled to bursting with tiny minnow and sardines. These fish he left to dry in the sun, then put into sacks and stored against the time when grazing was poor and the goats had need of them. So good were Ibrahim's catches of these small fish that his father thought he might send some of the sacks down to Saffina where they would fetch a good price as camel fodder.

And, contrary to Ibrahim's fears, the people of Jaheel had not been critical of him for leaving his work in Saffina. It was part of the village's isolation that it saw itself as an entity complete in itself; the next village as another whole — another country — with different ways, values and oddities. To comment on these separate villages was to discuss the world. This microcosm did not envy Saffina its power station or the rest of its development. That would come later. Now oil lamps were enough and grey-beards could still remember a time when fish-oil had been the only source of light. Also, the tortuous tracks their fathers had used were good enough for them too. Jaheel, like the very primitive and the very sophisticated, felt itself to be all in all — but would never have considered the question: Why are things so different in Saffina? A shrug and a tag: It is as God wills.

For several weeks Ibrahim felt only an exultant relief that all his premonitions of disaster and disgrace had come to nothing. He went through his daily round with a new certainty about his place in the village; a new faith in the decency of its people.

But something stayed strange. Like a traveller securely surrounded by his dearest possessions but convinced that something is missing, though not knowing what or even why the thought had struck him, Ibrahim felt different but could not fathom the reason.

One manifestation of the change in him was that he had become less gregarious than he had been before and spent a lot of his time alone, not mixing with the other young men of the village when they talked around a lamp or fished from a boat under the almost impertinent light of the stars.

But, more importantly, Ibrahim had lost his powers of reverie.

The people of Ibrahim's village and, indeed, people similarly placed all over the world, have an ability to accept with stoicism the humdrum day-to-day activities of life. In former days, before he left the village for Saffina, one could have spotted Ibrahim in the Wadi Kabir with his goats. All day long he minded them and for most of the time he would sit perfectly still, his shepherd's crook supporting his headcloth spread tent-like to protect him from the sun. He would stay for many hours so and never notice the passage of time. He was not asleep, or in any trance-like state. But neither was he bored. He had not known the meaning of the word then. This reverie, for there is nothing else to call it, came upon Ibrahim and his kind whenever hours of fixed, unchanging activity came around — and most of life was thus spent.

But in the months that followed his return it dawned on Ibrahim that somehow he had lost his people's gift, though he could not express to himself exactly what had been lost. Hours that had passed so effortlessly previously now dragged their feet interminably. The heavy Japanese watch he had bought and learned to use in Saffina did not help him. Rather it was a constant reminder of his new boredom — a life so different from the one he had had with Nicholson, when every day was a novelty.

Winter approached and the boy's boredom grew from an ache to a fever that made him jump and fidget and sulk his way through his days.

It did not take Ibrahim's father long to notice the boy's restlessness and debate its cause. No answer came to his mind and at last he went to the mosque to talk to the muezzin about it.

"Not all men are like you, Abu Ibrahim," the muezzin told Ibrahim's father. "They cannot wait until they are half way towards the Garden of Allah before they marry. Perhaps the boy is in need of a wife. He must have seventeen or eighteen years by now, isn't that right?"

Ibrahim's father thought hard. "Something like that, yes. He can grow a beard."

"Well, then, it's time. He's ripe for the marriage bed. No wonder then that he is sad and sulky all alone on the tree."

But Ibrahim's father said, almost to himself, "But he's a youngster."

"Abu Ibrahim, may you have long life!" replied the muezzin. "You will never see Ibrahim as anything else but a youngster. For his manhood speaks to you of your own failing powers."

"I'm a long way from being a greybeard!" said Abu Ibrahim, stroking his grey beard.

"Of course you are. But if it is not as I say, tell me why the boy is pining so. Tell me that."

"It is as you say," replied Ibrahim's father. And he began to search for a suitable match for his only son.

A week later Ibrahim was called aside by his father and told of the marriage that had been arranged for him.

"Moona Al Alawi is the one I have chosen for you," his father told him. "She is from a good family who own two boats in Jaheel and an orchard of thirty prize palms near Wadi Beni Omar. Her father and brothers assure me that Moona is beautiful in both body and soul. I trust that you will bless me for my choice, both now and in later years."

Ibrahim gazed at his father and said, "Thank you, father. I hope that I will prove a good husband to Moona and that we will have many children to delight your later years."

And as he spoke the prescribed words he reddened inwardly for the hypocrisy that was tripping so readily, like a sweet poison, across his tongue.

68

He did not care for the idea at all. Not at all. But he dared not show his father any opposition. The decision had been made and in Jaheel it was the last and the greatest decision a father takes: to choose his son a wife. For a son to go against such a decision was not only unthinkable, it was also "shirek", that is to say, an act that grossly interferes with God's plan for man, cuts straight through the traditions of family and social order. To a good Muslim, marriage is as necessary as Baptism to a Christian. And long tradition has dictated that parents make the choice of partner for their children. To remain unmarried is to say "No" to the truth as revealed to man through the Prophet.

Ibrahim bowed before his father and thanked him. In his heart he pondered ways of escape.

As his father reminded him of the duties of a husband, the boy plotted. As the old man talked of dowries and feasts and contracts, his son wondered if Nicholson would take him back. As his father debated which goats to fatten, his son shouted to him silently, "I cannot marry! I cannot marry! Old fool! I cannot marry yet!"

And, at the same time, he hated himself for his rebellion. His heart burned with ferment. Ibrahim felt that if someone were to lick his heart now, they would immediately drop down dead.

The following day Ibrahim attempted to sort out the predicament he was in. He forsook the fishing boat and spent the time alone with the goats in the Wadi Kabir, indulging in fruitless one-sided conversations with them.

The concept of shirek was well known to him. It was a state of mind, a poison of heart. His doubts and fumbling rebellion were in themselves shirek. Fear of any sort was shirek. For fear of a man dilutes that fear which is due to God alone. Now Ibrahim feared his father. Would it then be a good act to not fear and confront his father with his unwillingness to marry? But he could not do it. So what to do? Run away? Run back to Saffina? No. Yes. Ibrahim was lost.

So completely had the pattern of Islam become woven into the fabric of life in Jaheel that it was impossible to say where religion ended and secular began. The mosque and the market place interconnected and the breaking of a purely secular tradition could never be viewed as an act (at best) of brave non-conformity, or (at worst) as an abnormal but run-of-the-mill event. To toe the line of society was to toe God's line.

Ibrahim watched the goats meandering over the flat valley floor and felt himself breaking into pieces as the split rocks at his feet had broken under the wind and rain of centuries. He marvelled at how easily his single, straight life had become split by the experiences of the last few months.

Only last year he had walked this valley behind his goats, his mind only on them and on Jaheel behind him. Then nothing broke up his reverie and the old devil of desire or impatience could be brushed off with a song or a few pebbles thrown at the goats. Now he felt years older and could only look down at the ground and wonder how the integrated youth of recently could have walked there.

He made his way to the base of the cliff wall of the valley where a small pool of water hung, a tear on the chin of the rock face. Behind this a cave had been carved right through the cliff to the sky above, from where daylight funnelled down.

He jumped across the pool, careful to avoid the hornets that swarmed there. Inside the throat-shaped entrance to the cave it was cool and damp. He shivered as he scrambled up the slurry of stones, starting his ascent towards the sunshine, which gushed now where water had gushed during the rains. He got half way up, and sat down, his back resting against the sheer face of rock. Beside him a small bush grew, bereft of sunshine except for a brief span which hit it once a day from the head of the funnel far above it.

This had long been one of Ibrahim's favourite places. He sat and tried to calm himself. He looked at the bush. It had been here since he had started coming here as a small child. It never seemed to get any larger, but its spiky leaves were green, fragrant when squeezed. It had managed to flourish in its small way by keeping a low profile; by not asking too much of the sun or the moisture. Its seed had landed here in the hollow and had miraculously germinated and just as miraculously survived. Like the people of Ibrahim's village it had flourished close to the soil and was known only to its soil and its roots.

Ibrahim planned his escape. Where to go? There were two possibilities: Saffina or the Capital. But the Capital was a far country. It struck terror into him. Saffina was far enough. It was big enough for a start.

He would return to Saffina. He worried about how he would manage. He worried about his father's and Jaheel's reaction. But he had to go.

Ibrahim, without thought or feeling, strode over to the little green bush and grasped it by the throat. With all his strength he pulled at it until it came screaming out of the soil of the Wadi Kabir.

As Ibrahim prepared for his departure from Jaheel, the whole village set about preparing for his ceremony of admission to the village as a full member, one of its proud male grown-ups; the village's guarantee of vigorous continuity.

As he collected together a few belongings, stealing away to hide them in the cave, his father tethered three goats outside the house. There they would remain in idleness, fattening on the richest food the village could afford, until that day when their idleness would be disturbed, and, tethered by the hind legs, they would be taken out and hung from a beam, their bleating throats cut, their blood falling to the ground and disappearing into the sand.

The presence of the goats started things moving and villagers came to the house to offer their contributions to the feast. Eggs, a sack of flour, another of rice, all arrived at the door of the house. Hameed Nasr donated several crates of soft drinks, though he had made no secret of his contempt for Ibrahim since the boy's sudden return from Saffina.

Those families too poor to contribute nevertheless sent their children with any scraps left over from their meals. These too would be fed to the goats and so, indirectly, contribute to the wedding feast.

Ibrahim, a bulge of belongings under his robe, had to step over gifts whenever he went to the cave to add to his store of luggage. They reminded him of the act he was about to commit as did the greetings of the people he met along the

71

way. The whole village conspired to tie him to them as he fought to free himself.

He decided to leave two nights before the ceremony was to take place but he could not decide which route he should take to Saffina. Either he could walk south as he had done the other time; or, he could take the route up the Wadi Kabir through the mountains and down to the plains of the Interior. From there he might be able to get a lift on the track that led to Saffina. He would be less likely to meet anyone if he took the inland route. He decided on this.

The moon had not yet risen when Ibrahim left Jaheel and made his way to the cave. He stumbled in the darkness and hoped he would not tread on a scorpion or a snake. By the time he arrived at the cave his fear of so doing had taken hold of him because one side of his nature expected that God might allow such a thing to happen as payment for what he was doing.

From the mouth of the cave he emerged with his belongings wrapped in a cloth. He could see the few lights of Jaheel a little to his left. Not only could he count them but he could say to whom each light belonged. Then he turned his back and started to make his way up the Wadi Kabir.

In the darkness the cathedral sides of the valley stood out from the sky like the place where shallow seas meet the depths.

He tried to forget his village and the shame that would push his absent name into the dust, kicking it there with gossip and story-telling until it rotted. He was helped to forget by the roughness of the terrain. He slipped frequently over the large stones that littered the valley floor and soon his ankles were bleeding, his feet a mass of pain. And in pain came forgetfulness. He concentrated his mind a foot ahead of his feet and at last attained a kind of peace.

Soon he was climbing the valley floor up into the forbidding fastnesses that barred his route to Wadi Beni Omar and the Saffina track beyond. This was the difficult part, the cause of most of Jaheel's isolation. He himself had never been this far up the valley. Traditionally it was the home of the Beni Omar and he remembered stories of the old days when their tribesmen fiercely guarded access to their lands and only let strangers pass on payment of large sums. Numerous were the tales of people from Jaheel slaughtered by the Beni Omar; understandable people's reluctance to venture into the area — even though King Fadl had attempted to stop all that sort of thing.

Then, from the direction of Saffina, Ibrahim heard the sound of a huge explosion. The sound echoed around the walls of the Wadi Kabir. He stopped, wondering whether the explosion had anything to do with him. A silence alive with the memory of the noise buzzed round his head like flies. Then he heard another bang coming from the same direction. The echoes again . . . Then the silence. Birds in the valley woke and flew around, dark ghosts against the sky. Dogs barked in the nearby village of Wadi Beni Omar.

What could it be?

Then that thought was pushed from Ibrahim's mind as he stole past the village in the approaching dawn. He heard the Call to Prayer from the village's mosque: "Awake everyone! It is better to pray than to sleep! Awake! God is Most Great!"

Ibrahim did not heed the call. It no longer applied to him. Alone and a stranger to the village and to himself, he kept his thoughts on escape.

Shortly before noon he arrived at the track to Saffina.

7

Nicholson had been about to fall asleep and sleep the sleep of the just when his two small gelignite charges exploded within seconds of one another and blew up the oil storage containers at the power station.

He was able to go to his verandah, be seen by everyone else in the compound, rumpled and tousled, and also witness the burning down of the new power station.

"I did not burn it down. I burnt it up!"

Nicholson had applied these words of Alexander the Great to his own exploits of that night. He had burnt up the symbol of modern Saffina just as Alexander had burned Persepolis, the symbol of Persian Power. Not a bad night's work. There was no fire brigade in Saffina to rush to the rescue, nothing that anybody could do but watch the show and make pious Islamic ejaculations of the "What a pity!" variety.

He did his perceived duty. With a barely-suppressed giggle in his voice, he barked that his men should form a human chain of buckets, while keeping a weather-eye out for insurgents. "The devils are back!" he told his bedouin guards. Then, duty performed, he raided the top of the fridge and poured himself a large glass of precious sherry. The almost unbearable sweetness of the sherry exploded on his palate with the flavour of merry guilt. It was the taste of his rich aunt's parlour.

As a child he would excuse himself from the fidgeting boredom of adult company and sneak a quick swig from the sherry bottle. Then, Nicholson the child would feel the liquid fire him and make him different. After a slug of his aunt's sherry he could wander off into her overgrown garden and play cruel games with cats and birds; with insects and worms.

"You shouldn't persecute the cat like that, you wicked boy!"

"He likes it, Aunt! See, he's coming back for more! He's nuzzling my knee and purring!"

The night before, Nicholson had been alone and sober. After a light meal of salad and Perrier, he went into his living room and sat down behind the keyboard of his harmonium. There he started bashing out Bach. After playing a passable rendition of *Jesu, Joy of Man's Desiring*, he got up from the instrument and turned on his hi-fi system, pushing the record button and placing a cordless microphone on the rosewood top of the harmonium.

He picked out *Abide With Me* and then turned to *Leaving on a Jet Plane*. Anything sounded decent on the harmonium, he always thought. All one needed to do was bang the keys with enough conviction. He had fooled Bob Hepworth like that, sitting him down with a drink and announcing that he would treat him to a few solo pieces for the harmonium written especially for it by Benjamin Britten. Then, with great aplomb, he had randomly selected weird chords and cheeky individual notes from top and bottom register.

Hepworth had sat dreamily sipping his drink and preparing an appropriate comment.

"Well, what do you think?" Nicholson had asked.

"I don't usually go for this modern stuff as you know well. More a James Last man myself, but . . ."

"Yes?"

"Well it does have a certain grandeur. Like the last night of the Proms."

"Thank you."

He had not let Hepworth in on the secret. Hepworth was fooled because he was an incorrigible fool beyond redemption.

"Lead kindly light, amidst the encircling gloom! Lead thou me on! The night is dark, and I am far from home," sang Nicholson to the accompaniment of his harmonium. The faithful cordless microphone picked up everything.

Newman's hymn was his favourite, but Nicholson's light and Newman's were very different beacons indeed. Nicholson saw light at the end of the tunnel of faith and delusion. He had throughout his childhood pushed himself through the tunnel keeping his eyes always on the prize of light at the end. Despite cuffs and blows and the world's attempts to keep him in the dark, Nicholson had emerged into the light of a strange new knowledge. Nothing existed on planet Earth beyond his own self interest. There was no God to be placated and the love and duty and virtues that flowed from the dried-up source in the sky, he abjured. Nicholson elevated selfishness to the level of a faith, seasoned it with pragmatism and ate it like a sacrament his every waking moment. His faith could not come out into the full light of day. It had to be hidden — and here the pragmatism came in — but any veneer of respect and honour and loyalty he knew to be role-playing. It was just something he had to do to lubricate his passage through a benighted world. His Way, his Light, was something very new. It was the next step in the Ascent of Man. His was not the ignorance of the first conscious beings on Earth, the people who gazed fearfully into the dark where the light of their campfires ended and calmed their howling children with tales of kindness behind the stars. Had the very first weavers of myth been aware of the lies they were telling? Had their repetition of their lies slowly pushed their lies into the heads of the new seers until they came to believe them themselves? No, Nicholson did not identify with these people. These people, our first erring parents, whose original sin was the telling of kindly, soft lies to their children to stop their fear of the dark, had been the ones who had entered the tunnel into the darkness, a darkness that had lasted up to now — up to Nicholson — and which would, no doubt, continue for decades, centuries, millennia still. The beauty of it was that he, Nicholson, *knew* the lies of the world. He could thus play his game according to his own rules. Monotheism was dead. Long live Monomania!

"I do not ask to see the distant scene . . . One step enough for me." Then Nicholson launched into *The Vicar of Bray* — smiling at the appropriateness of that too — and followed it with a selection of sea shanties.

Tiring of the harmonium at last, he sat down in his favourite chair and read a thriller for a couple of hours.

Yes, it was important to make sure that he won through. That was what tonight was going to be about. If some unpleasant steps were necessary to ensure that everyone asserted that his presence in Saffina was necessary, then so be it. He had not seen Hepworth since the night he had floated his ideas. Almost certainly he would have either forgotten, or thought Nicholson was joking. Well, by morning he would know different.

How would he react? Nicholson felt quite certain that he would be able to say, "We do it like this," and Hepworth would follow, like a duckling follows a piece of rag it thinks is its mother. One merely had to say things with enough conviction — no, conviction was the wrong word; machismo was better — to people like Hepworth and they would fall into line. One might have to bawl it a number of times to get it into the thick grey-matter, but it was worth it. Once there, it stuck and would not be changed. It was the lynchpin of Nicholson's belief. Say it loud: "Jesus was right; Mohammed was right; Hitler was right; Churchill was right; the Falkland Islands belong to us; I'm OK, you're OK; never give a sucker an even break; the cat enjoys the string round its neck, Aunt!"

The novel engrossed him. When he looked at his watch it was two a.m. Everyone sleeping like babes. Everything quiet. Just the job.

In his bedroom he stripped off to his underwear and unlocked the door of one of his built-in closets. Hanging neatly in a row was a selection of Arab garments in different colours and fabrics. These he had acquired over the years. He seldom wore them now though they were much more comfortable than trousers. He chose a brown, oil-and-blood-stained one he had often worn on undercover operations during the Civil War. It had been given to him by an insurgent whom he had treated kindly during interrogation. After such a gift, the only thing the man had had to offer, it had grieved Nicholson to take his pistol and place it against the back of the man's neck. He had taken care that the man should not know what was about to happen to him. It seemed the very least he could do.

Finally, he took a black-patterned headcloth and put it over his head, not, though, in the manner of Ras Al Surrans, but as the insurgents had worn them. He gathered the ends and pulled them round his face, concealing everything but the eyes. Then he inspected himself in his full-length mirror. From a drawer he took out a pistol, and placed it in his thick leather belt.

Stealthily now, feeling he already needed to exercise caution, Nicholson tiptoed out of his bedroom and into a small store-room next to the kitchen. There he unlocked a cupboard and took out the two explosive charges he had set up earlier in the day. They were small affairs, nothing elaborate, connected to a digital timing device. He consulted his watch and carefully set the charges to go off in two hours' time. That should be plenty, he thought.

Then he turned on the tape recorder and waited to hear his rendering of *Lead, Kindly Light* which would convince the servants, should any awake, that he was up and about. He was ready and left the bungalow by the seldom-used rear door. Just outside the house he found the place between the barbed wire that John De Lobo had widened when he took a short cut to go fishing, as he had done most days. He wondered fleetingly what John was doing back in Delhi. He saw him behind a counter surrounded by the fumes of hamburgers. "Silly boy" he told his vision of John.

Once outside the compound it was easy enough for Nicholson to creep over the road and across the wasteland to the power station. The installation had been built so hurriedly that there were no security fences in place. The metal posts were there but the wire had not arrived. The guards, a couple of Hepworth's delinquents, would be curled up asleep in their huts a hundred yards to his left.

Nicholson, keeping to the shadows but feeling all his precautions were unnecessary, reached the first storage tank. He snapped the charge to it. The powerful magnet engaged and made a dull tinging sound. He blenched at the sound. He would have to be more careful with the other charge.

Fifty yards separated the two tanks and in that area was a

portakabin belonging to the company which had been brought in to maintain the power station. No lights showed. The Bangladeshi and Lebanese workers must have gone to bed hours ago. Reaching the second tank, he was careful to place the charge gently against the metal surface. He used his head-dress to dull the sound and was about to remove it when he thought that if some fragments of an insurgent's head-dress was found after the explosion, it would be all to the good. But would it survive? Probably not. He changed his mind and eased the cloth from under the charge. He started back to his compound, discarding the cloth on a bush some distance from the power station.

He was back in his house less than twenty minutes after leaving it. He listened to the recording of his harmonium playing for a minute, standing still and panting in the middle of his living room, then he turned it off. It had probably not been necessary anyway. He looked out of his window at the sleeping compound. Nothing stirred.

Back in his bedroom he stripped and showered. Then he got into his nightclothes and read the thriller for a while. He looked at his watch. Half an hour to go. He turned off the light and waited for the bangs which would be heard in the Capital Area and tell him that he was wanted, needed . . .

8

Peter Drury was far away from Saffina when the power station was destroyed.

After more than a month in Saffina he had begun to understand how everything worked or did not work. He now knew what a difficult job he had undertaken. The challenge he had accepted so readily in London had turned into a cross of impossible weight in Ras Al Surra.

It had taken him a week just to find out where the schools in the Eastern Region were located. The area under his charge was, he guessed, about the size of Wales, a crescent shaped piece of terrain, bounded to the east by ocean and to the west by the Rub Al Khali, the Empty Quarter. At once he had started to plan his first trip around the area, a reconnoitre to ascertain the problems. It was with a feeling of great relief that he left the education office after his first confusing week there and set off in his Landrover to see what was what.

What was what had not been a pretty sight. The schools of the Eastern Region of Ras Al Surra did not have any books. Nobody had told him that. Indeed, it was difficult to get anybody even to admit the fact. Where were the books, he asked. In the Capital Area, he was told in words spoken through wide smiles. When would they arrive? The teachers looked towards heaven.

The schools were like gypsy encampments, the children sitting on the floor while sweating, unhappy teachers did their best or did not do their best to impart knowledge. The teachers then returned after school to asbestos prefabs, carbon-copies of his own, except that each one was inhabited by upwards of eight teachers. They did not enjoy the benefits of a generator. They ate sitting on the linoleum floor around a table of spread newspapers.

Into this demoralised group the new inspector would intrude. He mentioned lesson plans and visual aids and new horizons in linguistics and the teachers looked at him as if he had just arrived from the moon.

"What can we do? We are in prison here!" they told him. And that was true enough. They were. The children were willing but there were no books, no materials, no desks. He made that his first priority. Before he started inspecting classes he would have to be Mr Bountiful to the schools under his charge.

While on this trip he accepted the hospitality of the teachers. In Sabab, a windblown place on the very rim of the Empty Quarter, his Landrover refused to start. The teachers had lined up alongside it to bid him farewell, but no farewell was possible. He could not get the Landrover to help his getaway. Everyone looked under the bonnet. The cause had been found; he needed a new fuel pump. But where could he find a new fuel pump in Sabab? Of course he could not, and he had been forced to wait there for ten days until one arrived from the Capital.

His time in Sabab had been heartening, however. He had got to know an Egyptian English teacher called Mister Shukry. At first the man had not made much of an impression on him, but, during his enforced stay, he went with Mr Shukry to his classes and saw that the man was a dynamo of a teacher who, through play-acting and enthusiasm, was managing to teach his poor boys well. Also, he did not close his mind when Peter brought up theory.

At one point Mr Shukry said, "It seems to me that we must go near our boys and say the sentence again and again. Only in this way can we assure them of the good English saying. It is imperative that we bring the wind of the world into the small air of the classroom and say to our boys, 'Look boys! There is the world's wind! Taste it! Smell it ! Feel it!'"

Peter had nodded happily. His own thoughts entirely. He had stayed close to Mr Shukry during his days of waiting and gained both courage and a feeling of optimism from the presence in the Region of such a decent fellow.

When he finally got on to the track that led to Saffina he felt inspired. He was tired and he wanted desperately to get back home. But, remembering Mr Shukry and the needs of his kids — and multiplying the children he had come to know in Sabab by one hundred to give him some idea of the area relying on him — he sighed and took the track north, towards the Capital. He must have books. Without books and materials he could not start his real job.

He spent two weeks in the Capital in the company of another inspector who had charge of the schools in that area. During the day he spent his time going from office to office pleading for books. He got lots of promises. They would be sent. "When?" "In God's good time."

During his time in the Capital, Peter toured the place, looking upwards at the mad architecture — some Japanese architect's notion of what was "Arabian". He shook his head as he rubber-necked. The airport aped a bedouin tent in concrete. The spotless toilets when he found them had sketches in each stall showing how nice people used western toilets; the Museum of Arabian Culture and Artifacts resembled "a cardamom container" — whatever that was; the Ministry of Foreign Affairs had a wing which was supposed to represent a traditional dagger, pointing outwards — towards the sea.

He thought of Saffina and its easy people; his prefab; his private pool near the track behind Saffina, the pool he had discovered that first day and had returned to so often since for consolation and the kissing bites of the impertinent fish. The Capital was a foreign country with little or nothing in common with the poor country behind it from whence he came and in which he knew his loyalties lodged.

Finally, he was taken to see the king's newest palace and was so appalled by the sight of the monstrous piece of concrete dwarfing the rest of the small Capital centre that he threw a tantrum. He gesticulated and shouted to the other inspector and said that it was monstrous that such a building existed in a country where children had neither books nor desks. Who in thunder did the king think he was anyway? Just a Rachman landlord of a tatty Third World country.

The other inspector led him away, murmuring "Shhhh!" Peter, feeling foolish, said he had better be going home.

On the way back to Saffina, looking with affection at the watchtowers and tiny dwellings of the villages he passed, feeling he was somehow coming home, he cooled down. It was stupid of him to get wrought up. He should know better. Trips into Khartoum had had a similar effect on him while in Sudan. There too he had railed against the leaders of countries who seemed to be completely oblivious to the plight of the people they ruled. It was as if they were determined to make their capitals ape the places they visited in the West. Did these rulers sigh as they left Manhattan and seek to recreate it in deserts and mangrove swamps and in the middle of old, sleepy, traditional villages? On state visits it was said, the king of Ras Al Surra had ten-foot-high fences erected to mask any sights of poverty which would wound the VIP's eye. Truly, these rulers belonged to an international nationality of other corrupt leaders. They were worse — far worse — than Colonialists: for these new rulers turned their backs on their own.

"If I were a king I would be the last person in my country to have a car, a house, books for my children," Peter Drury told himself with conviction.

Then he laughed away the thought and concentrated instead on swimming in his pool and returning to the prefab.

On the night of the explosion Peter Drury was back in Sabab. He had told everyone in the office that he was going to make another inspection tour, but really he wanted to see Mr Shukry and spend more time with him. He rolled up in his Landrover and threw himself on Mr Shukry's hospitality. The man had smiled a smile which split his face wide open and then opened his arms wide, saying, "We do not have many things, dear my inspector! But what we have is yours!" And he had taken him in.

Peter had been extremely grateful; grateful in the way a child lost in a busy shopping precinct is grateful to the lady who takes him by the hand and, gazing over the crowds of shoppers, says: "I'll find your mum for you. Dry your eyes!" In return he helped Mr Shukry make visual aids, taught some of his classes, and talked endlessly to him about Egypt and the strange confusing country that Ras Al Surra was fast becoming to Peter. Also, around Sabab there were high, conical hills. These he climbed.

On his way back to Saffina, the day after the explosion, he saw a young Arab walking towards Saffina along the track. As Peter passed him the lad turned and waved at his Landrover. Then, in the driving mirror, in that time when he was trying to decide whether or not to stop for him, he saw the Arab drop his belongings and slump down next to them by the road. Peter pushed the brake hard and reversed back to where the Arab was sitting disconsolately.

"Where are you going?" he asked the youth.

"Saffina. Would you take me?"

"Certainly. Get in."

Peter glanced at him as he started up. "You look tired. Where have you come from?"

"Jaheel."

"Jaheel? That's a long way from here. You came over the mountains?"

"Yes," said Ibrahim. He reached into the pocket of his robe and took out a cigarette, lit it and smoked hungrily. He reached into his pocket again and offered Peter one.

"I don't," replied Peter. "I used to but I stopped."

Ibrahim nodded.

They went on in silence. Peter watched the lad smoke. He had noticed that Ras Al Surrans smoked in the same way as some women smoked at home. The cigarette was a prop, a means of display, a tool which said, "Here I am! I'm OK. I'm independent," but which also spoke of insecurity and worries.

"Why are you going to Saffina?" Peter asked.

Ibrahim shrugged.

"Work?"

"Maybe."

"What's your name?"

"Ibrahim. And you?"

84

"Peter."

"What's your job?"

"I am a teacher."

"A teacher . . ." said Ibrahim. He threw the stub out of the window and asked, "Are you English?"

"Yes."

"Where do you live?"

"Saffina — well, near Saffina. Between Saffina and Bilad Saffina."

Ibrahim nodded. Then he asked, "You need a boy?"

"Er, how do you mean?"

"I need a job. I have experience as a houseboy."

Peter did not know what to say. He did not feel he needed a houseboy and said so.

"Please, Sir. I will work hard for little money. And you can teach me English and I teach you Arabic."

Peter had heard that before. "But I already speak Arabic."

"Yes, but I can help you here. You don't know the people in Saffina. I can shop and get the best price for you. Please, Sir."

It irked Peter to hear himself addressed as Sir. He did not feel he merited the title. But more, he did not feel sufficiently old to be so addressed. It crossed his mind that, perhaps, he was becoming old enough. To Peter there did not seem to be much difference in age between Ibrahim and himself. He wondered if he looked in the mirror enough; if he really knew what he looked like. When he had returned from the Sudan, more skeletal even than was usual for him, his mother had gasped and exclaimed, "What have they done to you? I hardly knew you!" He had laughed at her and, while home, had co-operated by eating everything on his plate.

The desperation in Ibrahim's voice moved Peter, but he held back. A houseboy in the place would mean that he couldn't pad around the place in the nude, or, as he did more usually, in damp underwear.

"Where are you going to stay in Saffina?" asked Peter, hoping to change the subject, but his ploy did not work. "I don't know," replied Ibrahim.

85

They did not speak again until the Landrover had begun the last part of the trip, heading east back towards the coast.

Peter began to weaken. After all, he had not made any friends in Saffina up to now. He had seen Nicholson and Hepworth, though he had not known who they were, had not even been granted the courtesy of a wave as they zoomed by him on the road in Range Rovers. He had heard that a Save the Children nurse was working in Saffina, but had had no sightings. Once, too, at the very beginning, he had presented himself at the hospital in the hope of meeting the American matron. Mr Nasser, the postmaster, had recommended that he get to know her. "A good woman," he had said. But this good woman had been out about her good works and Peter had not had the courage to go back. So, who did he have that he could call a friend? Had he not just pushed himself on to Mr Shukry because he was desperate for company? He looked at Ibrahim and wondered whether the youth would provide that company.

At last he said, "Look, if you have nowhere to go you can come and stay with me. I warn you, though, my place is not a palace. It isn't very comfortable. Maybe when you see it you will decide you don't like it."

"Thank you, Sir!" And Ibrahim grabbed Peter's right hand from the steering wheel and kissed it.

Images of Robinson Crusoe and Man Friday came into Peter's mind. With distaste he pushed them away. He wondered what he was getting into but told himself that he had not made any long-term commitment. He was merely doing what he had heard any Arab would have done for him, what Mr Shukry had done for him just now in Sabab: offer a stranger hospitality. It was the Arab custom that had most appealed to him and he had found, thinking of the way Mr Shukry had taken infinite pains to entertain him, that it still existed. The time had come to show that he was entering into the spirit of life in Ras Al Surra.

"I don't have much to offer, but you're welcome to what I have. My house is your house," Peter told Ibrahim.

★

Hepworth drove into Nicholson's compound at speed that day, around noon. The power station continued to burn, sending a plume of thick black smoke high into the air over the Interior. Hepworth had seen the smoke while on patrol. He had been camped about thirty miles out of Saffina.

He found Nicholson sitting in his office.

"Have you seen the power station?" he gasped as he exploded into the office.

Nicholson looked heavenward and shook his head sadly. "God, you're thick, Hepworth!"

Nicholson's Indian secretary chose that moment to turn from his ledger and smile at Hepworth. He had not heard his boss' reply. Hepworth thought he had and that he was laughing at him.

"Get that cocoa out of here right now!" he told Nicholson.

Nicholson gestured to his secretary to leave. The man did so, quietly closing the door behind him.

Nicholson turned on Hepworth. "Never again use the word cocoa in my presence! And never, never tell me what to do in my own office! Is that clear?"

Hepworth glowered. "I didn't use the word cocoa until you taught it to me."

Nicholson ignored this. "You'd better sit down," he said.

Hepworth sat down and gestured towards the burning power station which could be seen through the office window. "What happened?"

"Sabotage, I reckon. Don't you?" said Nicholson, serenely.

"You don't mean . . ."

"No, I don't mean that the insurgents are back, but that is how it will appear, won't it?"

"But if the insurgents aren't back then how . . .?"

Nicholson nodded and signalled with his hands to get Hepworth to bring his thoughts out into the open. It took a while; then Hepworth's mouth fell open:

"Not *you*?" he asked, quietly.

"Yes, me. Little me. All by myself. What do you think?"

Hepworth crumpled. "You didn't, did you?" he asked without hope. He looked to Nicholson like every loser who

87

had ever discovered his loss, every softie who had discovered that the world was hard.

"Yes, I did. I told you what was required. I have started the process."

Hepworth hid his head in his hands. "What a stink there's going to be! What a stink!"

"On the contrary, old boy. On the contrary," said Nicholson. "The government will be in a state of shock. It's the sort of thing they *dread*. You don't imagine that they will suddenly become all bold and brave and come down here to clean things up, do you? I will be very surprised if they do. No, I expect they will remember that they have a loyal Research Department and a reliable Desert Regiment. I am now sending a distressed memo to the powers-that-be. In it I will say that we suspect a resurgence of insurgence. I have been warning them about the possibility for quite some time. I shall assure them that we will do all that is humanly possible to prevent further incidents. In a day or two the telex will begin to clack. It will clack for ages but the kernel of the government message will be, 'We're shit-scared! Do something! Please accept an increase in salary and an extra Range Rover with our compliments!' Yes, I expect that is how it will be."

Hepworth, his head still in his hands, bemoaned his lost innocence. When Nicholson had finished he cried, his voice breaking, "Tell me it's a joke!"

Hepworth's reaction worried Nicholson somewhat. It was time to play tough, to raise his voice, to rub it in. "We discussed this, Hepworth. I have a tape to prove that we discussed it. Go away now and think about it, but centre your thinking on what must be done next. We've only just begun, Hepworth, old son."

"I don't believe I'm hearing this," moaned Hepworth.

"You sound like a character from one of those soap operas that are perverting and rendering unproductive the evenings of the labouring classes back home," said Nicholson, his mind running ahead to what would have to be done should Hepworth prove to be a liability.

"How's the Beat the Baby nurse?" he asked, trying to improve the other man's mood.

Hepworth had stood up and was gazing forlornly out of the window. "She's frigid," he said flatly.

"Frigid? And she a nurse? Are you sure you're making the right approach?"

.Hepworth did not answer. He continued to gaze at the burning power station. "What happened to those men who lived in the portakabins?" he asked.

"Didn't stand a chance, I'm afraid. Both storage tanks went up more or less simultaneously. It would have been very quick. They wouldn't have known what hit them," Nicholson said brusquely. "Still not to worry. I've mentioned them in my memo. Their families will be handsomely compensated."

Hepworth turned round and gazed at Nicholson steadily. He looked, Nicholson thought, like a beaten bulldog.

"Come on, Hepworth! Snap out of it! We can't have you going round looking like a wet weekend." And he added, "We've got work to do! That little bonfire is just the start. We must keep up the momentum. Have you seen that English teacher, by the way?"

Hepworth shook his head forlornly. He fumbled in the pockets of his uniform jacket, searching desperately for his cigarettes. His hands shook uncontrollably.

Nor did they stop shaking as Nicholson, his hand as steady as a clay tablet, held out a sandalwood box of cigarettes. Then, from nowhere, appeared an almond-shaped flame from Nicholson's Dupont.

Hepworth bowed towards the small flame and lit his cigarette. Its smoke at once stung his eyes and pricked his tear ducts.

9

Peter Drury left for work at the Education Office the following morning with a spring in his step. He was looking forward to seeing everyone there and to finding out if there was any news about his English textbooks.

He shared his office with a Mister Abdul Wahhab Nasawi, the Egyptian expert on visual aids. Mr Nasawi had been good to Peter and had taken time when he first arrived to introduce him to everyone at the Education Office. But, when Peter arrived that morning, he found a note on his desk from Mr Nasawi.

"Where are you, my dear? I hope you have not deserted your post! (I joke.) I must take my works of visual education to the very end of the Earth! It grieves me to leave the little comforts of Saffina for the cruelties of the desert. But that, my dear, is the price we must pay to take education to the ignorant! God keep you! Abdul Wahhab Nasawi (Head: Visual Aids)"

The Education Office was a very loose ship indeed. There was nominally a Ras Al Surran in charge, but he was almost always absent. The other employees were mainly Arab expatriates from Palestine, Jordan, Egypt and the Sudan. Peter felt a bit bashful around them, wondering what they made of him and whether the Balfour Declaration, Suez and the British influence in Ras Al Surra, came bubbling up into their minds whenever he made an appearance.

But, quickly bored with his own company, he forced himself to approach a colleague in the next office. It soon filled up with other employees with time on their hands and Peter found, as he had so often before — but seemed incapable of really taking in and remembering — that he was treated, handsomely, as a friend and colleague.

He told everyone that he was expecting books, but this was greeted with some scepticism. Everyone wanted to talk about the dreadful happenings of two nights before.

"The Godless communists are back among us!" exclaimed Mr Siddiqui, the Sudanese inspector of Arabic, a very tall, impossibly thin man with two diagonal lines carved into each cheek. These gave his face a majestic appearance. Sitting at his desk writing, eyes down, his head still, Peter would gasp at the face of Mr Siddiqui, at the smooth, uniform colour, the high cheek-bones, but, above all, at the aura of timelessness and agelessness. He felt that he was looking at the face of "Man", and not just at the face of "a man", Mr Siddiqui, an inspector like himself, an ordinary chap with an ordinary job to do.

"Couldn't it have been an accident?" asked Peter.

"No accident! No accident! The rebels are back, my dear," replied Mr Siddiqui with certainty. He gestured round his office. The new air-conditioner in the wall lay lifeless, the ceiling fan had become a snoozing bar for flies. "And, as you see, Peter, the twentieth century, such a welcome guest, has not consented to stay with us long. This morning at the Education compound there was much gnashing of teeth, my dear! I had purchased my wife the rice cooker she has always wanted. Also an electric lamp of great beauty from the Capital. Imagine our sadness. There is much weeping in Saffina, my dear. Many are the wives who are cursing their new electric gadgetry."

"Yes, it's a miserable thing to have happened," said Peter.

"It was your big mistake, Siddiqui, to bring your poor wife to such a terrible place," remarked Mr Ahmed, the inspector of Arithmetic. "Women are tender blooms and must be protected from the harsher realities."

"Where is your wife, Mr Ahmed?" asked Peter.

Mr Ahmed smiled. "She is minding the children in Gaza."

"But isn't there er . . . trouble in Gaza?"

Mr Ahmed continued to smile as he said, "Everywhere there is trouble. Here there is trouble. There there is trouble. Even in England there is trouble. I am sure that even in paradise there will be trouble."

"Shame on you!" replied Mr Siddiqui piously. "In heaven everything is peace and quiet and much loving of houris."

"Then there will be trouble about who gets which houris. The Iraqi president will want the one with the breasts like melons and Khomeini will want the same and he'll send his revolutionary guards to make sure he gets her."

Mr Siddiqui said nothing, but frowned and looked disapprovingly at Mr Ahmed.

"If there was bloodshed in the Holy City of Mecca — Muslim slaying Muslim — and my Uncle Abdullah saw the whole thing, then, believe me, there would be trouble in paradise." And Mr Ahmed nodded his head briskly to show that the conversation was at an end and that he had won the argument hands down.

Towards the end of the morning Peter went into his stifling office to catch up on his work. He had not been there for more than ten minutes when a beautiful black girl entered the office dressed in a diaphanous robe that resembled a sari.

"I am one of your!" she stated.

"Oh yes?"

"Yes, I am teach in Zarut Girl School. Where are you?"

"Where am I?"

"Yes," replied the girl. "We wait for and wait for but no English inspector."

"Oh, I see! I'm sorry, but to tell you the truth I did not know there *was* a Girls' School on Zarut. I'm Peter Drury, by the way."

"Pleased to meet you. I am Batool Al Chanri." And she flashed a smile of ebony and stars at Peter, then covered it modestly with the cloud of her long, dark hand.

"Sit down, Miss Al Chanri."

"You're welcome!" replied Miss Al Chanri setting herself down, like a slowly deflating hot-air balloon, her chiffon dress settling around her form.

"Tea?" asked Peter.

"No, thank you. I am drinking tea before I am come here."

"Right-ho."

There was a long silence between them. Batool looked

steadily at Peter. Peter gazed back, then looked away. He was aware that this was the first female he had spoken to outside a school staffroom since his arrival in Ras Al Surra. But somehow he could not describe Batool Al Chanri as "a girl". She, in the same way that Mr Siddiqui was "man", was "woman" and totally beyond his reach and his grasp for reasons of religion and culture, and, above all, beauty.

"How can I help you? You say you're the English teacher at Zarut Girls' School."

"Well, really I am chemistry but when I am come they ask, 'Who is speak English?' I put up my hand and they say, 'Go to Zarut Girls!' But my English is bad. Yes?"

"No," replied Peter. "It's fine. Now tell me how I get to Zarut Girls' School. I'll be happy to come and visit you."

"It is a journey of much travail," replied Batool, like some nineteenth-century English phrase book.

"But I must come," countered Peter.

Batool gave him directions and then looked suddenly sad.

"I am from Khartoum," she said.

"Are you?"

"Yes. Do you know Khartoum, Mr Peter?"

"I know it a little. It is a lovely city. I once worked in the West of Sudan, near the Chad border."

Batool's head made a complete vertical revolution on its slender, seamless neck. "So beautiful, Khartoum, Mr Peter!"

"More beautiful than Saffina?"

Batool pushed out her bottom lip and pulled the edges of her mouth downwards. She said nothing, but she did not need to. The look was an eloquent reply.

"I see," said Peter. He told Batool that he would visit her school the following morning, God willing. Batool left happily.

The office was impossibly hot and Peter was very relieved when he heard everyone leaving. He quickly followed suit, wondering what his strange companion at home had been doing with his morning.

★

93

As Peter drove back to his stifling prefab, a Bell 205 helicopter flew low overhead. It momentarily terrorised him, its stealthy approach unexpected, its unbearably loud, cackling engine jolting him, adding to the feeling of unease brought on by the news of the power station's destruction. But then he saw what it was and wished, as it rapidly shrank towards the horizon in front of him, that he was inside.

The pilot, Ken Kendal, had flown down from the Capital early that morning, and, if all went smoothly, would be flying back there in the evening to his villa near the international airport. The night before, as a matter of routine, he had checked his charts. It was a long way to Saffina, but the helicopter ate up the miles, mangled them in minutes with its inexorable rotors. He would pass dhows and coastal vessels which would take two days to make the trip he was making in two hours. He saw the route the new road was following, shown on the chart as an intermittent red line. Friends had tried to drive down the track in a car. They had lost their back axle in Abna. It was a remote bloody spot all right, but soon it would be an easy drive. When that happened, and when the branch roads joined the main trunk, it would spell the end of his time in Ras Al Surra. Other, cheaper forms of transport would replace his expensive presence. Ah well, perhaps something else would turn up. He would regret leaving, but he would be taking a lot of wonderful memories with him.

Kendal always loved the flight down and usually took a route which followed the coast, keeping to a low altitude, low enough to see what there was to be seen, high enough to avoid any detail in the terrain that would distract or dishearten him. There would probably be enough to dishearten him once he had arrived at Saffina and had started ferrying Joanna and her hospital orderlies to the remotest villages in the area.

Joanna, seated next to Kendal, palms sweaty with anxiety and excitement, watched the tiny Landrover below her and then concentrated her attention on the looming mountains ahead. This part always scared Joanna. On her first trip the pilot had confessed that he had not been certain that the helicopter would make it over the peaks, so thin was the air, so peculiar the eddying of the winds.

It was the first time Kendal had been her pilot but Joanna had liked him as soon as she saw him. "If he were a few years younger . . ." she allowed herself to think as she helped the orderly aboard and handed Kendal the boxes of medicines.

"If she were a few years older . . ." Kendal thought as he greeted Joanna and settled herself down in the helicopter.

They had flown over the still-smouldering ruin of the power station. Kendal shook his head. "A bad business," he said.

"You're telling me," Joanna shouted back. "It took us an hour to get the hospital's generator working. It was chaos!"

"They're alarmed in the Capital, I can tell you."

"I bet they are!"

They stopped talking as the helicopter approached the sheer face of the mountains. The passengers concentrated on willing it up to the required altitude so that it could slip over the ridge. After some circling and loud complaints from the rotors, it did so.

Below them a vast plateau stretched, a blank face that seemed to cover the whole Earth. It was pock-marked in places by perfectly conical hills from which swirled patterns on the ground like the stream of sparks from a Catherine Wheel, marking the flow of water across the terrain during the brief rainy season — water which quickly drained away. The helicopter swooped down to a more comfortable altitude. Joanna felt her stomach rise and with it a feeling of elation intruded. This was how a bird must feel.

The helicopter made for a small settlement in the centre of the plateau. Kendal landed in a deserted place near a flagpole from which the red and yellow flag of Ras Al Surra fluttered. There was not a soul to be seen anywhere. Then, out of the mud-brick dwellings, from behind the dunes, Joanna saw a lone figure. Then another. Some children ran towards them. Soon the helicopter was surrounded by a hundred or so ragged people.

"There's your clinic, Joanna," said Kendal. "Look, I've got to find the Sheikh of the village and give him a letter from the government. I'll be back in twenty minutes."

"Twenty minutes!" exclaimed Joanna, surveying the humanity gathered around the orderly and his drugs. "Twenty years more like."

She did what she could. It was never as much as she would have liked. She dropped eye-drops into the milky irises of trachoma victims; she placed antibiotics into the hands of people with sores and infections; she gave aspirins to old men who complained of tiredness; she pinched the children and gave pictorial health literature to mothers . . . Then the orderly came to tell her that the allocated drugs were finished. She waited around, talked to the people as well as she could manage, and felt useless.

These clinics were better than nothing, she knew, but only just. Mary-Anne had once likened them to the putting of a Bandaid on to a spurting artery. To be effective, every fly-blown village in the region should have had a clinic — would have, given time. In the interim, however, these rushed, near-panicked sessions would have to suffice.

Trying to close her eyes to the symptoms she saw in the faces of the people who besieged her, Joanna waited anxiously for Kendal's return. The people pleaded for her help in a language she could barely understand and she found herself shrugging until her neck began to ache, pleading with the orderly to tell them that they would return soon. Then, quite suddenly, she was imagining herself back in Britain, and, like Peter Drury longing for a W. H. Smith, longed for a Boots. At this moment, she thought, she would give her right hand for a branch of Boots. Here, now, set down like a genie's palace among the scrub and sand-dunes.

She walked around the helicopter and the people followed her at a distance. Her favourite pantomime had been Aladdin and she remembered, as a child, shouting out her wishes to the fat genie who had appeared from behind a sudden, startling puff of dry ice: "A doll's house; a doll with lots of changes of clothes." Then, suddenly silent, she had mouthed her third wish: "Make my Mummy get better."

She had got her first two wishes, but the third had been beyond the ability of the genie of the Lamp. Mummy, in hospital at the time of the panto, had never left it. She had been playing with her doll when her father had come in and told her that Mummy was in heaven with Grannie and Grandad and God and Tiggy, the cat.

Joanna never played with her doll again.

An only child, she had lived with her dad; come home from school each day to cook a meal for him; alternated homework with ironing and dusting; grown up fast. She knew at twelve that she wanted to be a nurse and had never changed her mind. At twelve she also knew whether Dad had changed his linen and which shirt went with which of his suits. She trained at a local hospital, in Chester, and, after her SRN, went straight on to Midwifery. Boys had not figured much. There had not been time. Dad, forty-plus at her birth, had retired on the day she had received her Midwifery diploma. He had mooned about the house for a year, attempting to turn his hand to household tasks. He burned stews and shrank shirts. Then she had come home one night to find him comatose at the foot of the stairs. Joanna had tried to kiss him back to life. She had biffed his chest with her efficient fists but to no avail. Dad had died and she could not pass the foot of the stairs without tears welling. Soon she could not bear the house. She put it up for sale and applied for the post in Saffina with Save the Children.

Then Kendal was back, accompanied by a veiled woman who was carrying a baby.

"I think we've got a case of Smallpox here, Joanna."

Joanna looked at the baby. "Yes, I think we have."

Mother and baby were taken aboard the helicopter to be flown to the hospital in Saffina.

The people gathered round, some with their hands out in a begging gesture. Then the rotors started and the crowd rushed back. They crouched and hid their eyes from the dust churned up by the helicopter's slipstream. When they took off, Joanna could see, through the dust, a circle of cowering people.

The woman with the baby was shrieking with alarm. Joanna tried to calm her. When she looked down, the plateau was as flat and blank as when they had approached it. There was not a sign of life anywhere.

"Bleak bloody spot, eh?" said Kendal.

"Hell," replied Joanna. "I'm worried about Smallpox, though. I hear there's a case on Zarut but the mother won't bring the baby to the clinic. I suppose I'll have to go over and have a look."

Kendal nodded. "Those buggers in the Capital don't know they're born."

"No, it's a different world up there. Where next?"

"The back of the back of beyond," smiled Kendal. "Um Hoot."

"Ah, yes. Um Hoot," sighed Joanna.

Peter Drury arrived back at his prefab to find Ibrahim cooking fish on a small wood fire built a couple of yards away from the front door. He had also rigged up a primitive tent which stretched from the wall of the house and was cleverly hung by string pulleys to a nearby Mashwaq tree. Under this shade Ibrahim knelt by the fire watching the fish intently.

"Well, I can see what you've been up to!" exclaimed Peter as he carried his briefcase from the ticking Landrover to his front door.

"Fishing," replied Ibrahim, hardly looking up from the fire.

"You mean you've been fishing this morning! How did you get to the sea?"

"On foot. And I walked back too. I caught three fish like this. It didn't take long."

"Well! That's wonderful. I don't have anything in the house. I had been going to go to Bilad Saffina to buy a tin of Chinese vegetables. But this is much better."

"Speak English please," said Ibrahim.

"Ah, yes. English," observed Peter.

He taught Ibrahim "fish", "fire", "lunch", "stick", and "fan" — Ibrahim was using a piece of cardboard to fan the fire. Ibrahim repeated the words again and again. Then Peter went into the prefab to change. He saw at once that the place was different: his clothes and books had been arranged into tidy piles; there was not a speck of dust anywhere; the bathroom was spotless. Even the mirror, which had had a manufacturer's label stuck to it, was now clear.

Delighted, Peter wandered from room to room. Everything was spotless. The mattress and sheets he had given to Ibrahim were neatly arranged on the floor of the bedroom at the back of the house. Wrapped in a sarong, Peter returned to the door.

"Thank you, Ibrahim. The house is very clean."

Ibrahim frowned. "English. Say it in English, please."

"Thank you, Ibrahim. The house is very clean," Peter said in English.

Ibrahim repeated the sentence. He pointed to the prefab: "House". Peter nodded. Then Ibrahim made a gesture, rubbing his hands and looking at them happily. "Clean," he said.

"Test me!" Ibrahim said, returning to the fire.

"What's that?" asked Peter, pointing to the fish.

"Fish . . . that's fish."

"What's that?"

"Fire . . . that's fire."

Peter continued to test Ibrahim on his memory and was amazed that he did not make even one error. He had an exceptional memory.

"Very good!" exclaimed Peter.

"Thank you, Peter," replied Ibrahim in English.

Peter badly wanted to ask Ibrahim what he was doing here and why he should choose to stay with him. He had half expected that the lad would have left by the time he got back from work and was strangely pleased and surprised to find him there. He had not seemed over-impressed by his bare home — nor by the corned beef sandwiches Peter had prepared for them for the evening meal. Nice then that he had

99

decided to stay around a while, a big bonus that he had worked so hard for his keep. It was a good feeling to share again, to have somebody to think about, to trip over, perhaps to argue with. Solitude had been descending into loneliness.

The two ate the fish with their fingers in the shade at the front door. It was hot but under the meagre awning it wasn't too bad, almost pleasant. And the fish was wonderful, like no fish Peter had ever tasted, almost like a succulent chicken, but with much more flavour.

They ate in silence but after the meal, when they had washed, Ibrahim said, in English, "You teacher, yes?"

"Yes."

The boy nodded. "Fish, fire, lunch. What's that? Stick fan, thank you, the house is very clean," he said and looked at Peter expectantly.

"More? You want more? You're insatiable!" laughed Peter.

"Yes! More! What is insatiable?"

Peter told him in Arabic.

"Yes, I am insatiable."

Peter was not sure he was ready for all this enthusiasm. His neat bedroom beckoned him for an hour's snooze. But he did not feel he could let the lad down. It was not often that he came upon anybody so keen.

He sighed, bowing to the inevitable, and went into his room to find a copybook. Then an idea occurred to him. He grabbed his cassette recorder and returned to the front door.

With Ibrahim watching his every move, Peter wrote the alphabet in the copybook. He drew little arrows to show the direction the pencil should move. Then he turned on the cassette recorder and slowly spoke the names of the letters on to a cassette. He showed Ibrahim how to work the machine and then said, "Learn them. I'm going to take a nap."

Ibrahim nodded.

"If I'm not up in a couple of hours, give me a call. We can go for a swim," Peter told Ibrahim as he left him.

He slept and dreamed of the mountains of Wales. He was climbing scree but it did not take any effort. He seemed to be flying up it and feeling the joy of reaching the summit. Then he was climbing again and reaching another summit and surveying another vista. The feeling of triumph as he came to the end of each climb, all in his dream ridiculously easy, was intense. Triumph after triumph passed before his sleeping eyes. The kingdoms of the world were laid out below his feet and he could resist all temptations. He did not want to possess any of them. Merely to see them from on high, earning the right so to do by his effort, was enough.

Ibrahim had to shake him to wake him up.

"What do I say in English when I want to wake you up?" he asked.

"Wake up! Time to get up!" he told Ibrahim in a daze.

Then he mimed realistically, waking up and then, after a pause, getting up.

Ibrahim watched him closely.

Scratching himself, Peter went to the bathroom and poured water over his face. Then he went out to the porch.

The sun had lost some of its power and was edging towards the horizon, from the perspective of the prefab anyway, over the nearby flat upland. He looked down and saw that Ibrahim had been practising his alphabet. He had filled page after page with letters, and, as Peter turned the pages, he noted with pleasure and amazement that the letters became better and better.

"Very good, Ibrahim!" he said, genuinely pleased. "Time for a swim. You've earned it."

"Where are we swimming?" asked Ibrahim in Arabic.

"In the sea, of course. Near Saffina. We can go in the Landrover."

"No. I don't want to go to Saffina."

"Ah, you don't." Peter scratched his head. "Well then, we can go to the wadi."

"Where's that?"

"Back towards the interior."

"Good."

Peter grabbed a towel and they got into the Landrover and headed along the track.

Ibrahim said, "A, B, C, D, E, F, G, H, I, J, K, L, M, N, O, P, Q, R, S, T, U, V, W, X, Y, Z."

"Very good. You're amazing!"

"Amazing?"

Peter translated.

"I am amazing and insatiable."

"Yes, you are."

Peter taught Ibrahim all the words he could think of on the way to the wadi. The boy repeated them and there they stayed in his brain like a fly stays on sticky paper. Peter had heard how phenomenal the Arab memory could be, but he had never encountered anything like this. Teaching Ibrahim would be no trouble at all. He would do it with pleasure. After all he had the time and Ibrahim was company.

They reached the wadi. Peter stripped off his sarong, and, naked, dived into the water. He swam down for a couple of strokes and then let the water take him slowly up to the surface. The sun percolated down through the water. The little fish nibbled at him as if he had never been away. It was cold. It was still heaven.

He surfaced to see Ibrahim, stripped of his dish–dash but wearing his underwear, making tentative moves to lower himself into the water. Peter splashed him, then grabbed his leg and pulled him in. They fought one another in the water, ducking and surfacing and fighting for breath. But Ibrahim soon tired of the water and got out. He sat in the sun at the edge of the pool while Peter went on with his swim.

The best thing about the place was the clarity of the water. He could swim down and see everything as clear as day. Down he went again and again, each time he stayed down longer, hoping he would be able to panic Ibrahim. But when he came back to the surface Ibrahim just said, "Good."

Then, on one of his dives, he saw that there was a hole in the steep side of the pool. It was quite wide and he felt he could almost go along it. He wanted to. He thought he detected light at the end of it. But, he thought, he had better have a fresh supply of air before attempting to swim along it — and returned to the surface.

Ibrahim had started washing his dish-dash in the water of the wadi. He looked up and smiled at Peter. Peter lifted his face to the sun for a minute or two, feeling very happy and content. His bloodstream now thoroughly aerated, he dived down and made for the hole.

He was in it and then, with no effort at all, he was at the end and at the surface of a little side pool. So porous was the rock that the water had worn through and formed a tiny pool, the shape of a water font at a church door, on the other side of the rock face. Yet, between this pool and the main pool, a wall of rock fifteen foot high and quite sheer intruded.

Pleased with his discovery, Peter started to climb to the top of the rock. It was not as easy as he thought. Being naked, the hot rock scorched him. He had trouble getting a grip on it and it took a while to reach the summit. When he did so he found himself looking down on the larger pool and at Ibrahim gazing into the water, looking worried.

Peter did not say anything, but launched himself from the top of the rock. He landed in the water a hair's breadth from the boy's nose.

Ibrahim looked at Peter, not believing what he saw.

"I'm a jinn, Ibrahim!"

"You're not a jinn, Peter! You're a joker!" replied Ibrahim. "Where did you go?"

Peter, leaning on the edge of the pool, still in the water, said, "Come in and I'll show you."

After some persuasion Ibrahim swam down behind Peter and through the hole to the small pool behind.

"Isn't it amazing!" exclaimed Peter.

Ibrahim nodded. "I am amazing. It is amazing."

They swam back through the hole. Peter towelled himself dry, Ibrahim got back into his dish-dash, which had already dried in the warm wind.

"Come on, Ibrahim, we'll go home and get your English course started," said Peter, happy and cheered to have a companion, feeling fit and cool and glad, in every fibre of his being, to be alive.

★

Peter taught Ibrahim for three or four hours that evening. Then, wanting to get to bed, he recorded what he had taught on the cassette player and left Ibrahim with a candle to study by. Ibrahim reverently carried his copy book and pen into his room. Then he turned:

"Good night, teacher," he said.

"Good night, Ibrahim," answered Peter.

Peter Drury, a happy teacher, brushed his teeth and lay down on the mattress. "Good night, teacher," he thought. Much better than "Sir". That title would do nicely. He felt worthy of it tonight. Like an engineer, he was building in Ibrahim's mind a complex machine which would change his thinking and widen his horizons. Each day a new pipe would be added, a new cog for Ibrahim to turn to his own uses. There was satisfaction to be had in the slow construction of the great machine of Language. He sighed, content.

His oil lamp was within reach and gave him sufficient light to read by. He picked up *Small is Beautiful* and started to read.

Then he heard a banging on his curtainless window. A little concerned and wary he took the oil lamp and went over to the window, sliding it open.

"Yes? Who's there?" he called out in Arabic.

"You're a bloody sitting target! I could have shot you dead — easy as anything as you sat reading that bloody book! The name's Hepworth, head of the Desert Regiment. Sorry it's taken me so long to pay you a pastoral visit but there you are. Rushed off our feet just now as you can imagine."

Peter could see Hepworth's shadowy face in the light of the lamp.

"Nice to meet you, Mr Hepworth. Would you like to come in?"

"Captain Hepworth, actually. No, I've come to invite you for a nightcap up at Research with Simon Nicholson."

"Research?"

"Not surprised you haven't heard of it. Good thing too. You're not supposed to. It's a bit hush-hush. Get some clothes on!"

104

Peter was not certain he wanted to venture out with the strange apparition that was Hepworth, but he felt he would welcome the chance to talk with English people.

"Right-ho," he said.

He pulled himself into a shirt and trousers, shuffled into his flip-flops and went into Ibrahim's room. "I'm going to visit the house of an Englishman in Saffina. I'll see you in the morning, Ibrahim."

Ibrahim had been crouched on his knees, copying letters into his book. He looked round and asked, "Which Englishman?"

"Simon Nicholson. Why?"

"Nothing," replied Ibrahim. "I'll see you tomorrow. How do you say that in English, please?"

"I'll see you tomorrow."

"Thank you, teacher. I'll see you tomorrow."

"OK. I'll see you tomorrow."

Peter left the house hurriedly. Hepworth was waiting at the front door.

"Got someone staying, have you?" he asked.

"Yes," replied Peter.

"Who?"

Peter hesitated. He was tempted to tell Hepworth that it was none of his business. He was already sure that he did not like the man one little bit. "A friend," he said. "Your vehicle or mine?"

"Mine," said Hepworth curtly, annoyed that Peter had not given him the full facts about his companion.

On the way to Nicholson's house, Hepworth took time to give Peter some cautionary advice. "I should have come to see you earlier . . . wearing my Desert Regiment hat of course."

"Well, I have been a little short of European company. Still, all the people at the Education office have been very kind."

"Arabs?"

"Arabs and Sudanese, yes."

Hepworth sniffed and continued: "Yes . . . well . . . I should have given you a talking to earlier. What I want to say is that it's bloody crazy them sending you here. You don't have the necessary security arrangements stuck out there in that god-forsaken shack."

Peter felt a little put out at hearing his prefab described as a shack but said nothing.

"I suppose they thought everything had calmed down and that it was safe to send you but you've seen what's happened to the power station. Things are hotting up again."

There was a tone of relish in Hepworth's voice.

"Yes, I suppose it is rather worrying," said Peter.

"Have you got a gun?"

"A gun! Me? No, I haven't."

"I'll give you one — for your own protection."

"Really, Mr . . . Captain Hepworth, I don't think it would be appropriate. I have to visit schools. I haven't even got chalk for the teachers or books for the kids. I can't see that a gun would be the right thing at all — unless I use it to get the government to get off their arses."

Hepworth said nothing but increased his speed. The Landrover flew dangerously over the rutted road.

Then they were on the track going parallel to the ocean. Hepworth honked his horn and flashed his lights as he approached Nicholson's compound. The guard opened the gates briskly. Hepworth saluted and gunned the Landrover to its parking place.

Peter saw the man he supposed to be Nicholson emerging from the door of the bungalow. He was wearing a white dish-dash and held a drink in his hand. He was tall, about thirty-five years old and reminded Peter of a missionary priest. His long, rather beakish face, the weak chin, had an air of asceticism about it.

"Nicholson," said the man, holding out his hand.

"Peter Drury. Nice to meet you, Mr Nicholson."

"Call me Simon."

Nicholson offered Peter a drink. He asked for a gin and tonic and drank it appreciatively. It was wonderful to taste alcohol again, especially this drink. He savoured it as he talked to Nicholson. Hepworth opted out of the conversation, falling on a week-old copy of *The Daily Telegraph*.

"Are you settling down all right?" Nicholson asked him.

"Yes. Fine, thank you. There are problems of course but they're to be expected. We need endless things for the schools and they're hard to get. The government is a bit on the slow side."

Nicholson leaned forward in his chair, interested. "What do you need?" he asked.

"Well, books for one thing. There's hardly an English textbook in the whole region. Chalk. Blackboards. That sort of thing."

"I'll see what I can do."

Peter was impressed. "If you could that would be wonderful."

"The Council have pushed you into a pretty rum place. No electricity out there, is there?"

"No. I have a generator but it's so noisy that I prefer to do without it. Anyway the whole of Saffina is without power now the power station has gone. It could be worse."

"So all in all you're quite happy?"

"Yes. I'm making friends among the people at the Education office. People there have been very kind."

"You travel around a lot?"

"Yes. I have the whole Eastern Region to cover. It's quite an area."

"It certainly is. Another drink?"

Peter could not believe he had emptied his glass so fast. "Yes, please. I'm sorry, I rather guzzled the first one. It's so nice to have a good drink with some ice in it."

"Yes, it is," said Nicholson.

He handed Peter another drink, and said, "You do realise that Saffina and the whole Eastern Region is a very dangerous place?"

"Well," replied Peter, "I hadn't, but Captain Hepworth here has been telling me about the er . . . problems."

Nicholson laughed loudly. "Problems! Hardly the word I would use. We're in the midst of what promises to be an ongoing crisis, Mr Drury. If I were you I would give some serious thought to your position here."

This was such a sudden turn around in Nicholson's attitude that Peter really did not know what to say.

Nicholson took advantage of the other's silence to say, "Well I can see that from your perspective things do seem to be going on quite happily. However, even you cannot have failed to see what has happened to the power station. I am in a position to know about these things. 'Research' is the local name for 'Intelligence'. I am the bod who is expected to have his finger on the button — and I think I do. Believe me, there are people here who are fermenting violent revolution against the government of King Fadl. These people will stop at nothing. They have no respect for human life. Do you know that seven expatriate workers were killed when the power station was bombed? And bombed it was. I am sorry to say this, because nobody wants peace to reign in this region more than I do. But it is my considered opinion that you should think about leaving here before anything dreadful happens."

Nicholson sat back in his rattan chair and sipped from his drink. He watched Peter with interest to see how his words were sinking in. Hepworth had looked up from his paper to observe the scene.

Peter did not know what to say. The gin was working its magic and he wondered if it was the alcohol somehow perverting his judgement so that he could not take seriously what the men were saying. He looked around the room. The rugs, the Kuwaiti chests, the private electricity supply, everything spoke of power and authority — backed up what Nicholson had been saying to him. He would be a fool not to believe this powerful government man — wouldn't he? Yet something deep inside him distrusted Nicholson and his henchman, Hepworth. It was all too pat, somehow. The way Hepworth had sneaked up on him at home, like the school bully trying to alarm the school swot. Perhaps this evening had been a plot between bullies. "Let's go and put the wind up the brainy bonce in his prefab." After what he had seen in the schools and villages of the Eastern Region, there was something distasteful about Nicholson with his power and possessions. He felt he was sitting in a time warp, a throw-back to an

England he kept trying to tell himself had died. In the Sudan, whenever any Sudanese had tried to make him guilty about the past he had said that England was not like that any more. England was just an island that happened to have a language that the world wanted. But had that been true, after all? He had only ever half-convinced those Sudanese.

What were these two doing here anyway? How could they be living here, like this, at the fag-end of the twentieth century? Nicholson said he wanted peace in Ras Al Surra. But did such a man ever want peace? Was not his finger always itching to be on some trigger? By what right did they lord it over the Ras Al Surrans? Peter thought of Batool and the Sea Captain and Mr Shukry in the Interior and Ibrahim poring over his alphabet at home. Did these people present a threat? Did these people feel there was a threat? But there was no denying the fact that someone — and someone who meant business — had blown up the power station. Peter looked into his gin and tonic, not knowing what to think. Then up into the blue eyes of Nicholson. He had never seen bluer eyes.

"Well, you've given me some food for thought, Mr Nicholson. Simon."

"Just doing my duty, Peter."

They talked for a while about Zarut, the place where Peter would be going the following morning. They talked about Wales. Nicholson talked about soft, green, lacking-moral-courage, Britain and expressed the hope that Mrs Thatcher would make it a country fit for gentlemen once again. Peter had a third drink and remarked that if a gentleman is defined — as Cardinal Newman had defined him — as "One who never inflicts pain", then he doubted it.

Nicholson was silent. Then Hepworth grew restless and said that he would drive Peter home.

At home Peter found that Ibrahim had fallen asleep over his book. He snuffed out the candle and pulled a blanket over the boy. He looked down at him and thought, "I'm going to teach you English!"

Then he went back to his room, stripped off his clothes and lay down on his mattress.

"Well . . ." he began, wondering if he should try to think about what had happened that evening. He decided not and fell immediately asleep.

Very early the following morning Nicholson passed by Peter Drury's prefab where both Peter and Ibrahim were still curled in sleep.

He drove on, through the oasis of Bilad Saffina and along the track that led to the Desert Regiment Camp. At the gate he tooted to wake up the snoozing guard, thinking what a poor show Hepworth presided over. Then he pulled up outside Hepworth's quarters and walked into his rooms.

Hepworth lay naked on his bed. A whisky bottle stood, three-quarters empty, by the bed; a whisky glass snoozed on the pillow next to his head.

Nicholson watched Hepworth for a long moment. God, he was hairy, he thought. Hair everywhere but on his head. And three colours: white, red and black. It was not a pretty sight first thing in the morning but Nicholson stood fascinated by this vision of a body in the very act of going to seed, closing and locking the door on life . . . a house on a hilltop, slowly slipping, starting its journey downhill to the little yew-fringed cemetery in the valley below.

He tiptoed over to the bed, and, very carefully, reached under Hepworth's pillow. His hand touched the revolver. Slowly and deftly he pulled out the gun, and paused with it lying in the flat of his hand. He held it out in front of him and aimed it at Hepworth's head. Then he cocked the trigger.

The click roused Hepworth. He puckered up his face, like a baby deciding whether it was time for a cry. He opened his eyes. What he saw when his stuck-closed eyes opened appalled him. Nicholson was smiling behind the revolver.

"Simon! What are you doing? Don't!"

Nicholson laughed heartily and lowered the revolver. "You're never too old to learn a new lesson, old chap. I got this out from under that bald pate of yours. If I can do it then anybody can do it."

"Yes, I suppose you're right. I must be more careful,"

replied Hepworth, covering himself with a crumpled sheet. "I'll just pour some water over myself. Back in a mo. Turn on the coffee machine. The boy will have charged it."

He went to the bathroom and stood under a cold shower. He was shaking and it was not only from the effects of the whisky he had drunk after returning home. No, it was the apparition that had confronted him upon waking which had really upset him. He felt that that picture of Nicholson pointing a gun, on the surface only a joke, was in reality a picture he had seen before at the darkest point in the night when dreams became dark visions of empty bank accounts; of putting on a shirt in a doctor's surgery having been told that the pain that anguishes will only let up in death; of Nicholson, tired of him, calling him yesterday's man, cocking a revolver and firing a bullet into his pleading face . . .

He wished the water were colder, but slowly it settled him down. The water told him as it tingled and enlivened him that it was just one of Simon's jokes. That was Simon all over. He towelled himself down briskly and put on his dressing-gown. Yes, Simon was as mad as a March hare. During the civil war he had been notorious for his sick sense of humour. He had once held a drunken colleague down and forcibly circumcised him with a Swiss Army knife because the fellow was going to have to "go native" on a spying foray. Oh, he could be a bastard all right! But it might have saved the chap's life. Nothing like a foreskin for blowing one's cover! Nicholson had been cruel in order to be kind. Yes, that was it. Now was like then. You always remembered a lesson learnt with pain.

"I should be more careful with the revolver, Simon. Good of you to point it out," he managed.

Nicholson nodded. "Thank your lucky stars it was me and not some cocoa out for blood," he said, handing Hepworth a mug of coffee.

"Too right."

Nicholson sat on the bed while Hepworth brushed his hair and climbed into his uniform.

"What did you make of that English teacher?" Nicholson asked.

"Bit of a wet sort of cove, I reckon. Probably queer too."

"What makes you say that? Why do you think he's queer?"

"I reckon he's got some Arab lad in the house with him. I heard them talking just before he came out with me to your compound. Couldn't understand what they were saying but the fellow was definitely an Arab."

"You don't say."

Hepworth drained his mug of coffee and poured himself some more.

"What did you think?" he asked.

Nicholson offered his mug for a refill. "He seemed a standard sort of Brit Cow bod to me. Not a bad sort. A bit of a second-rater. But I can't say I caught any whiff of pansy about him."

"Do you reckon he'll take the hint?"

"I doubt it. I think we'll have to scare him a bit more before he runs, don't you?"

"I suppose so," replied Hepworth unhappily.

"And that's what I've come to see *you* about. Come and sit down by me, Captain Hepworth. You are shortly going to have greatness thrust upon you!"

Hepworth, now unexpectedly reimmersed in the darkest of his dark dreams, approached the bed and sat down next to Nicholson. Obediently.

10

"Are you sure you don't want to go to Zarut with me, Ibrahim?" Peter asked.

It was 7.30 a.m. Ibrahim had got up before Peter and made him breakfast of fried tinned beans, bread and tea. They ate together, using the floor of the living room spread with a cloth as a table.

Peter had told Ibrahim where he was going, asked him if he would like to accompany him, but Ibrahim had refused, rather vehemently. Then Peter had tried to find out a little more about Ibrahim, where he came from, what he was doing in Saffina, what his plans were.

But to each question Ibrahim merely shrugged and finally Peter desisted.

"Maybe you will tell me when you can tell me in English," he suggested.

Ibrahim smiled and nodded at that.

Peter took fifteen minutes to review the work he had done with Ibrahim the previous evening. He had remembered everything. The book was now half-filled with capital letters and Peter thought it would soon be time to introduce him to cursive script. He held back, however. Soon enough books would come from the Capital. He would give him one or two writing practice books then. Better to concentrate on spoken English.

"Did all go well last night with the Englishman?" asked Ibrahim as Peter was gathering his things together before leaving.

"I think so. I got a little drunk."

Ibrahim scowled. "Alcohol is very bad."

"Yes, I suppose it is, but it is also very nice."

"And Mr Nicholson. Did you like his house?" asked Ibrahim.

It seemed strange that the boy should remember Nicholson's name, but then Peter wondered why he should wonder. Ibrahim did not forget anything he had been told. "Yes, it is a splendid house. It makes this one look like a slum," he said.

Peter left the prefab and drove towards the Education office. As he drove memories of the meeting with Nicholson and Hepworth came back to haunt him. He began to see strewn rocks near the road as hiding places for rough insurgents who would kidnap him and kill him. As he passed them and each proved harmless he wondered to himself how much he should worry about the situation. The two men were not fools. They had experience in Ras Al Surra. They would surely know whether the place was safe or not. Also, the power station had been destroyed. Yet his instinct told him that he was not wrong to see Saffina as a safe place. Peter generally trusted his instincts. He had found in his climbing that he somehow "knew" whether a foothold would support him or let him down. He had not once been wrong.

After reporting to the office and telling Mr Siddiqui that he was going off to Zarut to visit the Girls' School, he drove through the old centre of Saffina, past the fish market and out to the channel that separates Saffina from Zarut.

On the way people waved to him and Peter waved back. The man in the flimsy post office, Nasser, stopped him, gave him a letter from home and started to chat. As they talked Peter's fears completely evaporated as moisture does into anti-damp crystals. Nasser asked him how his work was going, was happy when Peter told him about his fight for books, saying that the Prophet had said that all good Muslims should seek knowledge as far away as China. He had a son, he said, and was anxious for him to do well.

Peter left Nasser and continued through the untidy high-walled alleys that lay between the centre and the jetty. These were decent people. These were "folk". The easy chat he had just had with Nasser could have taken place in any post office anywhere. These people wanted what was best for their families. They were close cousins to the beautiful ragged people of his village in the Sudan. They did not mean him any harm. No, if there was harm, that harm would be more likely to come from the barbed wire compound of the man with the too-blue eyes.

He left his Landrover next to the Customs house near the jetty. The little outboard ferry boat was on the Zarut side and he waved his arms to attract the attention of the boatman who was chatting to a group of old men. The boatman did not seem to notice.

As he waited another vehicle pulled up and stopped beside his. Out of it stepped a vision of a young nurse in a white uniform. Peter felt himself suddenly tense up. He did not know why this happened, had never known why. He wondered, if she came over to talk, would he be able to reply coherently — or would he babble? Would he be like he had been when leaning against those pub bars in small Welsh villages? Girls came up and spoke and he, tense and over-eager, wearing his virginity like a clown's red nose, had talked too much about things they did not want to hear; had watched their eyes glaze over; had known that, once again, he was coming across to them as a hearty type emitting a masculine, yet sexless, odour.

The nurse marched straight over to him and smiled. He lost much of his anxiety then and thought everything might be all right.

"Hello. I'm Joanna Marchant. Now, let me guess. You're the English teacher."

"So you *do* exist!" exclaimed Peter. He had heard talk of an English nurse but was beginning to doubt the truth of it. "I'm Peter Drury. I am a teacher really but here I'm an inspector."

"What do you inspect?" asked Joanna. She spoke the question in a brusque manner which put him on edge again, made him feel, somehow, that he was lying.

"The schools of the Eastern Region."

"Are there any?"

"Over twenty."

Joanna's driver, carrying a heavy bag of medical equipment, came and stood next to Joanna, who introduced him to Peter. The man, whose name was Sa'ad, was very black, with a navy-blue patina to his skin, and looked severe. He shook Peter's hand unsmilingly, then shouted over the creek to the boatman who was still talking to his friends. At once the boatman got up and made for his boat.

"How long have you been here?" Peter asked Joanna.

"Couple of months. What about you?"

"About the same time. Funny we haven't met."

"Yes," agreed Joanna, "but I've been very busy. Rushed off my feet in fact. Have you met the other two Brits?"

"Hepworth and Nicholson? Yes. Funny thing, I met them last night."

Something in Peter's voice must have hinted to Joanna what he thought of the two.

"Yes. I know what you mean," said Joanna. "An odd couple."

"Yes."

The ferry boat was heading over to Saffina at last. It looked in danger of being swept up into the creek behind, so strong was the current of the incoming tide. But the boatman did not seem in the least concerned and sang a meandering song which reached Peter and Joanna and caught them in its mood. The song was about fishing in the deep ocean; about pirates and women left weeping at home. The rushing waters accompanied the sound which was rough and moving.

"The last corner of Arabia," sighed Joanna.

"Yes. We're lucky."

Joanna shrugged. "I think in the future we will look back and think we were lucky. Now it's all a bit . . . well . . . *real* somehow."

Peter nodded. "Why are you going to Zarut, Joanna?"

"Two reasons. We've heard that there's Smallpox there. Also I'm looking for Tayaba."

"Tayaba?"

"Yes. Tayaba." And Joanna smiled at Sa'ad who beamed, and whose character in that beam underwent a seachange. "Tayaba is a baby who weighs less than three pounds. The mother was persuaded to give birth to her in our clinic. You've never seen anything like Tayaba. The tiniest bit of life in the world. A face of an octogenarian. Folds of skin hanging down with absolutely no flesh under it. Well, I put her straight into intensive care. Last night I found that some damned silly orderly had let the family take her home. Imagine! So I'm off to search for Tayaba. What about you?"

"I'm paying a visit to Zarut Girls' School."

The ferry arrived and Joanna, Sa'ad and Peter got on. The boatman sang them all the way across to Zarut.

"It's a rum sort of place," said Joanna as they started to walk across the sand towards the village, a façade of high mud-brick houses interspersed with the flotsam of shacks made from palm fronds and clapboard. "You know there's no drinking water over here? None. Every drop has to be carried over. And no electricity. Even when we had a power station Zarut wasn't deemed important enough to get any of it. Zarut is the slum of Saffina."

They followed Sa'ad across the sand.

"What do you think happened to the power station?" Peter asked.

"Search me," replied Joanna. "Hepworth came round to me full of horror stories about the rebels. It could be true, I suppose. I know there has been a lot of trouble in the past. But I don't know. It all seems too peaceful."

"Exactly what I think."

Sa'ad was calling out at the door of a tiny hut. Then he lifted a sacking cover over the doorway and went through, ushering Joanna in after him.

"I suppose I'd better be off," said Peter.

"No, you come too. You may learn something," replied Joanna.

Inside, the hut was dark and smelled of babies and goats.

Tayaba lay in a corner of the room. Her father sat next to her fanning the tiny creature to keep the flies off her. Tayaba's mother was nowhere to be seen.

Joanna picked Tayaba up and started cleaning her. Then she reached into her bag for a piece of gauze and wet it with some water, feeding it to Tayaba, who sucked hungrily.

Peter looked on helplessly, captivated by the huge eyes in

Tayaba's tiny old head. Some children had found their way into the hut and were gawking at the scene. Tayaba's eyes wandered over them, seemingly with great interest, but with sadness too, like a princess trapped in a strange, grotesque body. Peter could hear waves breaking in the distance. He felt suddenly sad and lost.

"If we can just keep her from getting the runs she may pull through. She's really a fine specimen, despite her puniness." And Joanna looked up at Peter, who was starting to cry. "One baby's enough to deal with at the moment, thank you very much!" she exclaimed, and set about preparing an injection for Tayaba. "Where's her damned mother? I need her here!"

Peter asked the man in Arabic and the man shrugged and replied that she had died during the night. His voice was flat. He did not seem sad. He was completely matter-of-fact about the event.

Peter told Joanna and Joanna said to Tayaba, "Poor kid!" and held the tiny claw hand.

Joanna injected Tayaba, who did not cry out, and momentarily thought of Peter's tears. They were natural. A month or two ago she too would have cried, had cried, but now she was tougher. She had come out to clean up Ras Al Surra, to piff-paff its diseases away with the cutting edge of her skill and her character. She was learning that progress was the act of walking up a down escalator. One rushed for the top at first but quickly got into the way of looking back and finding reassurance in not being on the first step, about to be tripped up by the bottom edge. In Peter's tears she saw her own. She liked him for his tears. She didn't yet know him but had seen enough to make her want to know more.

Peter Drury, for his part, was intensely moved by Joanna. He watched her pick up Tayaba and wrap her in a little blanket from her bag. He thought how nice it would be to be picked up by Joanna and taken care of. But, he thought, she probably had a man at home, and, even if she hadn't, he could not imagine that she would be in the least attracted to him. Women just weren't. In the mountain cottages during week-end climbs Peter had always been a male wallflower, clutching his pint, chatting with other men, while those who could, did unseemly things behind settees. Girls always seemed to become silly when he started talking to them. He wondered if they saw something in him that he couldn't see. If they did he wished they would tell him. But, of course, they never told him. They just glanced sideways at their girlfriends, giggled, played with their fringes and mentioned, pointedly, Roberts and Iains and Tonys left at home, worried and forlorn, standing guard over their bottom drawers and Building Society accounts.

With her back to him, still cradling Tayaba, Joanna said to Peter, "Tell the father we're taking her back to the hospital. She can't stay here. There isn't a hope in hell for her here."

And Peter told the father, who seemed not to care. And Tayaba, her head resting on Joanna's shoulder, stared knowingly and long into Peter's moist eyes.

Peter left Joanna at the jetty. She had decided to take Tayaba straight back to the clinic and would return to Zarut in the afternoon to check on Smallpox.

Half an hour later he found himself seated in the tiny staffroom of Zarut Girls' School chatting happily with six female teachers. They pushed Chinese shortbread biscuits and Pepsis and milky teas in his direction. They flirted with him innocently and made him feel like a film-star. Was this the treatment Arab men got from their wives? If it was, he quite envied them. However, he suspected that it wasn't.

At last he was able to get away and go and see Batool Al Chanri's class. The school was situated in an old, single-storey building very close to the high water mark. From where he sat Peter could see the ocean. In the distance dhows rose and fell on the swell. Batool had to raise her voice to be heard over the crashing waves outside the glassless window.

Batool introduced him to the children in the class. They turned in their seats to gaze at him.

"Greet dear our inspector, girls!"

"Good morning, Sir! Welcome, Sir!" cried the girls, in harsh falsetto.

Peter squirmed.

"Now sing, girls!" shouted Batool.

And the girls sang:

"I'm H–A–P–P–Y! I'm H–A–P–P–Y!

That means . . . that means . . . I am happy . . . I am happy

To see you . . . to see you today!"

"Thank you girls! Oh, there's more?" shouted Peter, as the girls launched into a second verse.

"I'm G–L–A–D! I'm G–L–A–D!

That means . . . that means . . . I am glad . . . I am glad

To see you . . . to see you today!"

"Thank you, girls!"

"For nothing!" the girls shouted back.

Then Peter, the inspector of English for the Eastern Region of Ras Al Surra, sat back and watched Batool teach a wonderful lesson based on prepositions. To help her she used a picture drawn on an old sheet that she had pinned to the wall. Then she placed objects under, on, over, between, behind, on top of, next to, beside other objects and had the girls make up sentences.

The inspector felt a lump coming to his throat and thought of Tayaba. Would she make it far enough to sit in a class and learn as these children were learning? Or would she become a sad little bundle to be taken out to one of the sand-blown cemeteries? He prayed for Tayaba and for himself.

Tears welled up in his eyes when a little black girl in the corner of the room mistook "in" for "on". The class began a barely audible jeer, quickly stifled by Batool, who quietly explained the difference to the girl until she got it right. "If only my books would come!" thought Peter. "I'll pour books into the schools! I'll make sure they lack for nothing! I'll get the kids pen-friends in Britain! I'll . . ."

Then the lesson was over. He made his way back to the staffroom with Batool.

"I am sorry for the lesson. But what can we to do? We have such little here!" sighed Batool.

"I think you're wonderful!" said Peter.

Batool smiled at him and the smile dazzled him. Then, perhaps knowing that her smile held more beauty than a thin, too-tall Englishman could bear, Batool covered the smile with her dark right hand.

Peter turned away momentarily and closed his eyes. He saw Batool's smile behind his eyelids, as, having turned off the light last thing at night, one sees the light still.

He turned back to Batool. "Books! I'll bring you books!" he promised.

When Peter got back to the Education office it was about time to go home. He felt ready for a nap, the alcohol of the night before was taking its toll. But, on entering his office, he found a scrawled note: BOOKSES IS PRESENT, Mr Ahmed.

Peter whooped with delight and ran straight to Mr Ahmed's office at the other end of the corridor.

Mr Ahmed, dressed in a horizontally striped jacket and vertically striped trousers, greeted Peter enthusiastically, grabbed his arm and pushed him down into a chair. Then he shouted, "Rabiah!" to the teaboy, who appeared and took Mr Ahmed's order for tea. Rabiah had never appeared when Peter called. He was lost in admiration for the man and his admiration grew when Mr Ahmed said warmly, "Your bookses are here. You are lucky. There is nothing for History or Geography or Arabic. But for English there are bookses."

"That is good news! Where are they?"

"In the storeroom. They came this morning. Are you friend of the king?" He looked at Peter quizzically. "I think you are!"

"No, I don't think so. I think it's just pure luck."

Rabiah returned with the teas, closely followed by a tall, thirtyish man wearing shirt and pants, but sporting a fedayeen headcloth in a blue and white pattern. He listened as Mr Ahmed and Peter chatted, then, having ordered Rabiah to bring him a cup of tea also, grinned and said, "Have you understood the lesson?"

Mr Ahmed, who had been speaking English with Peter, lapsed back into Arabic like a man who sighs into his home after a heavy day at work.

"This is Mr Drury, our new inspector of English," he said. "And this is Mr Titi," he told Peter. "Mr Titi is an engineer."

The three sat down, and, once Mr Titi's tea had arrived and Rabiah was safely out of the room, Mr Ahmed said in English, looking to both right and left like a child doing kerb-drill, "We are in prison here in Ras Al Surra. I have a family far away but here I am a eunuch. Israel has my home. We used to own vast estates but now the Israelis have put up apartment blocks on them. Never trust Egyptians, my dear. All are snakes in the grass or peasants. The Ras Al Surrans are not bad people. Simple. A little crude. We are here to help."

"Have you understood the lesson?" asked Mr Titi in his impeccable English.

"Do not notice Mr Titi, my dear," said Mr Ahmed. "He is doing a joke. He speaks no English except that one sentence."

"But that sentence is wonderful!" exclaimed Peter in Arabic.

"Have you understood the lesson?" asked Mr Titi proudly.

Peter looked at his watch. He drank his tea down and told Mr Ahmed and Mr Titi that he wanted to see his books. They protested that his visit to them had been too short, so Peter sat down and asked if there was any news from Mr Nasawi.

"No news is good news," said Mr Ahmed in a funny tone. Peter did not pursue the subject. Probably, he reasoned, there was some friction between the two Arab brothers. He got up to leave. Once again they protested that it was early. But everyone always did that whenever anybody wanted to leave.

"Badree! Early!" the host would exclaim, in despairing tones.

"Badree min umrak, in sha'allah! Early in your life, God willing!" the departing guest, shuffling into sandals at the threshold, would reply.

Peter left, wondering if he would ever be able to sit and talk as the Arabs talked. Conversation was their greatest form of

122

expression. Like their lands, it did not stay still. It could not be accurately surveyed. It blew away on the wind.

The bookstore of the Education office was situated some way away, about two hundred yards along the coast from Nicholson's compound.

Only one man, a guard, was at the bookstore when Peter arrived, but he opened up the warehouse for him readily enough and watched as Peter rolled up his sleeves and started to sort out the books.

It took Peter three hours with the help of the guard to count and sort the books into tidy piles. He was delighted by the work, relished the feeling of sweat trickling down him and the mental effort of counting all the books carefully and accurately. All of them had bright colours which he knew would please the children. He saw himself carrying them around the Region and imagined the whoops of delight when the children received their copies of *Living English for the Arab World, Hamad the Diver, Green Island.*

At around 4 p.m. he finished his task. The other workers at the store were returning now from their afternoon break and were amazed to see what he had achieved. The guard, whose name was Othman, gave them an account of the work that Peter had done. He mimed the lifting and counting and carrying, smiling at Peter and calling him "My Brother". Finally he hugged Peter to him, lifting him off the ground and telling him he was too thin.

Peter, for his part, was unashamedly proud of his achievement and moved by the praise of the guard. This was work and useful work too. He could not believe that anybody in the world could have had more job satisfaction that day than he had had in the bookstore of Saffina on the eastern shores of the Arabian Sea.

Dripping sweat he drove away from the storeroom armed with a piece of paper that inventoried the books, in the knowledge that the following morning he could commence distribution.

He had also taken a set of books for Ibrahim — the first student in Ras Al Surra to attend Evening School.

11

Nicholson had heard that Peter Drury's books had arrived before Peter. He retained a man in the Education office who, in exchange for a weekly pittance, daily reported on any happenings in the world of Education. Almost always this information made Nicholson snooze, but he was mildly interested to hear about the arrival of the English books.

"That will please dear Mr Drury," he said to himself.

He left his office at noon and looked from his verandah at the Education storeroom. He had never liked the blank-walled building. He smiled and thought what an easy target it would make. Even Hepworth would be able to manage.

Over lunch Nicholson wondered why it was that he was so different from other men. He had little in common with anyone of his acquaintance. Hepworth was beneath contempt. Drury was wet and unutterably boring. The Scoutmaster type. A poppy-seller possibly.

What was it people lacked that he, Nicholson, had? He considered this as he drank his port at the conclusion of an excellent lunch.

He had received a conventional Church of England up-bringing from doting middle-class parents, of whom he was the only child. He had sensed very early on that he was different. He listened to fairy stories but knew they were lies, childish deceits. Of course he did not show the adults that he had tumbled to their wiles. It had been the same with religion. He had knelt in the boring pew between his parents and been absolutely certain that everything he heard and witnessed was plain untruth.

As he grew up he saw his contemporaries rejecting Christianity, but, and this had been incomprehensible to him, they hung on tenaciously to great swathes of the morality that went with it. Nicholson had not done this. He rejected such wet behaviour totally. After all, if one had thrown out the baby, why should one hang on to the bathwater — and, not only that, set up the bathwater as an icon? The Great of the world — the top politicians, the rulers, the successful heads of corporations, the great train robbers, the gnomes of Zurich, pop singers, art dealers, anybody with a will or a tendency to succeed had one thing in common: they made up their own version of what was "good". He embraced this philosophy and found when he tested it that it was correct. If one were ruthless enough one would succeed. But one had to for ever be on one's guard against the intrusion of "decency" and "altruism" and "compassion". These qualities were the gallows on which many an aspiring superman swung.

After lunch he contacted Hepworth over the radio telephone and told him to come to the compound immediately. Hepworth, somewhat peeved, had asked why.

"I have a little job for you to do," Nicholson had told him in his driest tone of voice.

Othman, the guard at the bookstore, stood in the dark outside the main door of the building. A worn prayer mat lay in the dust in front of his feet. Facing west, he raised his hands level with his head, bowed and knelt. Then he bent forward on the mat and touched his forehead to it in adoration.

It was the last prayer time of the day and the man had not missed one. In fact he could not recall a single day in his life when he had missed his prayers. Those prayers divided the paragraph of each day with necessary punctuation, without which it would have become meaningless.

He stood up, his lips reciting verses from the Koran. He then repeated his bow and his gestures of worship.

Perhaps he had sinned in his life, but God understood his sins — expected them almost — and would forgive him as long as he stayed faithful and submissive to Him until death. Anyway, sin was far behind him now, almost the actions of a different person completely. Before he had settled down he had been a sailor. Many had been the temptations in Bombay,

Zanzibar and the ports of the Malacca Straits to which he had journeyed. He had not been immune to the charms of the loose women who haunted the dhow harbours. He had sinned but he felt confident that Allah would forgive him. He had been a fair husband and caring father; he had not drunk liquor or smoked hashish; he had never once broken the Ramadhan fast; he had not sought to discover the secrets that belong only to God. His God would not hold his human frailties against him. He had submitted himself to the will of God. And submission to God is the very first thing for every Muslim. Does not the word Islam mean submission?

When Othman had finished his prayers he carefully folded his prayer mat and took it into the tiny office where an oil lamp burned. Carefully he placed the mat on a shelf. Then he returned to the open air and wandered over to the sea.

He saw the dhows of Saffina moored off the entrance to the creek and shook his head. There were not so many as before. Those beautiful ships, for which Saffina had become so famous, were now being replaced by metal-clad bulk carriers that brought the goods Ras Al Surra needed to the large new port in the Capital. The once majestic, all powerful, dhows had been reduced to the rôle of coasters, merely bringing goods down from the Capital area.

He knew many an old sea captain who was dying a slow death sailing endlessly up and down the same piece of coastline. The boredom that change brings was sapping his people's soul. The new wealth of oil was destroying the old wealth of fish. Balls of oil-tar destroyed nets and poisoned beaches. And human beings were polluted too. Children wanted things which he had never dreamed of. They wanted to travel. They wanted the easy life.

Once the guard had taken his wife to the Capital area. There he had seen many things. He had wanted to hide his wife's face, not so that others would not see her, rather to shelter her from the sights he was witnessing. They had had to dodge cars driven too fast by both Arabs and foreigners; they had had to witness Arabs imitating the ways of the foreigners; the king's palaces; the pretentious government buildings — he did not take any pride in these things. He just tried to leave as soon as he could. He did not like the place. The food there tasted bad. He felt that, in the Capital area, his countrymen were losing their souls.

Then, on his last day there, he saw a Saffina dhow by the side of the road, placed on a plinth like a graven image, a mere decoration. What was it doing there landlocked? He saw that the timbers of the boat were grey and cracked. He shook his head and returned to Saffina as quickly as he could.

During the Civil War he had kept quiet, but, secretly, he backed the rebels. They were good Muslims and were fighting Jihad against the corruption in Ras Al Surra. Friends of his, less fortunate, had been more vocal in support of the freedom fighters and had disappeared. Young men had melted away from Saffina to join the fighters in the mountains. They had either died or had fled abroad. He remembered them in his prayers.

Recently things had become quiet. The guard looked over to Nicholson's compound and cursed the man. He was still hunting out anybody who was anti-government. He did not have too much success because the people had long ago learned not to voice what they felt.

The burning of the power station had excited Othman. It was a sign that not everyone had accepted the new order. Perhaps there was some hope there. He had not allowed his wife to buy any foreign gadgetry and he had been proved right. Devoutly he hoped that the wicked regime would die, just as the electricity had died.

And yet . . . and yet, that morning he had seen the Englishman working in the heat of the storeroom, sorting out books. How he had worked! It was as if he was working for the good of his own children, not for the children of strangers. And how thin he was! What sort of wife would let her man get so thin? No, he was not like the other Englishmen. He was more like Mary-Anne at the hospital. She was as crazy as an oryx but such a kind heart. And the English inspector was like that. He was keen to help the children of Saffina . . . Ah, life was confusing. Not like the old days at all.

The guard sat on the ground outside the office in the dark and tried to think of other things. His son wanted to stop fishing and go off to the Capital. Othman was fighting him but he doubted that he would win. Parents were losing battles with their children all over Saffina . . .

The guard slept.

Hepworth, holding a Molotov Cocktail made with a Perrier bottle, crept in the dark along the shore towards the book storeroom. He felt fearful of what he was about to do, but more fearful of what would happen if he did not do it. Nicholson had read the riot act to him, had told him that he was already an accomplice and that the consequences of not going along with the plan they had both devised would be dire indeed.

He stopped and tried to control his breathing. This was just another operation, after all. What he was doing was no worse than other things he had done. It was just that he had got used to the quiet life, the easy option. Nicholson was right. He must try to see what they were doing as necessary.

Hepworth could see the outline of the storeroom nearby. He crept up the bank and walked slowly towards the building. He looked around but did not see anyone. Reaching into his pocket, he took out his Dunhill lighter and lit the Molotov Cocktail which he lobbed through the window of the storeroom.

The bottle smashed and exploded with a sheet of flame right in the centre of Peter Drury's English books.

The guard was suddenly awake. He saw the flames and saw the figure of Hepworth in the light of the flames. He stood up and shouted, running towards the figure.

Hepworth did not move. He was shocked. Nervousness had made him forget about the guard. He stood facing the man who unleashed a torrent of Arabic at him and then raised his arms to hit out at Hepworth.

Hepworth shielded himself from the man's blows. Othman could only wonder at his own anger and feel shock at seeing the Englishman in the act of burning down the bookstore. The flames were taking hold. The guard kept asking why as he aimed blows at the foreigner.

Hepworth shielded himself from the blows of the man. "Silly old buffer!" he thought. He reached out and with one hand grabbed the man by the throat. He squeezed and watched, detached, as the guard's eyes bulged and his cries were strangled. Then he heard shouts from Nicholson's compound and knew he should make off. He knew that Nicholson would be watching the fire from his verandah. He mustn't waste any more time. People would be gathering. He gave his other hand to the job of throttling the guard, who, in the midst of panic, hoped that God was seeing this and taking note. Before Othman lost consciousness, he wondered why this government man was destroying the work of the government. Life did not make any sense any more. Why the books? Books are holy. . . .

Hepworth let go of the man and watched with some satisfaction as he dropped into the dust like a sack of potatoes. He remembered the knife that Nicholson had given him, and took it out of its scabbard, thinking to bury it in the guard's chest, but was startled by the sound of an alarm bell. He dithered on the spot for a moment, then replaced the dagger in his belt.

He ran back to the shore and dived into the dark sea and swam out, away from the shore. From a distance of three hundred yards he could see the fire blazing. The water was warm. He felt he had the best seat in the house for viewing the bonfire. He would wait there in the water for a while and then make his way back to Nicholson's compound, sneak under the wire and shower. Nicholson would be sure to offer him lots of liquor.

Hepworth, immersed in the water watching the mayhem he had wrought, felt reborn.

Ibrahim had been at his books when Peter arrived back late in the afternoon. He at once set about preparing a meal, more fish, which he cooked on the fire near the front door.

Peter waited until they had eaten before presenting him with the books he had taken from the bookstore. Ibrahim was delighted and demanded to make a start.

"No, please, Ibrahim! I'm really tired! Let me have a sleep and I'll teach you afterwards."

It was already getting dark when he went into his bedroom and flopped down on to his mattress. It seemed almost obscene to be resting at this time of day. He wondered if, after this, he would be able to sleep when bedtime came around. Still, if he could not sleep, he would read. His reading had fallen by the wayside since coming to Ras Al Surra. He had started *Riding the Mountains Down* without first finishing *Small is Beautiful*. He could not settle to reading somehow.

As he dropped off he thought of his pile of books in the storeroom. It was nice to think of them there, ready and waiting for him to start distributing in the morning.

Ibrahim woke him up after an hour. He came in holding a lamp in one hand and his copybook in the other. They had a cup of tea and then Peter set about teaching him. That night he concentrated on the sounds of English. It mystified Ibrahim that one letter could have more than one sound; that the spelling of English words seemed to depend on whim more than on logic.

Peter tired of teaching long before Ibrahim tired of learning. Ibrahim, he felt, had to be a phenomenon unique in the world. Students could never outdo teachers! Teachers, almost by definition, ran students into the ground. He let the hours and minutes of his classes increase hoping that at some point Ibrahim would hit an unsurmountable pain barrier. It had yet to happen. Peter always gave in first — when he felt that, instead of salty water, he was sweating letters.

Once again he broached the subject of Ibrahim's past and his plans for the future. At first Ibrahim was reticent, saying that he had thought they would wait until he could tell Peter in English, but now he started to tell Peter his story.

He spoke baldly in short, staccato sentences. He did not once describe any of his feelings in the midst of the occurrences, but Peter felt that he was able to fill those in for himself. It was a sad story that Ibrahim told. Peter knew enough about Arab society to know that the youth had taken steps which would utterly exclude him from the tight world of home and hearth. It scared him when Ibrahim said, "My father told me to marry. He arranged the match. I did not say anything. I ran away. I came to Saffina."

Ibrahim finished his tale with a shrug.

Peter wanted to ask him questions. He still did not know what Ibrahim was planning for himself. Probably nothing. Planning was not something he would ever have been called on to practise. He also wanted to ask him about how he felt about his former employer, Nicholson. "No man is a hero to his valet." Ibrahim would be able to give an opinion on that vexed topic. Still, that would have to wait. He had not expected to get so far that night. The subject, now broached, could be returned to when the time was ripe.

"Well," said Peter, "at least there are plenty of lizards here. You should feel quite at home."

Ibrahim smiled.

And it was true. It hardly mattered when you looked at the walls of the prefab; there was always a lizard. Peter had not heard that they were "good" but he did know that they ate up flies and mosquitoes and that was good enough for him.

It occurred to him too that what Ibrahim had done was what people in the West did all the time. Youth revolted against adult authority and went its own way, perhaps crawling back home, prodigal, perhaps not. He had not thought that such things happened away from the pampered parts of the world. Perhaps they did, after all. Ibrahim was not alone in his prodigality. Peter felt tempted to tell him so, but that could wait too.

The two returned to the English books. So intent on teaching and learning were they that neither noticed the glow in the sky over Saffina.

"One each!" exclaimed Nicholson.

He had been out with his men attempting to fight the fire. Of course it had been a hopeless task. He had organised a human chain of buckets from the compound water tank. Nobody could say that they had not tried. He had been appealing to the Capital for years for a fire-engine but without result.

In all the confusion the wretched guard had been left where he had fallen. It was only when it was obvious that the building was beyond saving that the ambulance had been sent for. The body had been taken away. It seemed certain that the man was dead, but Nicholson thought it strange that there was no blood. He had told Hepworth to stab the man, had given him a special dagger with which to do the job. Still, that was a detail. He had stood with his men and surveyed the husk of the building; had exchanged the commiserations of comrades with them, while noting with no small satisfaction that he now enjoyed an uninterrupted view from his compound right the way to Zarut. Things would soon be just as they had always been.

"Yes, one each," replied Hepworth. He was emerging from Nicholson's shower, wearing Nicholson's Eau Sauvage Extrême and one of his newest fluffy American towels, towelling down his upper half with the one Nicholson kept for drying his face.

Nicholson ignoring these lapses on Hepworth's part, clapped him on the back and said, "Good work!"

Hepworth stuck out his chest. "It was nothing, Simon. I don't know what I kicked up all the fuss about. I suppose it was that I was out of practice. But undercover work is just like riding a bicycle really. One never forgets."

"And you got the guard?"

"Yes. No trouble. I forgot about him in the hurry and he came right at me — wizened old bugger. I did the Hepworth Turkey Lock on him. One hand, like this." Hepworth held out his arm and throttled Nicholson's towel.

"I think I get the idea. So that's why he didn't bleed?"

"That's right. Didn't use the knife, I'm afraid," confessed Hepworth. "It all happened so fast."

Nicholson frowned. "Pity. That dagger in his ribs would have pointed the finger straight at the insurgents. That kind of dagger has a handle that is only found in Tazuk, where many of the rebels come from. Where is it by the way?"

"In the pocket of my pants. I'll get it in a mo," replied Hepworth. He did not like Nicholson's tone. Why, it was as if the beggar didn't trust him! Hepworth felt his fist tighten. He looked at Nicholson's thin neck. He could squeeze the life out of him in a minute. He wouldn't, of course, but it was nice to know that he could if he wanted to.

Hepworth went into Nicholson's bathroom and put on his uniform. He looked at himself in the mirror and thought himself no bad sight all in all. There was still plenty of go in him yet. He was in his prime.

He handed the dagger to Nicholson when he came out.

Nicholson did not thank him but asked him if he'd like a drink.

"Would I! Roll it in!" replied Hepworth enthusiastically.

They sat down and drank two drinks in quick succession. Then both went out to view the results of their night's work. A few people had come to watch the scene of desolation.

"Books burn wonderfully," said Hepworth.

Nicholson nodded. "I think we should go to the hospital to enquire after the guard. It wouldn't do if we were thought to be slow in following up every possible lead."

"It's pointless, Simon. He's dead. Nobody can survive the Hepworth Turkey Lock."

"I'm sure you're right," replied Nicholson impatiently, "but we're not supposed to know that. We didn't have anything to do with this dreadful deed, remember."

They drove over to the hospital. The American missionary sister, Mary-Anne Sissons, was in her office when they arrived. She had been writing a report on the death of Othman and was feeling very down. She had known Othman and his family for many years; had helped his wife to give birth to several of her children; she had, in her young, naive days, even tried to convert him to Christianity. That had been a waste of time. The people of Saffina could not be converted. Not in the twenty years of her presence in Ras Al Surra had she converted one Saffina native. Not one! It depressed Mary-Anne sometimes. Still, she had been of use in other ways.

Tonight, though, she felt useless. Othman had been brought into the emergency room. The orderlies had tried to revive him; had massaged his heart, tried mouth to mouth resuscitation. She had been informed and had rushed in. She tried to revive him herself and he had seemed to be coming out of it.

"Come on, Othman! Come on!" Mary-Anne had told her dying friend. "Don't leave me here to tell your wife! Get better! Please!"

Othman had opened his eyes for a moment and looked at her with an expression of horror. His lips had moved and she put her ear close to his mouth to try and hear what he was saying. At first she could hear nothing that made any sense to her. Then she heard what he was saying.

"Ingleezi! Ingleezi shaytan!" ("The Englishman! The Englishman is a devil!")

"Why? Why?" asked Mary-Anne. "Why is the Englishman a devil?"

But, his mouth open wide, Othman had lain back and died. Mary-Anne prayed for her old friend and had then left him to the Muslim orderlies.

"We've come to see the guard, matron," announced Nicholson.

"I'm sorry, Mr Nicholson, you're too late. He's dead."

"Thank you, matron," said Nicholson coldly. "I won't take up any more of your time." He and Hepworth left the office.

For a long moment Mary-Anne looked without seeing at the report in front of her. Then she got up, reached for her aerosol can of Lysol and started spraying the room.

The next morning, before the tears clouded his vision and he had to look away, Peter saw that nothing remained of the bookstore. The roof had caved in, the walls collapsed inwards. In the midst of all this the charred ashes of thousands of pieces of paper sat serenely in high piles. The breeze blowing from the sea caught the top pages and blew them away in single charred sheets. They eddied high in the air, and disappeared into the desert.

A hand touched his shoulder. "Such desolation my dear!" said a deep voice.

Peter turned and saw Mr Nasawi, his long-absent office

mate, standing there in a shiny, navy-blue safari suit, a smile on his lined, pale face.

"Tears, my dear?" asked Mr Nasawi, his face now mirroring Peter's.

"Yes, I'm afraid so, Mr Nasawi," replied Peter, rubbing his arm across his face. "All my English books have gone up in smoke, I'm afraid."

Mr Nasawi nodded. He gazed at the wreckage and said, "It will throw the Education Department into even more chaos and mayhem than is customary here. For me too it is a great loss. My whole portfolio of visual aids for the learning of Arabic has returned to dust. It took me many months of much effort to compile."

"I am sorry."

"We are used to this sort of thing in Egypt, my dear. Like you English we too have looked to the sky and seen the destroyer."

"Yes, I know," said Peter, feeling that remote English guilt.

"We, like you, have had to learn the spirit of the blitz. Now the people of Ras Al Surra must learn it too. Still," and Mr Nasawi smiled broadly at Peter's gloomy face, "let us sing together and endeavour to pick up the pieces and start again, my dear."

"But I was supposed to deliver my books to the schools today. It will take me months to get a new supply." He knew his voice was coming out in a whine but did not care.

"The children of Ras Al Surra have waited hundreds of years for their books. They can wait a few months longer."

"So what happens now?"

Mr Nasawi curled his lip, looked to right and left and said, "It is all so simple, but so time-consuming, my dear. We will send our new order to the Capital. There it will sit under some official's teacup, but, eventually, it will be sent away to the suppliers. In six months the books will arrive."

"Not that long, surely?"

"That long, surely," stated Mr Nasawi.

Mr Titi passed by and said into Peter's ear, "Have you understood the lesson?"

Peter nodded and Mr Titi smiled broadly and disappeared. Mr Nasawi pulled Peter closer. "Do not trust Palestinians, my dear. Snakes in the grass, I assure you."

"Not Mr Titi, surely! You Arab brothers are a funny lot."

"It's true. We are a family full of feuds."

Then Peter suddenly remembered the guard. "What happened to that bookstore guard?"

"He was killed."

Peter felt his tears welling up again. To staunch them he asked, "You have been away for such a long time. I got your note, by the way. Was your trip successful?"

"It was a trial, a great trial, my dear. The accommodations and the bathroom arrangements are most primitive. Also, the teachers feud so much. It became most painful. The Egyptians in Waphi will not speak to the Jordanians. I spent much time as an envoy of peace. All most tiring. And now, of course, this."

Peter said goodbye to Mr Nasawi, who said, "When we embraced the Flame of Education, did we not burn our hands?"

Peter thought about that on his way to the centre of Saffina. In ten minutes he arrived at the market place. The fish and vegetable market were in full swing. Hundreds of people milled about, haggling, buying or just passing the time of day. Peter bought some vegetables and a scrawny chicken, impressed by the way things were going on as normal. It was consoling to see. He resolved to forget work that day and go home. He would give Ibrahim a long lesson, cook a good stew with the chicken. Perhaps, in the afternoon, they could climb a mountain.

As Peter made his way back towards the Education office and his Landrover, he thought of Batool in her noisy classroom by the sea and cursed the rebels. What was he going to do? Well, he would think about it tomorrow. Today was for distraction. Unlike Mr Nasawi, he did not feel ready to burn his own hand on the flame of education. Not today.

12

Mary-Anne Sissons had been unable to sleep. Upset and disoriented by all that had happened earlier in the night, exhausted and with her nerves set jangling, she tossed and turned in her bed for an hour. Finally she gave up the attempt.

With a sigh she switched on her bedside lamp. The light at once illuminated a photograph of her family and she found herself gazing at it. All the people in that photograph were now either dead or much changed. There she was in the centre smiling a very toothy smile at the camera. The blankness of her face never ceased to amaze her now, all those years later. She could remember her big brother saying, a moment before the photograph was taken and the blinding light flashed. "Make it good, sis! We want to remember you as the beauty you are."

Her brother's face in the picture looked down at her from the second row, the mouth still working from his utterance. Mother had turned round to shush brother Bill and had been caught turning, not quite ready for the picture. Her face was the tiniest bit blurred. Her brother and sister's children, all eight of them, had been single-minded and looked at the camera steadily and happily. Nathan, the eldest boy, then thirteen, had died in Vietnam. She looked into his face closely. Were the signs there? It often seemed to Mary-Anne that people who had died immediately became blurred in photographs and there was no mistaking the fact that Nat's image was less clear than those of his brothers and sisters. But had it always been like that? Hadn't it once been as clear as the rest and only taken on an insubstantial quality after his death?

Mary-Anne sighed and took up her book. It opened and the bookmark fell on her sheet. She saw, "O Lord, make me an instrument of Thy Peace" and turned it over. At this moment her life in Ras Al Surra seemed like a great ocean of wasted time. At this moment, with Othman dead, with seven corpses of foreign workers recently sent up to the Capital in body bags, with her own power of fortitude draining away into the desert, her whole life after the taking of the photograph looked like a gigantic mistake.

She had suddenly found herself tempted by the very worst of temptations: it occurred to her to question God's ways towards men. Not only that; she wondered sometimes if she even liked and approved of God any more. She knew she loved Him. He was far too deeply embedded in the centre of her existence ever to lose her love. But God, like an adored husband who cheats on his wife repeatedly and who comes home too late night after night year after year, strained Mary-Anne's tolerance to its limits.

She prayed. In her prayers she said, in the intimate way she used towards the godhead, "Well, all I can say, speaking bluntly, speaking my mind, is that I would not have allowed Othman to die like that; I would not have let those men burn up the power station. Had it been up to me I would have stretched forth my little finger and stopped it. You, I am told, set the world turning and care about every hair on our heads. We are, You say, worth more than many sparrows. I'm just saying that, if I were You, these wretched cruel things would not have happened. I should have put my foot down and interfered."

The day after the photograph was taken she had left her family at Fort Morgan Station and taken a train to Chicago. There she had been taught Arabic after a fashion and then put on another train to New York. Winter had been approaching. Snow flurries had guffawed against the windows. She had answered the enquiries of the other passengers about her destination: "I'm going to Ras Al Surra" — and she had been so proud to say the words. At last every childhood hope and ambition was being fulfilled. She was going to preach the gospel and help the sick in a land far away. She was going to answer God's call.

Ras Al Surra had been a fright, the Capital area enough to

make her want to turn round and run home. Then it had been a walled city, whose gates closed at six in the evening. She had had to wear a veil whenever she went out in public — but even a veil had not been sufficient to conceal from her the desolation that she had come to. African slaves on the harbour-side, chained and lost; loud, brutal seamen pushing her aside; people dying in the street; the cruel-sounding Call to Prayer; the religious policemen of the old king who beat people with sticks if they were slow to answer that Call to Prayer. She had been saved only by the presence of Florence Gill.

"You will probably not convert a single soul, Mary-Anne," Florence had told her on that first day. "Concentrate on helping those poor bodies. Concentrate on that and you will not waste your time."

And Florence, who had set up the Missionary Hospital in the Capital, had accompanied her to Saffina and helped her through those first awful months, working day and night to convert an old merchant's house into a clinic. Mary-Anne had slowly, by following Florence's every move, become more content. When the hospital opened its doors but nobody came to them as patients, the two women prayed together for a change of heart among the inhabitants. Then one day Othman, who had been working on the hospital, had fallen from a ladder, and, unwillingly, protesting and cursing, had been their first patient. They had mended him. Othman had discovered the power to heal of tender loving care and had gone out among the people of Saffina to spread the news. Soon the hospital was overflowing with Saffina's sick. And not since then had it looked back.

Florence had returned to the Capital, but, from there, had been a well of support to the still unsure Mary-Anne. Then she had been posted to Isfahan in Iran. Mary-Anne visited her on every vacation but when Florence died in 1976, Mary-Anne, never the most talented at making friends, had soldiered on in Saffina without mentor.

"Not their souls, their bodies," she had kept telling herself.

With the arrival of oil wealth the Ras Al Surran government recruited foreigners to work at the hospital. Indians and Sri

Lankans arrived who were more open to Mary-Anne's Christian message. She soon found that she had a group of three or four who would gather and share prayers once or twice a week. That helped. The hospital expanded. An Indian doctor arrived. A Catholic from Goa, and in spite of believing in the Bishop of Rome, he was a decent chap and a wonder in the operating theatre.

Mary-Anne had thought she would have to leave during the civil war. It had seemed that Saffina would become totally cut off from the Capital and that life would become intolerable. She saw the casualties from the war. They daily came into the hospital and the cruelty of their wounds and tortures spoke eloquently of what might have awaited her should Saffina fall.

But Saffina had not fallen and things had seemed to be returning to normal — until the destruction of the power station and the bookstore.

Mary-Anne read for a couple of hours but found it hard to take in what she was reading. Her mind would not settle. Sleep was as far away as ever. At five in the morning she gave up and put on her uniform to make her rounds. Joanna was in charge that night and Mary-Anne went off looking for her. She found her gazing into a cot in the children's ward.

"I don't think she's going to make it," Joanna answered Mary-Anne's enquiry about Tayaba. "We just can't stop the dehydration." Mary-Anne sighed.

Together they walked along the corridor to the adminis-tration office.

"It's terrible about the bookstore. Why that, I wonder?" asked Joanna.

Mary-Anne shrugged. "I don't know. You know the guard died, don't you?"

"No, I didn't. I'm sorry."

"Yes, it is too sad. He was my first patient here. Othman. Do you know what he said just before he died?"

"No. What?"

"He said, 'The Englishman is a devil.' Just that."

Joanna frowned. "Whatever could he have meant by that?"

"I don't know. I don't seem to be able to work out anything any more. Things are getting more and more mysterious," replied Mary-Anne.

A week later, when Peter arrived at the Education office for work, he found a letter waiting for him from Joanna:

Dear Peter,

I know it's funny my writing a letter to you when you live so near, but I have honestly not had a moment to myself in the last few days.

I'm sorry to have to tell you that Tayaba died yesterday. We just couldn't stop the dehydration and she slipped away last night. Still, thank you for all your help and support. I know you will be as sad as I am.

It has been a bad week for all of us. I was very much distressed to hear about the burning of the bookstore. I do hope that it will not set you back too much.

I thought it might be a good idea to try and raise our spirits a bit. How about coming round for dinner next Thursday night? About seven? I am going to invite Mary-Anne, the head of the hospital. She's been here for years and years. I am sure you will find her very interesting to talk to.

No need to reply to this unless you can't come.

Cheers!

Joanna

Peter's first reaction to Joanna's letter was a sense of shame. Tayaba had hardly impinged on his consciousness since the night the bookstore had burned down. But, along with guilt, now overlaid with more sadness, was the good news of something to look forward to.

He did not linger in the office for long. The place oppressed him. Anyway, the previous evening he had had an idea. He was off to test its feasibility.

During his lesson with Ibrahim the day before, the word "newspaper" had come up. He had explained to Ibrahim the concept of spreading news daily around the country using quickly printed materials. Ibrahim had started to listen to the news on the radio and had taken to the idea at once; had been interested to know that there were newspapers in the Capital. They had discussed the topic. Ibrahim had been assigned to write a simple article for a newspaper as his assignment.

Leaving his companion to get on with this Peter had gone into his bedroom to listen to the BBC World Service. Sometimes it came through loud and clear. Sometimes he could not hear it at all. On those days when he could not pick it up, Peter cursed Margaret Thatcher. On every night he had been in Ras Al Surra, Radio Moscow was as clear as a bell and he did not believe all the talk about the BBC being difficult to receive because of "disturbances in the stratosphere". If that were true then all radio services would suffer from it. Radio Moscow did not because they spent the required funds to make sure that they could be heard. Peter did not rate Radio Moscow very highly. A pity, he thought, that the World Service, with so much to say, had not the means to assure it could say it efficiently.

But that night he picked it up quite well and it was while he was listening to *The Pleasure's Yours* that the thought occurred to him. If the children had no books, perhaps he could fill the gap with a newspaper! The newspaper would contain lots of language exercises, games and activities. It would range widely and serve beginners as well as more advanced students. The first problem would be writing it. Well, he had time to do that. The second, and much greater problem, would be printing it. The Education office had nothing. Their ancient spirit duplicator had died ages ago. Still, he had plenty of skins to type on. Perhaps around Saffina there would be a working duplicator.

So, after reading Joanna's letter, he went to the hospital. An orderly there said that they had nothing, but advised him to try the post office. There, his friend, Mr Nasser, said that as far as he knew Mr Nicholson was the only man with necessary facilities.

Peter felt reluctant to approach Nicholson, but, taking his courage in both hands, he drove straight round to Nicholson's compound. The guard at the gate, seeing a European face, opened the gate to him immediately.

Nicholson was in his office speaking to an elderly Arab. He

greeted Peter cordially and asked him to sit and wait while he finished his conversation. The Arab was complaining about the way the builders of the road from the Capital to Saffina were using part of his land to store their heavy equipment. His land lay close to the road and the palm trees were being damaged by the equipment. Nicholson listened to the man and promised that he would attend to the matter. The man thanked him and left.

Then Nicholson turned to Peter. "You're still here then?"

Peter nodded.

"Sorry about your books. Can't be easy for you to do your job with no books." Nicholson was finding it difficult to keep a note of relish out of his voice.

"No, it's not. The schools are in a real pickle. That's really why I've come to see you, Mr Nicholson."

"Please call me Simon. How can I help?"

"Well . . ." And Peter told Nicholson about his idea for a school newspaper.

Nicholson scratched his chin. "Yes, I can see how it would be of help. Of course you can use our machine. It's not exactly state of the art though. We've got quite a good photocopier but I'm afraid I couldn't let you loose on that. Have you got the materials ready?"

"No, I haven't, but they will be in a couple of days. We've got the skins to work on. I've brought one with me to see if they are compatible."

Nicholson called his Indian clerk over and told him to see if the skin fitted on the machine. He came back after a few minutes to say that it did.

"Well, that'll be fine then. You just get everything prepared and we'll print them for you. We must all pull together in this crisis, after all."

Peter was cheered. "Thank you, Simon," he said, feeling angry with himself that he could ever have entertained uncharitable thoughts about Nicholson.

"Tea?"

Peter accepted gratefully and the Indian went out to fetch it.

"I suppose you must be pretty busy?" Peter asked.

"Busy? No more than usual. Why do you ask?"

"Well, with the acts of sabotage and everything. You must be working hard to find out who did it."

Nicholson laughed. "Oh, we know who did it! The rebels did it. But there's a great difference between knowing and finding. Especially here. All we can do is wait for them to put a foot wrong."

Something in Peter's expression made Nicholson realise that he was not believed. He continued, "The thing is, Peter, I am sure you would not expect me to tell you what we are doing. Take my word for it, though, that steps are being taken."

"Yes, I'm sure they are."

"And I trust that you are taking seriously the advice Captain Hepworth and I gave you. As you know I think it would be best if all you amateur expats upped and left. But, since you seem to be reluctant to do that, I do hope that you are being careful."

"Yes, er . . ." Peter did not know what to say.

"I mean, you living alone so far away from everyone is not too good, you know."

"I don't live alone," interrupted Peter.

Nicholson raised his left eyebrow while his right remained where it was. Peter had always wanted to be able to do that.

"You don't? Who lives with you?"

"An Arab chap."

The eyebrow jumped further up Nicholson's forehead.

"An Arab chap, eh? Are you sure that's wise?"

"Oh, yes. I trust him. He used to work for you actually."

"Really? What's his name?"

"Ibrahim."

"The one from Jaheel! Not *that* Ibrahim! So that's where he ended up! He's with you!"

Nicholson laughed hard and Peter could only watch mesmerised and taken aback by his reaction. Finally, between bursts of laughter, Nicholson managed, "You do pick 'em! God, whatever possessed you? You do *know* about him, don't you?"

"Know what?"

"Know that he's a pariah, an outcast, the lowest form of life?"

"I know he's been very silly."

Nicholson once again spluttered with laughter. "Silly! Silly! Well I suppose silly is one word for it. Silly will do nicely for a start." Then he sobered up and in a tone of sudden seriousness added, "However, mad, wilful, treacherous, cocoa-ish, rebellious, unfaithful, are words that more adequately describe him. You know he walked out on me, do you?"

Peter nodded. "He did mention it. Yes. In fact he's told me everything."

"Oh he has, has he! And you're keeping him as a 'guest' in your house."

"Well, he's not exactly a guest, he does work . . ."

Nicholson shook his head. "But he's *in* your house!"

"Yes, he's in my house," answered Peter in a clipped tone.

Nicholson leaned back in his chair. "Well I never!" he said.

The Indian clerk brought in the tea and Nicholson dismissed him with a wave of the hand. When the door had closed again he leaned over towards Peter and said, "Get rid of him at once! Send him away! I knew he had left Jaheel again. I have my sources there. If anybody were to find out that he's there and the news got back to Jaheel or Wadi Beni Omar then I wouldn't answer for your safety. The brothers of the girl he jilted would come and kill both of you without a second thought. You know, of course, that the shock killed his father. He died on the day of the wedding. The shame of it was just too much for him. I had thought that the wretched kid might have gone to the Capital and become a corner boy, just got himself lost. They can do that there. I would never have dreamed that he would return to Saffina. No, you get rid of him pronto. He's an albatross round your neck. Especially now."

Peter did not know what to say. It was the news of the death of Ibrahim's father that had stunned him. The boy definitely did not know. He already saw himself having to break the news. But what about the rest? What Nicholson was saying seemed to make sense. Honour might well demand the boy's death. God, what was he going to do?

Nicholson, seeing Peter's confusion, stepped into the silence. "Are you fond of him?"

Peter, suddenly snapped from his thoughts, replied, "Yes."

"A consolation to you, is he?"

"Yes."

And both his answers were true, but he noted that Nicholson was nodding and saw, too late, the implication behind the questions.

"But not like that!"

"Like what, old boy?"

"You know. That."

Nicholson looked at Peter hard. "Get rid of him!" he said.

If it was not evident to Peter that Ibrahim was suffering because of what he had done, this was simply because he did not share his feelings with his friend and benefactor.

Ibrahim did not quite understand his role in Peter's house. Unlike Nicholson, Peter had not provided him with tasks; drawn demarcation lines to show him how the land lay; kept his distance. It had been difficult for him to know where he stood, if, indeed, he stood anywhere. Peter seemed to have few routines. He did not pray, he seemed grateful when Ibrahim cooked a meal for him or tidied the easy, bare place. He did not treat Ibrahim like a servant at all. And, above all, he spent great swathes of time teaching him English.

What did his friend get in return? Ibrahim for the life of him could not think. It was all very strange and he was grateful for this strangeness. It made him feel as if he was a million miles away from Jaheel — in a peculiar country, a country far away.

Of course, common sense told Ibrahim that he was, in fact, an easy day's walk from home. He had only to look across the plain to the northern mountains to know that his feeling of being abroad was a complete illusion. So near, yet so impossibly far — a distance he could never span — lay home.

Home? When alone, Ibrahim would laugh at the word; a hard, unpleasant laugh that would have shocked Peter had he heard it. He knew that there was no home there. He would, if he ever did, return to Jaheel as a murderer returns to the scene of his crime. Home? There could be no home for Ibrahim. He had cut himself off from home forever by refusing to accept the rules of home.

That day, as on all the days when Ibrahim was left alone in the house, his thoughts were full of Jaheel. He wondered about his father and his friends. He ached to know how they were; to know how they felt towards him. Though he knew. Daily, he chided himself: "I could have married! I could have stayed!" And he thought how easy it would have been. Why had he left? He could not remember now. The thought wandered around his mind and made him nauseous with confusion. He was no longer the same person he had been when he left Jaheel in that he could not remember his feeling then. He could not recall the boredom and tedium of his days. He could not introspect accurately enough to place himself, in imagination, in that place and situation and answer the question: "Why?"

Ibrahim had made the same mistake twice. When, bored minding the goats in the Wadi Kabir, he had wondered how he could ever have left the interest and comfort in Nicholson's house, the reason "Because he killed a lizard" provoked then the same laughter that now the nearness of home provoked.

Neither Ibrahim, nor the people of Jaheel, had libraries of books to draw on; books that would surely have given him some comfort. He was not able to read a single book that would tell him: "I was like you. I had to run away. I made mistakes." He had become an adolescent, had put himself into that in-between state unknown in the society of Jaheel. One was a child and then, quick as a flash, or, at least, a wedding service, one was a man. Ibrahim had only The Book — the Koran — and the in-bred tales told round the fires at night. Those stories, kernels of rock-hard morality surrounded by a marzipan of humour and tradition, were, in tandem with The Book, a safe haven for those who were content to sail through their lives keeping to the shoreline. But Ibrahim had been swept out to sea by the current of the twentieth century.

When Peter came home after his meeting with Nicholson, Ibrahim could not read the confusion and distress beneath the outward façade of normality that Peter presented. He found it strange that Peter was so silent over the meal, was a little put out by not being offered an English lesson (for English to Ibrahim had become the best way he had discovered of drowning out the angry voices of home) but reasoned that Peter was tired.

Only when Peter emerged from his room after a two-hour nap and said to Ibrahim that he had met Nicholson and that Nicholson had told him some news about Jaheel, did everything begin to fall into place.

"What did he say?" asked Ibrahim.

Peter could not answer at first. He had not been sleeping in his room. He had been furiously trying to compile pages of his newspaper while his mind wrestled with the problem at hand. He was still not certain that he could repeat to Ibrahim what Nicholson had told him. He was not certain he possessed the strength.

"What did he say?" repeated Ibrahim.

Then Peter thought, "He has a right to know. He has a right." He said, "Nicholson says your father died, Ibrahim."

It was as if Ibrahim had not understood Peter's words. He cocked his head and asked, "What?"

Peter repeated the sentence and Ibrahim did not move a muscle. He merely stared back at Peter blankly.

In his head Ibrahim was repeating the sentence. He massaged it and even attempted to translate it into English but could not do it. "Thank you for telling me, Peter. However, for me my father died when I ran away from home. I have caused his death." Then he asked Peter if he could have an English lesson.

Peter was both alarmed and relieved at Ibrahim's reaction to the news he had given him: alarmed because it seemed totally unnatural; relieved because he had expected Ibrahim to scream and rush out of the house in the direction of Jaheel. Nothing in his experience aided him in this situation and the peculiar reaction, or lack of it, exhibited by Ibrahim made him realise how little he knew him.

They sat down at the table and Peter started the lesson. He postponed getting down to any grammar work and asked Ibrahim to read to him from a book of simplified Arab stories.

Ibrahim read in a flat, fluent voice:

"Nasruddin wanted to cross over the sea to an island. He went to the ferryman and paid the man the fare. He got into the boat.

"When Nasruddin and the boatman were half way across the water, Nasruddin asked the man, 'Do you know grammar?'

"'No, I don't,' replied the boatman.

"'You have wasted half your life!' said Nasruddin.

"After a short time, the boatman asked Nasruddin, 'Can you swim?'

"'No, I can't,' replied Nasruddin.

"'Then you have wasted all your life!'

"'Why?' asked Nasruddin.

"'Because we're sinking!' replied the boatman.''

Peter corrected Ibrahim's pronunciation, had him read the story again and then asked him questions to test his understanding.

"Why has Nasruddin wasted his whole life?"

"Nasruddin has wasted his whole life because he cannot swim and now he needs to swim or he will drown."

"That's right."

Ibrahim watched his teacher closely. "Teacher," he said, "you are sad. I know. Believe me, I am sad too. I do not look sad but I am sad. We have a story. Can I tell you?"

"Yes, of course."

Ibrahim reached for a page on which he had written a number of English words, together with their meaning in Arabic. He began:

"A young man lived in a small village. His name was Omar. One day he broke wind in the mosque. This is very bad and the people were angry.

"Omar left his village and wandered round the world for half of his life. He became very rich and bought a car and many houses. After thirty years he returned to his village in his big car. The village had changed and Omar did not know where his family's house was. He asked a small boy at the side of the road the way.

"'Where is Abu Omar?' he asked the boy.

149

"'Who are you?' asked the boy.

"'I am his son, Omar.'

"The boy laughed. 'Are you Omar who broke wind in the mosque?' he asked."

Peter nodded and Ibrahim, tears suddenly gushing from his eyes, said, "I am that Omar but my fault is worse." He moved back into Arabic. "Some things cannot be forgiven. I have broken one of the central rules of my people. I have betrayed the tribe. I am no longer a Muslim. I am no longer anyone's son. I am an outcast. You tell me that my father is dead. You are not telling me anything I did not know. To me he was dead from the moment I placed my feet on the road away from home that night. I knew then what I was doing and I did it. Now . . ."

He stopped and Peter waited but no further words came. "Now?" he asked at last.

Ibrahim shrugged. "Now is not then. It is foolish to contemplate. But now I wish I could make it then."

"Ibrahim," said Peter, feeling it was time to say what he had been thinking. "What you did was wrong. We both know that. However, I wonder if you are unique. You in Ras Al Surra are living through strange times. Everything is changing very fast and becoming complicated. You, it seems to me, went away from home where everything was simple and had easy traditional answers, to Nicholson's house. You were not prepared for the things you saw there; for the strangeness and attractiveness of everything. It is inevitable that it should make you a little crazy. We have a saying: 'How can you keep them down on the farm after they've seen Paree?' People all over the world are losing their contentment when faced with the possibilities of travel and city life. When I was in the Sudan village boys would come back from the local town with headphones on, wearing flared trousers and singing disco songs. They behaved for a while foolishly in the village. They strutted around, thinking they knew finally what the world was about. They felt contempt for the elders, feeling that they knew more than the elders ever would know. Nobody is immune to this. When I go home I will find it hard to fit in there because of what I have seen. Believe me, Ibrahim, you are not alone!"

Ibrahim nodded. "I think I understand. But understanding does not change anything for me. I can never go home. I have killed my father."

Then he looked up at Peter. His tears had dried on his cheeks, leaving salty tracks. "But what about you? You surely don't want me to stay? Not now!"

"I want what is best for you. I don't want to be alone here. Watching you learning English so fast has been very rewarding for me, has made me feel useful. Precious little else around here has done that for me. I just wish there was something I could do for you. There!"

And he touched Ibrahim's head.

"There is nothing you can do. I have a sickness: a stone heart, an ungrateful heart, a confused head."

Peter nodded. He thought of Nicholson's advice and resolved to ignore it. "OK, Ibrahim. Let's get going on English," he said.

"Give me an exercise book, a red one," said Nasser the postmaster, to his friend Abdullah the shopkeeper the following morning.

Abdullah, seated at the end of his counter, next to the window, on a high stool, barked an order to his ever-smiling Indian assistant. The man fetched a ladder and, gathering his sarong tightly around him, climbed up the steps past matches and Chinese canned vegetables and 3D postcards of the Ka'aba and winking women and lost kittens and unsold electric irons, to a stack of exercise books. He took a red one, cuffed the dust off it on his sarong and scampered back down the steps, handing it to his employer with both hands.

His employer did not acknowledge the gesture. He took the book and wiped the cover before handing it across the counter to Nasser.

"Anything else?" he asked Nasser.

"No, I don't think so," replied Nasser, looking around.

"You wouldn't like an electric iron or a rice cooker or an

electric incense burner, I suppose?" asked Abdullah, surveying his large inventory of electrical goods with some distaste.

"Not at the moment, no," smiled Nasser. "There's really no point until we've got electricity, is there? We are not all rich men like you, able to afford our own generator."

"Afford! Afford, you say!" Abdullah shouted. "I cannot afford any of this! All this unsold stock is killing my business and I'm in debt to several big men in the Capital who are becoming impatient with me! If this goes on, they'll make trouble for me."

Nasser had never known Abdullah to err on the side of optimism. He thrived on imagining that the very worst, if it possibly could, would always happen. The coming of the power station had allowed him to run the whole gamut of his pessimism, and, of course, for once his worst fears had proved to be correct.

Nasser smiled at him and did not comment. He liked Abdullah and knew him to be an honest man, a generous helper of the poor and a man who held Saffina's good close to his heart. He was also the muezzin at the Friday mosque nearby and had never been known to miss a call to prayer. Also, and this was rare, Abdullah's voice was a sweet sound to hear first thing in the morning. "Awake! It is better to pray than to sleep! God is most great!" Abdullah's call encouraged people to get up and pray. A voice less sonorous than Abdullah's made the first conscious thought one of resentment and rebellion. Nasser had heard many calls to prayer which just asked to have a fist shaken at them. But not Abdullah's. Abdullah pulled his heavy frame up the spiral staircase of the mosque five times a day and called, without the aid of amplification, across the white rooftops of Saffina. He was like Bilal, the freed African slave, who had performed the first call to prayer at the Prophet's command.

On a visit to the Capital, Nasser recalled, he had heard muezzins calling people to prayer from tens of mosques all over the city. Each neighbourhood had a mosque and each mosque had up-to-date amplification equipment. The sky became saturated by an unpleasant, stultifying cacophony which crossed neighbourhood lines. Each mosque, almost like competing creeds, sent its call too far. Like everything else in the Capital, it was overblown.

"You don't have any textbooks, do you?" asked Nasser, without hope. He had bought the exercise book for his son. It was all the child had to put into the Taiwanese bag he had got for him to carry his books.

"Sorry," said Abdullah. "You'll have to wait for those. If I'd known what was going to happen I'd have got some in. Could have made a killing. But as it is . . ."

Nasser leaned over and whispered, "You didn't know, did you?"

"Know what?"

"That the bookstore would be burnt."

"Nasser! How could you . . ."

But Nasser grasped Abdullah's hand and pressed it hard.

"I'm sorry," he said. "But I had to be sure. I knew, but I had to ask you."

Then Abdullah was looking past Nasser and quoting quietly, "'To speak of evil is to call up the evil doers.'"

Nasser glanced round and saw Hepworth at the other counter.

"Give me six batteries like this," they heard Hepworth say to the Indian assistant. "Fresh ones mind. The last ones I bought here died on me after a couple of hours."

The assistant, still smiling, brought Hepworth his batteries. Hepworth paid and left without another word.

"What you said . . ." began Nasser.

"What I said?"

"Yes, when you saw the Englishman you said . . ."

"What I said, I said," said Abdullah.

"Abdullah, my friend, may you have long life! We must go fishing together! We never go fishing together, not like in the old days," said Nasser, back to his normal room-filling voice.

"Well, I might as well go fishing as stay here watching my investments turning to dust."

"Good. This evening after the last prayer?" and Abdullah nodded.

13

There could be no denying now that Saffina was becoming dangerous. Since the burning of the bookstore, Peter had noticed that Hepworth's men from the Desert Regiment were very much in evidence around the town. They stopped him most days on his way to and from work. Their presence, however, did not reassure him. Rather it made him constantly aware of the invisible threat all around.

Daily he expected to hear from the Council man telling him to leave. But Peter still did not feel himself to be in any real danger. At work and in the town he was always well received. The Arab expatriates did not appear to be getting edgy, and he wondered why Nicholson and Hepworth should be trying to get him to cut and run. They should be pleased that a Brit was showing the flag, exhibiting a bit of "the right stuff", shouldn't they? Ibrahim, a captive who would not leave him alone with his dark thoughts in the prefab, who would not cut and run himself because he had nowhere to run to, was a great consolation to him. His presence in his house, his dependence on him, also stopped Peter from seriously entertaining any thoughts of leaving himself. For now he had more than merely himself to think about. And he liked that too.

That day after work he did not teach Ibrahim, however. He plugged him into the tape recorder and left him to teach himself while he went into his room and worked on making the newspaper, now christened *The Eastern Star*.

In the evening they ate outside under the stars and listened to the BBC.

Hepworth had called round, spoken a few words to him from his Landrover but had refused Peter's offer of tea.

"The fellow's still with you, I see," he said.

"That's right."

"Well, enjoy yourselves, lads!" he had shouted as he pulled away. He sounded his horn. The noise of his Landrover faded into the silence and the dark around the prefab. Some wild dogs, disturbed by the sound, barked for a while, but then they too were silent.

Hepworth's tone had left a bad taste in Peter's mouth and that taste combined with an equally nasty one from the visit to Nicholson. It was clear that they thought his relationship with Ibrahim was suspect. Their reasoning seemed to be hinting that there could be no explanation for his having Ibrahim in the house other than a sexual one.

Peter thought about that. A part of him felt that the Englishmen's reaction was their problem rather than his, but then he thought that it might be his problem too. Was he attracted to men? Perhaps the answer was yes. He felt comfortable around men, valued his friends, especially those — and there were several — who shared his status of male wallflower. But he could not for the life of him imagine kissing any of his friends or — and he smiled at the thought — going to bed with them. He knew the mechanics and did not think he was attracted to any of the acts he had heard about. Peter Drury expressed his love of his friends by helping them up the difficult part of rocks and then not mentioning that they had needed his help; by buying them pints when they were skint; by staying by them when they vomited up his largesse, and by seeing them safely tucked up before he left them. He knew himself well enough to know that he was a great big sexual don't know, a late bloomer whose petals were in danger of falling away before he was picked. Peter did not admit to himself that he was a virgin. It was not that he did not realise that he had never managed to "have it off", to "go the whole way", to "lose his cherry" — though he never had. Rather that he did not think the term applied to chaps.

One of his favourite programmes, *Anything Goes*, had started on the BBC. Some lonely expatriate in Dhahran, Saudi Arabia, had asked for *Brothers in Arms*. Peter, looking up at the stars, started to sing along with Dire Straits.

Ibrahim listened, then asked Peter to write down the words for him. Peter sighed and said he would.

"Peter," asked Ibrahim. "Why don't you have a wife?"

Oh God, he thought, now we come to it.

Peter laughed. "*You* ask me that! You of all people!"

"Yes, I know. But I have told you that I am an outcast. I was supposed to marry but now I cannot. With you it is different. You can choose for yourself. But you haven't."

"No, I haven't. I will, Ibrahim. But if I married I couldn't travel and I want to travel."

"When will you stop wanting to travel?"

"I suppose when I want a wife more than I want to travel."

"When will that be?"

"At this rate in a couple of months."

Ibrahim did not see the joke. "You are not happy travelling in Ras Al Surra?" he asked.

"Well, it's interesting but I am not happy with my work."

"Why?"

He felt the polite answer he always made to such enquiries coming up in his throat like bile. He swallowed and decided to tell Ibrahim what he felt. There was no one else to tell and he was tired of exchanging mere pleasantries with his companion. It wasn't fair on either of them.

"Well, I'll tell you, Ibrahim. The bookstore has been burned and it looks like I'll have to wait months for a new supply. OK. If Ras Al Surra was a poor country I could accept it but on the news tonight you heard that King Fadl has just arrived in London on his personal Jumbo Jet to buy a dozen warplanes. Well, maybe you need the warplanes, I don't know. I also hear that King Fadl is just about to move into his third palace. One palace is necessary. Two is a little much when the country is in the state it's in. But three? Well it is an outrage. It's an outrage because the king is not doing the things he should do. He's not doing his, to use the title of one of your textbooks, *First Things First*. You saw how Nicholson lives. You see how I live. I have not the least idea what Nicholson does but it angers me to see him so pampered while I and everyone else in Education, not least the children, suffer. It's not that I want to live in luxury. I

156

don't. It's just that the difference in our conditions speaks volumes about the priorities. Nothing in this world requires more care, thought and effort, than the education of children. I think the level of civilization of a country can be judged by the way that country treats its children. When I went to the Sudan the people who sent me gave me a long talk in London. They said I must look straight ahead at my own job and not look around at what was going on in the country as a whole. Most of the time I managed to do that; partly because I was in such a remote place and out of sight. My village in the Sudan was much less developed than Saffina. But even there I got angry when government officials visited in their Mercedes cars, lighting their cigarettes with Dunhill lighters and talking to me about how, when in London, they stayed at all the most expensive hotels. It seemed to me to be wicked when I was there on a very low wage and my children had no paper to write on."

Ibrahim nodded but said nothing. Peter took a gulp from his glass of tea and continued.

"Of course this is the way the whole world works. I am learning that the hard way. I will become tired of travel because I am not able to block these thoughts out of my mind. I think I can understand the rebels here. If I were Ras Al Surran I might be one. I hope I'm not shocking you but it does seem strange to me that you should be content to see your country run by the British. Fine if it was well run. Less fine, indeed downright despicable, when it is run by self-serving cronies of your king."

He waited for some reaction from Ibrahim but nothing came.

"Are you there?" Peter asked, craning his neck into the darkness.

"I am here."

"Are you angry? I think maybe I was too honest."

"No, I am not angry. You are my friend. But I do not understand everything. You make me feel ignorant."

"Well, maybe you are ignorant about some things, Ibrahim. But you know many things I will never know. You know how to catch fish, tend animals, track, survive. You know many things which the English have forgotten. And," he added, "you are willing to learn. Many in England are not willing to learn, to open themselves up to other cultures. They have lots of books and opportunities but do not use them."

"Why is that?"

Peter shrugged. "I don't know. But believe me, Ibrahim, you would put most English students to shame."

"But we in Ras Al Surra are forgetting our knowledge, I think. When I returned to Jaheel from Mr Nicholson's house it took me a long time to remember my skills. Had I remained away for much longer they would have disappeared. But I am knowledgeable enough to see my ignorance and what is happening. I can see that my state, my wretchedness, is something which has hit me first in Jaheel but it will shortly hit others. My disease will spread around my village like a plague. I think many people in Saffina have the plague already. My knowledge no longer works for me. It is a dhow with a hole in it below the waterline. That is why I am trying to acquire new knowledge. Look! I can tell you a story. That is something I can still do. Would you like to hear it?"

Peter was delighted. "Go ahead!" he said.

Ibrahim began. "I will tell you a story about a wise man called Joha. One day Joha said to the people, 'What am I going to say to you?'

"The people replied, 'We don't know.'

"Joha said to them, 'You are ignorant people and I do not speak to ignorant people.' He went away.

"A week later he came back and asked the people, 'Do you know what I am going to say to you?'

"The people looked at one another and answered, 'Yes, we know.'

"Joha responded, 'Well, if you know you don't need me to tell you.'

"He went away.

"A week later he returned and said to the people, 'Do you know what I am going to say to you?'

"The people looked at one another and smiled.

"Half the people said, 'Yes, we know!'

"The other half said, 'No, we don't know.'

"Joha said, 'So half of you know and half of you don't

158

know. If that is the case then the wise can instruct the ignorant.'

"And Joha went away. He did not return."

"What does the story mean?" asked Peter.

"It means many things, Peter. But you must not ask me the meaning. If you ask, I shall go away."

"Ibrahim, you must not go away!" laughed Peter, resolving to put the story into his newspaper, even though he did not understand it.

They were silent. Then Peter, seated in the dark, heard Ibrahim crying. He sat helplessly for a moment feeling useless, a poor friend. He knew what he should do, what friendship demanded that he do, but for a minute sat frozen listening to his companion's convulsed weeping. Ibrahim's tears were catching and Peter felt himself breaking down too and thinking, as he always did whenever moved to tears, of his Sudanese kids. Then slowly and awkwardly, thinking of the leers of Nicholson and Hepworth and hating himself for thinking of them, for being so split and selfconscious and cold and English, he moved across to Ibrahim, giving rein for the first time to his sorrow. He put his arms around his friend and patted his back, gently, as if burping a baby. He was surprised at himself and moved at how, once the effort had been made and the risk taken and the scoffers ignored, all anxiety ceased.

"My father! My father!" cried Ibrahim. "I have killed my father. I am as good as dead myself!"

"No, you're not! No, you're not! Your father understands your confusion, Ibrahim. He can see you now and he has forgiven you."

And Peter rocked him there on the step.

Late that same night, Nicholson, dressed in his poorest Arab outfit, his skin stained dark brown, pushed and cajoled a donkey through the maze of streets of Saffina. The donkey carried a small load on its back.

"Little donkey! Carry Mary safely on her way," whistled Nicholson through his teeth.

In the dark houses he passed nothing stirred. Through one of the unglazed, barred windows the sound of reassuring snoring reached him. He arrived at the central market place. Some rats darted across the empty square.

"This is what is called in the trade 'Keeping up momentum,'" Nicholson told the donkey amicably.

The donkey said nothing.

"Simon Nicholson, Gentleman and Thug at your service," Nicholson added. The donkey still said nothing. It stopped and Nicholson hit its haunches with his fists which sent it cantering off.

As he did this, Nicholson saw himself at a point-to-point, a child, sending off a gas balloon with his name and address on it. He saw himself watching the balloon meandering up towards the threatening clouds; his orders for it to fly farther than all the other balloons rising to it like an invisible ray from the gun of Flash Gordon. The balloon, he had believed, was under his control. It felt itself free but it was not free and would win for him. The following day his mother had answered the telephone and been informed that her son had won £50. "It got all the way to Snowdonia!" the man had said. Mother had rushed in to tell him. He had not been surprised.

For a long moment, Nicholson leaned against the wall of a shop, surveying the deserted square and the donkey meandering through it, sniffing the rubbish, no doubt pleased no longer to be pushed and prodded.

"Let's see if you can find the best possible target all by yourself." He had intended to tether the donkey outside the post office. It had pleased him in the planning to think of that damned devious fellow, Nasser, having his life thrown into chaos. There was something not quite right about Nasser. Nicholson had compiled a thick file on him. Nasser was deeply involved in anti-government activities, Nicholson was certain of it. But the stories that filtered through to him did not add up to hard-and-fast proof. And to take in someone as influential in Saffina as Nasser demanded more than circumstantial evidence.

Watching from his wall, Nicholson suddenly changed his mind. It was foolish to let the donkey roam free. But then, as he was about to step out into the square, he heard voices from the small house next to the shop. He heard a match struck and the light of a lamp spread its rays from the barred window across the square. Still, there might be time to get the donkey and tether it. Nicholson made his way around the slash of light that cut across the square. As he caught hold of the donkey's bridle it took fright and began to bray loudly.

"Shhh!" Nicholson commanded it, aware as he did so that the voices from the house were continuing. The braying was the last straw. He turned and fled out of the square, back to the darkness, then along the beach, to his compound.

Silence slowly returned to the square. The donkey wandered around the market place for a few minutes more. Near the door of the main mosque, it found itself some greenery to eat. It stopped and gorged happily on carrot tops — little knowing that it was partaking of its last supper.

The bomb blew up the Friday mosque of Saffina. One of the minarets was totally destroyed, while the other one lost its top half. The remains of the donkey were splattered over the entire wreckage, adding insufferable insult to unbearable injury.

The people of Saffina mourned. Businesses did not open on the market square the following day. Fish catches were left to the flies. The people did not mill about staring at the scene. They merely approached the mosque, gazed at it for a moment or two and then retreated from the scene, as if to watch it for too long would further insult their holy building.

The mosque was well over two hundred years old and had been built by a merchant seaman who had become rich importing coffee and spices from Mocha, Zanzibar and the ports of India and Malacca. The mosque had been his memorial and his gift. He had spared no expense to decorate it: blue tiles were imported from Isfahan; carpets for the interior woven in Nain and Qom. But the greatest treasure of the mosque had been its stained glass windows. These the explosion completely destroyed.

Hepworth went to survey the damage on Thursday morning. He too had paid a very short visit to the scene of devastation for, when people saw him, they pointed at him and acted as if he were in some way responsible. A child threw a stone.

"Control your children!" he had shouted at the people as he retreated, but the people merely stood and watched him.

The people of Saffina were thinking thoughts that would have shocked and unnerved Nicholson and Hepworth had they been able to see into their minds. They were thinking that never, never at any time during the civil war had the rebels attacked a mosque. It had not been their way. The power station, perhaps even the bookstore, but a mosque, never. The rebels stood for Islam. They called their fight Jihad. They told the people that the wealth coming from the Capital was an idol sent by a vain, cowardly king to seduce their hearts and minds from the Truth. And, thinking back to the times of war and the propaganda of the rebels, and now, looking at the ruin of their mosque, the people of Saffina wondered if they were being punished for accepting the king's mercenary representatives and distracting consumer goods. The cars broke down and needed foreigners to fix them; imported gadgets fell apart and could not be repaired; everything, day by day, was costing more and nobody wanted the skills Saffina had to offer.

The feeling that they deserved what had happened fermented with the thought that the insurgents of old, many of whose members they had known and grown up with, would never have done this deed. And if not them, then who?

Hepworth went to the hospital and warned everyone not to go to the market that day. He met Joanna and asked her to go to the Desert Regiment Camp for a swim in the evening. She said she was having Peter and Mary-Anne round to dinner.

"You don't want a fourth?" Hepworth had asked her without hope.

"No, thank you," replied Joanna, not even making an attempt to be polite.

"Well, suit yourself! And I wouldn't go shopping in the market if I were you."

"Went last night, thanks."

He stormed in on Nicholson. "Well you've really done it this time!"

Nicholson nodded.

"Is that all you've got to say?" asked Hepworth.

"Blame the donkey."

Hepworth was appalled at Nicholson's attitude. "Blame the donkey! Blame the wanker who drove the donkey I say! What could have got into you? We planned that you tether it outside the post office and leave it at that. But no, not you! If you want my opinion, you're losing your grip, old boy!"

"Well, I admit in retrospect I could have done better."

"Done better! Done better!" fumed Hepworth. "This isn't some damned public school's end-of-term lark, you know. This is the world of adult education." Hepworth felt the balance of power was shifting. Ever since he had set fire to the bookstore and killed the guard his old confidence had returned. And Nicholson's star was waning. Definitely. He could feel it in his bones. "There's one hell of a lot at stake," he went on, relishing the feeling of turning the knife. "Your pathetic effort of last night sets us back. Any fool will tell you that the rebels would never have sabotaged a mosque, for God's sake."

"I think we should move on to the next phase," said Nicholson quietly.

"What's the next phase? Bomb Mecca?"

"No. Nothing like that, although I would like to keep bombing Mecca as an option if all else fails. The watchword is 'Whatever is necessary'. It is time to show that the foreigners are not immune to attack. So far it has just been the Arabs who have got it in the neck. Now it is time to make a sacrifice from among our own kith and kin. If the destruction of the mosque — a mosque, by the way, to which I was really quite attached in a detached sort of way — has made people question who is to blame. A death among the foreigners would soon redirect their thinking, especially if that foreigner had done a lot of good for Saffina."

Hepworth was interested. "So who gets the short straw?"

"It seems quite clear. The Yank woman. She's known to

everyone. Been here years. If she gets done in they'll be back on our side in a flash."

"Why not Joanna? She really pisses me off!"

"Well, she may piss you off but she hasn't been here long enough to make a difference. Nurse Sissons on the other hand, has won the king's award for industry, or whatever they call it. She's our very own Mother Teresa. Do her in and you cause a stir."

"Yes, I suppose so. Got a plan, have you?"

"One is forming. One is forming."

"Well make sure there's a part in it for me."

"Oh, I will, Hepworth. I will," replied Nicholson pacifically.

He offered Hepworth a drink and changed the subject. "How's the love life?"

"Non-fucking-existent," replied Hepworth. "That Joanna woman is frigid. Today she told me she was having a dinner party for Nurse Sissons and that inspector cove. She actually said that I wasn't invited. Imagine that!"

"Where is the party?" asked Nicholson.

"At her place, I suppose. No, I haven't had a leg over for ages. I'm not going to risk it with the whores around here. They're probably riddled with AIDS. No, it's all a bit bleak. Much winding of Seikos I'm afraid. How about you?"

"I can turn it on and off."

"Ah, yes. So you said."

"Look," Nicholson asked, suddenly quite intense, "there is something you can do for me. Spy around that inspector's house and see if his chum has gone. I told him to chuck him out. I'll be interested to see if he has."

"Well, I can tell you now. Saw them together last night. Having a cosy little tête-à-tête on the front step of their little love nest," said Hepworth, mellowing somewhat under the influence of the alcohol.

"Ah, well, in that case, young Ibrahim may have a role to play in the Grand Plan that is forming."

"No donkeys this time, Simon!"

"No donkeys," replied Nicholson, looking at Hepworth,

smiling sweetly and thinking how well a halter would suit him.

Nicholson was watching when Peter Drury arrived at the hospital compound the following evening. Through his binoculars he saw Peter stop his Landrover outside Joanna's bungalow, adjust his tie in the wing mirror, smooth down his wayward hair, and, armed with a small tin of Quality Street bought that morning, walk over to Joanna's door and knock. The door opened almost at once and Peter disappeared.

"Now he'll spend five minutes apologising for only bringing a tatty tin of Quality Street," Nicholson thought, turning away from the binoculars on a tripod.

He turned on his video and television and sat down to watch part of *The Jewel in the Crown*. His mother had sent it out week by week some years before and had kept enquiring how he was enjoying it. He had enjoyed it. He continued to enjoy it on this, his umpteenth time of watching, though parts of it irritated him greatly.

His mother seemed to think that he lived a life similar to Mabel in Rose Cottage. And he did not disillusion her. Mother must be allowed her fond illusions. She had decided that her Simon was somehow working in the "mission fields", had been known to lament that "that common Bob Geldof" got all the attention while people like her son laboured in the thick of things far away from media attention. If that was what she chose to believe who was he to disillusion her? When illusions went so deep as, he felt, they went with his mother, it was a vain task to attempt to uproot them.

He had watched four episodes of *The Jewel in the Crown* this time around. He liked Merrick and wanted him to win. But he would not win. If Merrick had won the novel would never have been accepted by the publishers. If the real life Merricks had won, the British would still be in India and there would have been no story to tell. Daphne made him want to throw up. Daphne was everything that was wrong with the Colonies with her liberal notions. Nicholson agreed with the sentiments of a character he had heard in a play on the World

Service who had said, on hearing that a fellow had been made Bishop of Bombay, "Isn't that taking Christianity a bit far?" So-called Christian principles were what had destroyed the Empire. Christianity, he reckoned, could be tolerated as part of weekend life in the shires. On no account should it travel up to the city on a Monday morning. Its mildewed dogmas dampened the corridors of power, eventually causing them to crumble. Never should it be allowed out of the country. It was like foot and mouth disease.

He watched an episode and then reckoned it was time. He would not do the job himself. He had men especially trained to do this job. They enjoyed it.

Nicholson picked up the telephone and summoned his henchmen. They arrived, two exceptionally tall Arabs with the profiles of falcons. They came from a tribe who subsisted in the very heart of the Empty Quarter, who were notorious for their independence and contempt for the soft farmers and urban Arabs of the coast. Their brand of Islam was a hard Calvinism when compared to the soft Anglo-Catholic variety that had settled down comfortably along the coast.

While in Saffina these two men stayed on the compound, unless sent out on an errand by Nicholson. They had left their wives in the desert and returned to them for a fortnight every three months. In many ways they were like expatriates. Nicholson, however, did allow them to slake their appetites on prisoners. The threat of such a violation was often enough to make a prisoner tell all he knew. And if they did not, why so much the better; then Nicholson was able to turn the two bedouin on the prisoner. He could watch.

"Murad! Zayn! May God give you the strength!" Nicholson addressed his employees. "I have a job for you to do tonight."

The pair smiled.

"There is a small house in the desert between Nicholson and Bilad Saffina. In that house you will find a young man. He is from Jaheel and you will know his face because he used to work for me. He has done great wrongs and has caused much anguish to the good people of Jaheel. I want you to bring him here. While you take him feel free to upset the property in the house. If he does not come willingly you may use force, but do not kill him. Blindfold him and put him in the small cell by himself. And if you feel hungry you may use him for your pleasure. You must both be missing your wives."

The pair saluted and turned to go. "One more thing: do it now. I want him in the cell in three hours from now. No more. Is that clear?"

"It is clear," they replied.

Nicholson fixed himself a drink and went back to the video. He was pleased to see that Mabel had finally snuffed it. Silly cow. If she wanted an English cottage with roses all over the bloody shop, why couldn't she have had it in England? Why pollute a perfectly good colony with her doilies and secateurs? With wets like her around, it was no wonder we had to bugger off out. Ah, there was Merrick. That's better. A good chap, that Merrick. Pity he would have to get his come-uppance. But then in fiction they always did. Those poufter writers had to give their audience what they wanted and they wanted the bad to get it in the teeth.

He took a comforting shot of whisky and consoled himself that novels were not real life.

14

"You've gone to such a lot of trouble for us, Joanna!" exclaimed Mary-Anne, surveying the candle-lit table decorated with flowers and carefully laid.

"You certainly have," agreed Peter, quite relaxed after two glasses of sherry.

"It's an illusion, I'm afraid," said Joanna. "When we've eaten the soup I'll have to take your plates and wash them so that we can use them for the chicken. And I've only got three glasses so you'll either have to use the ones you've got or do without the wine."

"Wine! How do you lay hands on such decadent items?" Peter asked.

"It's quite simple really. I laid it down on my second night here. I bought a plastic bin, raisins and lots of sugar in the market and, following an ancient Save the Children recipe, concocted a brew."

"I'm sure it will be wonderful," said Mary-Anne. "How industrious you've been!"

"Just as long as you can keep it down," laughed Joanna in her practical manner, which could sometimes seem like rudeness and could so easily be rudeness, in the right circumstances.

They started to eat the soup.

"It's mainly from a tin but I tarted it up with some Ma Ling mushrooms."

The three continued to exchange pleasantries until they were half way through the chicken. It irked Joanna and Peter that neither seemed able to bite the bullet and talk about something more interesting.

But Mary-Anne was hard to get talking. Only on the night of the bookstore explosion had she opened up to Joanna and, since then, she had returned to her tranquil shell — smiling and approving of everyone and everything, but very much her own person. Peter, Joanna felt, would be quite happy to talk, but he was held back by Mary-Anne.

Finally, she could bear it no longer. Taking a large mouthful of wine she asked, "So are we going to survive all this?"

Mary-Anne looked at Joanna. "It's all really nice. A wonderful treat! I'm quite sure we'll survive it very nicely."

"I don't think that's what Joanna meant," Peter said.

Thank God! Joanna thought. "No I didn't. I was referring to what's been happening in Saffina."

"Well, to be frank, it's beginning to scare me," said Peter.

"Me too. It doesn't make any sense. Why would they blow up the mosque? You'd think they'd want the people on their side. That's not the way to do it."

"What do you think?" Peter asked Mary-Anne.

"Oh, my. I don't know. I haven't a notion. I honestly feel it's better not to think about it. Leave it to those who have the power. I'm sure Mr Nicholson and Mr Hepworth are doing their best to protect us. They've posted more guards on the hospital and elsewhere. I expect it will get better. It was much worse during the war." Mary-Anne returned to her chicken.

"Have they put a guard on your place, Peter?" asked Joanna.

"No, they haven't. Should they have?"

Joanna frowned. "Have you asked for one?"

"Well . . . no."

"You're very isolated out there."

"But I wouldn't have thought that anyone in Education would be in danger," said Mary-Anne. "During the war here the rebels only attacked military targets."

"But don't forget, they blew up the bookstore, Mary-Anne."

"I haven't forgotten. I suppose I was thinking out loud. It *has* been bothering me a bit. This time it's — oh I don't know — different. I have no time for insurgents and terrorist acts of any kind, but the rebels in the war — well, you could respect

169

them. They attacked the targets they hated. This time — it's just different. Much more ruthless and dishonourable."

"Tell Peter what Othman said!" commanded Joanna.

"Othman?" asked Peter.

"The guard at the bookstore. He was killed."

"I remember Othman. He helped me pack up all the books the day before the fire."

Mary-Anne smiled. "Did he? That was Othman. If he liked you, he'd do anything for you. And he must have liked you because if he hadn't he wouldn't give you the time of day."

"So Peter isn't the devil, then!" exclaimed Joanna.

"Joanna, don't!" pleaded Mary-Anne.

Joanna continued to look at Mary-Anne, who did not look back, but moved peas from one side of her plate to the other with her fork.

"Othman said something to Mary-Anne before he died," Joanna told Peter.

"Did he? I thought he had died at once."

"He was strangled but he did not die immediately. He died in the hospital," said Joanna.

Mary-Anne let out an audible sigh. "That has been bothering me too. Strangulation. It's not an Arab way of death. They don't kill in that way. Blood must be shed whether you are killing a chicken or a person. I remember when the Iraqis killed those poor Jews in Baghdad after the Yom Kippur War. They hung them. It was almost like killing them twice. A real insult."

Peter looked at Mary-Anne. "Are you saying that you think the killers may not have been Arabs?"

Mary-Anne shook her head. It was a gesture not so much a denial of Peter's question as an unwillingness to consider the implications of her thoughts.

"And Othman?" asked Joanna, suddenly, very hard. Hard to a point that Peter wanted to kick her under the table.

Mary-Anne put down her fork. "I always thought the English talked about the weather. It seemed a dumb topic of conversation until I gave it some thought. Here we are creatures on God's earth. The weather is the one thing that must dominate us as organisms. If flowers could talk they would talk of the weather. Because when you talk about the weather you talk about the most basic ingredient of life on earth. You paint quite a lot of your picture. Then it's only left to fill in the detail. Can't we talk about the weather?"

"Mary-Anne!"

She looked at Joanna, who was, Peter could see, not going to be placated. "Othman. Yes. Othman did say something to me before he died. He said, 'The Englishman is a devil' *Ingleezi shetan* in Arabic. He used the singular. However, you must remember that he was about to die, perhaps had already died. We revived him in the hospital. He had almost certainly suffered impaired blood supply to the brain. There may well have been brain damage. I don't know how much attention one should pay to his words."

"Good," said Joanna, gentle again. "Now we *can* talk about the weather."

Mary-Anne said nothing.

Joanna got up and cleared away the dishes, then came back from the kitchen with a huge trifle. "Now this I do really well. Unfortunately the cream is tinned stuff from Denmark and the custard is made with Nido but apart from that it's the real thing."

They ate in silence.

The Englishman is a devil, thought Peter. Perhaps he meant me. Maybe he saw my books as bad, that they would pervert the children. They were full of pictures and many Muslims don't approve of pictures. Oh, God how depressing!

After they had drunk their coffee, Mary-Anne excused herself saying that she had to go and make her rounds of the hospital wards. She thanked Joanna heartily, but was obviously still put out by the conversation they had had over dinner.

Peter helped Joanna to wash up.

"Mary-Anne can be strange sometimes," she said.

"Well you were a bit hard on her. Why didn't you just tell me about Othman if you thought I should know."

Joanna shrugged. "I suppose I thought she might have some ideas on the subject."

"Well, what are your ideas?"

"I don't have any ideas — just intuitions. And I wanted Mary-Anne to voice my intuitions."

"Well she didn't. So you voice them."

"No."

Peter snorted. "So why bring it up? Just to make me feel bad? It's not very nice to be called a devil by a dying man!"

Joanna stopped scouring the coffee cups and said, "No, you don't come into it. I'm sure he didn't mean you."

"Well who did he mean?"

"I don't know."

"Who do you *think* he meant?"

Joanna looked at Peter as if he were a very slow schoolboy.

"You mean Nicholson or Hepworth?" he asked incredulously.

"Right first time. That's my theory — no, it isn't even a theory. My intuition."

"And what makes you 'intuit' that?"

"Well, first of all, I agree with Othman's sentiments. I think they are devils from what I've seen of them. Second, given the context, I think they . . ." She stopped.

"What? Tell me what's on your mind?"

"It's nothing concrete. I have no evidence. I just feel that they — that they might have done all these things. I don't know why they would but I do know they're capable of it. They're straight out of *The Lion* or *The Eagle* those two, except they don't have any of the innate decency you found there. They're just mercenaries who have stayed on. This whole country is run by their sort — but they're especially powerful in the Eastern Region. Now why are they so powerful here? All the other areas have a civilian police force. But not here. Here the government still worries about the people's loyalty. Imagine you are them, banking a couple of thousand a month and living very comfortably. If nothing is happening to help you justify your existence, if expats like us who are paid pittances can come here and survive, if you see yourself being sent away to the dole queue in England . . . just imagine you are them, a you without any queer moral squint . . . what would you do?"

Peter thought for a long moment. He did not want to give the answer that occurred to him. "Try to justify my existence."

"How? No morality, remember."

"By making it seem as if there is still trouble."

Joanna threw one of the glasses into the sink. When she drew it out of the water it had a crack in it.

"Now I've only got two!" she cried triumphantly.

Peter felt suddenly very afraid. "Still, it's only an intuition. Surely the government would have tumbled to it by now!"

"To all intents and purposes they *are* the government, you silly boy!"

Joanna dried her hands, walked over to Peter. He thought for a moment she was going to smack him, but she kissed him.

"I'm scared, Peter," she said.

"Me too."

"But not of me?"

"Well, a little."

"Don't be."

"If you say so."

"You don't want to go home in the dark, do you?"

"Er . . ."

"No, of course you don't. Nurse has spoken."

And Joanna led her bemused patient towards the bedroom.

Nicholson's men, Murad and Zayn, parked their Suzuki jeep a hundred yards from the front door of Peter's prefab. They approached the building, guided by the slight golden light leaking out of the living room window. They looked through the window and saw Ibrahim bent over his copybook at the table.

He had been writing, "Mary, the girl with a blue dress on, is talking to John." He had already written twenty or so practice sentences and was pleased with the way they had flowed. As he wrote he could already see the bright red strokes and the

173

"Very Good" that Peter would write after he had read the work.

Ibrahim was never bored or unhappy when he was doing his English. Somehow hard study did what nothing else could do: blot out thoughts of home and the agony that lay in store for him just over the northern mountains.

He heard a knock on the door but did not get up to answer it. He knew that the oil lamp would tell tales on him, would show the caller that someone was home. Perhaps they had looked through the window already and seen him. But he was unable to move. He sat watching his pencil, poised over the paper and listened to his fearfully loud heartbeat.

The two men knocked again. One called out, "Ya, Ibrahim!"

He did not recognise the voice. It did not have the ring of Jaheel and that made him feel a little better. But still he did not move. Fear froze him.

Then Zayn's face appeared at the window, the nose pressed against the mosquito wire:

"Open the door, Ibrahim! Mr Nicholson wants you."

"Why does he want me?" asked Ibrahim.

"We don't know."

"I want to stay here. I have done nothing wrong."

The face disappeared and there was more banging at the door, then the sound of both men putting their shoulders to it. The pressure made the whole flimsy prefab shake. Sand, trapped in the roof space, rained down on to the floor and over him. Some was spreading over the copybook.

"I will come!" shouted Ibrahim.

The banging stopped.

Ibrahim blew out the oil lamp and started to stand up. Then he felt the pencil gripped hard between his fingers. In the dark he found his copybook and wrote, "I am with Mr Nicholson." And slowly, fear eating him up, he walked to the door. He fumbled, looking for the catch, and opened the door a little way.

Murad and Zayn caught hold of Ibrahim, pinioning his arms behind him. Murad slapped him across the face and punched him in the chest.

"What are you doing? Why?"

"You didn't answer the door at once! In future you will obey us at once!" Zayn shouted.

Zayn led him out of the prefab, keeping his arm locked tightly behind him. As he stumbled across the rough ground towards the jeep, Ibrahim could hear the sound of breaking glass and of furniture being thrown about in the house.

"Why is he doing that? The house belongs to the Englishman."

"Be quiet!" replied Zayn, giving Ibrahim's arm a twist. Ibrahim screamed.

He was put into the back of the jeep and his burning arm was handcuffed to one of the roof supports. Zayn left him and joined Murad in the house. More sounds of breaking furniture reached him. Looking towards the house he could see the darting light of a torch.

Ibrahim knew the men. He had seen them when he worked for Nicholson. But John De Lobo had warned him about them. "Be careful of them, Ibrahim! They do the dirty work for Mr Nicholson. You know why Mr Nicholson is in Saffina. He is here to find out about anybody who does not like the king. When he finds them he sends those two men to arrest them."

John had pointed out a windowless building joined to Nicholson's office and told Ibrahim that the "bad" people were brought to that building and interrogated. But Ibrahim had never seen anybody brought there. The two men who were now rampaging through Peter's house had always seemed to spend their time lounging on the verandah outside Nicholson's office.

Ibrahim pulled at the handcuff but the effort hurt his arm. If he could get free he could run off over the desert and easily lose himself. But, even if he could get away, where could he go? Now he had lost the safety of Peter Drury's house there was nowhere on earth for him to hide.

He stopped struggling and tried to be optimistic. Perhaps Nicholson only wanted to see him to find out why he had left. Perhaps then he would let him go. "I haven't done anything wrong!" he told himself. But then another voice came back and told him that he deserved anything that Nicholson wanted to do to punish him. Anything at all. He slumped down in the back of the jeep.

Murad and Zayn did not drive him straight to Nicholson's compound. Instead they took a track which led away from Saffina towards the mountains. But only for a mile. Then Murad turned off the track and drove over the rough scrubland for a few minutes. Finally they stopped the jeep in the middle of nowhere.

"Here?"

"Here."

"Why are you stopping here?" asked Ibrahim, terrified. "You must take me to Mr Nicholson."

"We know what we must do."

They took him out of the jeep and stripped off his clothes. Then Zayn held him down on his front and Ibrahim knew what was going to happen:

"Don't!" he told Zayn.

He heard a laugh behind him and the voice of Murad. "Are you not the Englishman's catamite? It should be easy for you."

Ibrahim felt the pain. He buried his face in the sand and screamed. Perhaps this, then, is what they wanted. After this they will leave me alone and let me go back to the house as if nothing has happened. But he could not go back to the house after this. Better that they kill him.

Murad finished and Zayn took his place. Ibrahim lay prone. He did not fight what was happening but just listened, detached, to the grunting sounds the man made behind him.

Part of him felt that he deserved this. So this is how it feels! He had done this to others while growing up but had always avoided being used in return. He recalled his own feelings, how he had felt contempt for the person so used, how, in his need, he had ignored the screams of the boy beneath him. It was his turn now. So much more than ever those lads in Jaheel had deserved it, Ibrahim deserved it. For those lads had merely been younger and weaker. He relaxed and let it happen. The pain brought him relief. He felt sure he would be left alone afterwards. The two bedouin wanted this and nothing else.

But when they had finished they threw Ibrahim's clothes at him and pushed him into the back of the jeep. This time they did not handcuff him but at once set off across the scrubland, back towards Saffina.

Nobody spoke.

The gates opened on Nicholson's compound. Ibrahim thought with misery of the first time those gates had opened. They clanged closed behind him. The jeep stopped at the door to the windowless building. Murad opened the door while Zayn bundled Ibrahim through it. They opened the door of a cell and threw him in.

The door banged shut behind them. Ibrahim lay on the concrete floor and heard laughter echo through the building before the heavy outer door slammed shut, leaving him alone with his thoughts and his pain.

"It's not working, is it?"

Joanna, sweat pouring down her body, saturating her hair and making it cling in thick wisps to her face, neck and shoulders, spoke to Peter from a long way off, from somewhere below him.

Peter lay on the bed. The sheet beneath him was wet through, his whole body covered in his own and Joanna's sweat. A pool of it had lodged in the hollows between neck and breastbone, between his ribs.

"No, it doesn't look like it. God, I'm sorry, Joanna."

Joanna's face appeared over his as a blur. He thought about reaching across for his glasses but it would mean saying, "Excuse me, please," and he thought it might be the last straw. He had also thought several times of accusing the wine of causing his impotence, but that seemed ungallant too.

Joanna looked down at Peter, thinking how much younger, softer, he looked without those dreadful National Health spectacles. But, above all, she wished she had not initiated this encounter. Why could she not have followed her instincts and let him be? Something had told her that it would be a disaster. She could not articulate what it was, but they were too easy together somehow. There just hadn't been that tension there which, in her experience, triggered off love affairs, or even a one-night-stand.

She blamed herself. Peter was nice, kind, decent, and, hopefully, discreet. She had desperately wanted to make love to somebody and to be made love to in return. Peter had been handy, so she had ignored her gut-instinct and pulled him towards her lair.

It had gone fine at first. A fine figure of a man had emerged from his British Home Stores ensemble — a rampantly sexy man in fact — but when it actually came down to it he had become impenetrably floppy in a priapic sort of way. Then he had reminded her of her old men in the geriatric ward, who, on being bathed, revealed themselves to be so well-endowed — were proud of the show they put on — but whose erectile tissue had spread and distended giving their poor, pooped, blood no chance at all to pump it up to the required psi. Her old men had enjoyed her making a crack. "I bet you were a ladykiller in your time!" she'd say, washing them down with a flannel. "I've had my share!" they'd croak back. And she, turning to rinse out the flannel in an enamel bowl, would stifle the tears, thinking of those bodies in their prime and immortality, and weep dryly for the way they had ended up — unable to remember their own names and addresses, their big, floppy, seen-the-world penises waving at the dust instead of pointing towards the heavens.

She manoeuvred herself off Peter and banged her head down on the pillow next to his. It felt wonderful to be on terra firma again. Her mouth ached, her whole body ached, from her fruitless exertions. But behind the memory of wasted time there was a deep tiredness which almost passed for satisfaction. She felt him stroke her back, a light touch. Any lighter, she thought, and he would not be touching me. She knew he was feeling humiliated and guilty and lost — just like her old men exposed by a blanket bath — and Joanna knew that she could not sleep until he slept too — and slept easily.

She reached out her hand to him and he grasped it gratefully and kissed it.

"How are you?" she asked him.

"I'm sorry, Joanna," he said.

"Don't be."

"I'm sorry I put you through all those . . . er . . ."

"Contortions?"

"Yes. Sorry."

"Can't be helped. Maybe you drank too much wine."

"Maybe," he answered gratefully.

"Or, it could be that you're nervous. Nerves are the worst thing for . . . for it."

"Are they?"

"Oh, yes."

"You see, it was my first time," he said quite matter-of-factly, surprising himself.

Joanna pulled her head from the pillow and looked at Peter, who was staring at the ceiling doggedly.

"Was it?" she asked hardly able to believe him, a picture like a succession of police mugshots of her own lovers passing through her brain and out again.

"Yes, I . . . er . . . somehow . . . never got round to it."

"How do you mean?" she asked him, thinking that one a bit lame.

"No girl ever seemed to want me somehow."

"And you were never able to convince one to take a chance?"

"No," he said. "I never could."

She didn't reply. Instead she turned over completely, lying on her back. The fan rotated above them as they lay, like bodies in a mortuary, not touching now. All that was missing, she thought, was the label tied to their big toes.

Then Joanna had a thought. She wondered whether Peter was gay. There he was, living in his prefab with some Arab chap. Could it be that? She dismissed the thought and mentally apologised to Peter. Then it was back. Two years in the Sudan and he had not done anything? He had said that it was his first time. Could it be that he was referring to heterosexual intercourse? Perhaps he was having all the men in Ras Al Surra? Perhaps he was a promiscuous homosexual who had spent two years in the Sudan having it off gutless with every lorry driver and tribesman who passed by!

179

Her imaginings were coming thick and fast now. She thought of the Listerine in her bathroom and ached to get up and pour the bottle down her throat and over her body. Instead, she let the fan mesmerise her for a few minutes.

Then she asked, "Have you *never* had sex before?"

"No," he replied.

"Not even playing about at school?"

"I went to a boys' school, Joanna," he replied innocently.

"Yes, but boys experiment at a certain age, don't they?"

"I suppose so. I never did."

"So, how do you . . . er . . .?"

"Well, I sometimes have dreams."

"And what are these dreams about?"

Peter was silent for a long time and she wondered if she had gone too far, if she had attempted to uncover things in minutes which he had buried for years.

But she need not have worried. After a long "Er . . ." he said, "Well, usually I can't remember them, but when I do I'm climbing with my mates. We reach the top of the mountain and . . ."

"Yes?" she asked.

"I wake up sticky," he replied.

She looked at Peter and he looked at her. It was a deeply serious look, though she could not tell whether, without his glasses, he was able to see her.

She felt a laugh starting, a post-fart-at-assembly laugh, which, the more she tried to stifle it, the more it would not be stifled. She gave up the attempt and exploded with mirth.

"Climbing with your mates!" she managed between guffaws.

Peter squinted at her and started to laugh himself.

"I've never told anyone before!" he said.

She tried to control her laughter. It seemed cruel somehow, but he was laughing too and each primed the other. Then she was gasping, trying to say something else, but had already been overtaken by the laughter her unuttered utterance was having on her. She resolutely bit the corner of her pillow for a moment, then, in a gruff, over-restrained voice that masked her panic at the onset of further laughter said, "Not even your mates?" and exploded again so violently that white snot exploded from her nose.

"Ooops!" she said and wiped her nose with the corner of the sheet.

"Ooops!" he repeated, sending her up.

She attacked him then, still laughing, played at smothering him with her pillow and he fought back and was on top of her suddenly, still laughing, and he bent down over her and seemed about to kiss the top of her right breast, but, instead blew a trumpet call on the soft flesh there which came out as a fart. And Joanna remembered the maternity ward at Queen Charlotte's and how she would blow on a baby's tummy in exactly the same way and get the baby laughing for the first time in its life.

He suddenly stopped laughing, however, and gazed down at her and listened to her and felt her diaphragm heaving and knew that something was happening.

She laughed on, then stopped because he had stopped and listened to the silence, broken only by the whirring of the fan. And then she felt something prickling down there, moving against her and knew why he was no longer laughing.

They were still, and silent.

He said with some urgency, his voice trembling, "May I, Joanna?"

And she, still feeling the movement and the heat and the stiffness against her thigh, replied, "Go on, then."

At five in the morning, Joanna ordered Peter out of bed.

"People will be going to the hospital mosque in a few minutes," she told him, "I don't want them to see your vehicle in front of the house. It would ruin my reputation."

He got up immediately, once again seized by his need to please Joanna. He pulled on his clothes and ran his hands through his hair, trying to push it into place and making not the slightest difference.

Joanna lay in bed. She looked a mess, very different from her usual neat self, but she managed a smile for Peter as he stood near the bed to bid her goodbye. Having done that, he shuffled on the spot and she knew he was about to say he was sorry again, and she did not think she could stand that. She had to restrain herself from snapping at him, but knew she could not listen to his expressions of regret one more time. She held out her arm to him. It was an action at once affectionate and restraining.

She added a small smile to the gesture and said, "I know what you're going to say, Peter, and I don't want to hear it. I just don't want to."

"But I er . . ."

"No. Not another word! Nurse has spoken! It is me who should be apologising. I was the one who forced you into it. So it makes no sense for *you* to keep accusing yourself."

Peter stood, unconsciously scratching his left ankle with the toe of the sandal on his right foot. He looked at the bedside mat as he replied. "Well, perhaps, I needed more time."

She wanted to say "You've had *twenty-seven years*! How much time does it *take*?" but instead she smiled and said, she hoped sweetly, "I just wasn't the right girl for you. It happens, you know!"

"Oh, no, Joanna!" he replied. "You were wonderful — are wonderful. It's me . . ."

"There you go again!" she said, her impatience breaking through. "I said there were to be no apologies. Look, you'd better be off."

"Right ho," he said quietly.

"But I'm free later in the day, Peter. How about getting Ibrahim to cook me some of that fish you say is so good? Shall I come round?"

He nodded.

"Say one?"

He nodded again, then he reached down and started scratching his ankle with his hand.

"You've got a lot of mosquitoes, Joanna. Much more than me."

"It's the creek, I expect."

"I expect so."

He dithered for a moment and she frowned at him, but smiling the while, and he took the hint, clapped his hands together once in a gesture of finality and said, "Bye, Joanna."

"Bye, Peter. Give my regards to Ibrahim. Tell him how much I'm looking forward to seeing him."

Peter drove out of the hospital compound. The day was announcing itself on the eastern horizon. Apart from the low hum of the hospital generators, everything was still. He felt suddenly light and cheerful and aware and the thought struck him that perhaps he felt so good because he was alone again and not confronted by the spectre of a beautiful woman — an infinitely complex collection of emotions and physical parts — who had lain there waiting for him to *satisfy* her. Of course, he told himself, Joanna had not asked for that. She had been kind and considerate and done everything she could to help him. But he was like a learner driver presented with the keys to Concorde and told to give her a spin at Mach 2. It was beyond him. He wanted to do it because he didn't want to disappoint anybody, to let anybody down. But that spark of daring, of need, had not been there.

He drove out towards the beach and remembered an old Doris Day film he had seen on television just before leaving home. Doris, an air stewardess, had been left to land an airliner. Doris had managed it. Had he, he thought, been a different sort of chap, he might have been able to accept the challenge too. Had he been Hepworth or Nicholson, he would have said, "Leave it with me!" and gone out with a light in his eye to show everyone that he was composed of "the right stuff".

Well, it did not look as if he *was* composed of the right stuff. He stopped the Landrover just behind the flotsam and jetsam at the high water mark. Was he still a virgin? Did penetration count? When they had laughed and horse-played on the bed everything had started falling into place. But Joanna's words, "Go on, then!" had reignited the cloud of fear that he thought had been dissipated. At once he was transferred from Peter Drury, erect and excited, to a nervy little lad sitting where the fan was and looking down at what his bony body was doing.

183

"You haven't a hope in hell! Satisfy a girl! You!" the voice had said over and over again. And the more he had tried to stifle the nervy little boy, the more the boy had protested. The boy had looked through all the sex manuals and quoted from them:

"You forgot to massage the clitoris! You've neglected every single one of her erogenous zones! You can't just hump away and hope to satisfy a *woman*, you know! Women are slow of arousal. You're not having a wank now! This is what the big boys do! Will you just *look* at yourself!"

And Peter had failed again.

And yet he did not feel sad. "Better to have tried and failed than never to have tried at all," he told himself, remembering that he had used that same proverb when consoling pupils who gave up the climb up Snowdon half way. The night had taught him something, he felt. What, he was not inclined to attempt to articulate just at that moment.

Peter sat on the bonnet of the Landrover and watched the mango sky lightening. But, suddenly, this was not enough. Looking to left and right, he stripped off and ran down the beach into the ocean. Then he swam out as fast as he possibly could—so fast as to blot out all thought—into deep water. The sea was almost cold, its surface unusually calm. He trod water and looked over to the east. The sun rose, almost to his command, at his whim. He applauded the sunrise, dived down, found to his delight capsules of icy water in the depths, tried to stay in them, then swam hard further down, aware that he was upside down, taking great vertical breaststrokes. He abandoned himself completely and let the water take him up slowly, slowly — to greet the splendid red surface of the ocean and the reliable ball in the distance.

He floated and watched as the sun rose and soon lost its redness, absorbed into the light of common day. In half an hour or so it would become a blur in the sky. It would no longer be a thing of beauty but a threatening mass that gave the impression of hurtling down on to Ras Al Surra.

Peter swam back towards the shore, then waded through the shallows kicking up the water. A sadness had descended upon him with the rising of the sun and the bleaching out of the colours of sunrise. It occurred to him that he did not really know what made the world turn. Most men would not have had any problem. Mr Shukry, Mr Ahmed, Mr Siddiqui, and probably Hepworth and all the men in Saffina lay with their women and made love and babies as if it were the most natural thing in the world. All those kids in all those classrooms and tents and under Sudanese trees were the products of that spontaneous lust for life. They did not talk about it much. They took it for granted. He, on the other hand, fretted and apologised and went hot and cold, flaccid and erect.

He dressed and drove back towards the prefab. When he arrived outside the front door he sounded his horn, expecting that Ibrahim would come to the door questioning his absence. Would he tell him about his night? Maybe he would. Then he noticed that the door was ajar. Perhaps Ibrahim was out.

He walked inside shouting his name, "Ibrahim!" But it froze on his lips when he saw the state of the interior. The whole house had been turned upside down: books and papers littered the floor, the fridge had been pushed forward on to its front; the mattresses and bedding had been thrown over, one of the mattresses climbing the wall.

Peter felt like following the mattress up the wall. He wandered around for a while, his head full of questions. All the last hours had been driven out by a vision of mayhem glaring back at him from the floor of the prefab.

He wandered through each of his wrecked rooms and tears clouded his eyes. Where was Ibrahim? Had people from his village come and taken him away? But they did not know he was there. He shouted his name again and again, knowing that, if by some remote chance the youth suddenly appeared, he could put up with the rest and not despair. He would run to Ibrahim and hug him and chide him for giving him such a fright and together they would set about tidying up. Peter would say, "It doesn't matter, Ibrahim, they're only *things* after all. The main thing is that *you* are safe".

His chin quivered when he thought of the night when Ibrahim had wept and he had reached across to hug him and comfort him and tell him he was safe. But he had lied to his friend. He sat down and surveyed the scene blankly. A grim spectre of revenge, destruction, insurgency and death hammered itself into his head. He felt like a hijacked plane passenger, powerless and sweating in a soft seat, watching in terror the triumph of unreason.

He felt he had to tell someone. But who? There was no police station in Saffina. Nicholson and Hepworth came to mind. He thought about going to them for a brief moment, but a picture of Nicholson's sneer and the conclusions he would reach and the advice he would give and the "I told you so's" that he would keep repeating sent this idea scurrying away. There was nothing he could do at the moment.

Peter started to tidy things up. He set about this task not so much because he wanted everything to be shipshape again as because he felt that, lying among the mess might be some clue that would tell him what had happened.

But an hour and a half later he stood, sweating and stripped to the waist, none the wiser about what could have prompted such a crazed attack on his house.

Five of the six sheets he had prepared for the newspaper had been screwed up and were unusable. Two of Ibrahim's textbooks had been ripped almost in two. He placed all Ibrahim's books on the table, and, as he did so, found the copybook wedged between the table and the wall. It was open at some work. Idly he read the twenty sentences, smiling to himself at their correctness, pleased to find some evidence of his friend's presence. He read the last sentence: "Mary, the girl with the blue dress on, is talking to John." And then, in a scrawl so unlike Ibrahim's usual careful hand: "I am with Mr Nicholson."

It did not seem like a panicked message in itself, Peter thought. But it alarmed him nonetheless, mainly because of the strange scrawl. Had Nicholson taken Ibrahim? And, if so, why? Peter could not think of any reason. He remembered the conversation with Mary-Anne and Joanna of the night before. Well, say that her suspicions were true, why would Nicholson take Ibrahim away? Perhaps Nicholson thought that taking Ibrahim would scare him and finally make him decide to leave

Saffina. Well, if that was what he wanted to do, he would not succeed. Peter decided he was not going to leave Saffina. Not now and not like this. He wanted Ibrahim back. How could he achieve that? He would ask Joanna. Yes, that is what he'd do.

Remembering that she would be coming at one, he continued to tidy up the house. There was nothing for them to eat. He took up *Riding the Mountains Down* but felt guilty to be reading a book. Perhaps Nicholson would keep Ibrahim for the day and then send him back. Perhaps everything would work out. He found it hard to believe, but allowed the hope to stay and got on with his book. And, as he read, he thought of the woman who had put up with him and tried her best for him and not teased him and not let him apologise and feel sorry for himself. He took some comfort from that.

"Joanna will know what to do!" he thought.

15

At midday Nicholson unlocked the door of the cell block and went in. He held out the key to Ibrahim's cell in front of him as he approached the door. Then he passed the tip of the key along his top lip, then the bottom. The light pressure made him tingle. He wondered how he would find Ibrahim once he had unlocked and opened the door. Most prisoners he visited lay on their sides, wombed, in the corner. A few stood straight in the centre of the room. Their attitude was crucial.

He unlocked the cell door. He was surprised to find Ibrahim sitting on the floor staring straight ahead of him. He did not look up.

"Stand up, please, Ibrahim! This is not a tea-shop."

Ibrahim stood up.

"Thank you," Nicholson said.

Ibrahim said nothing.

"I suppose you are wondering why I have brought you here. Indeed, I am surprised that you have not already asked me. But, on second thoughts, perhaps I am not surprised. Perhaps you know. Perhaps you feel you deserve to be arrested, buggered by your captors and imprisoned in this hell-hole. You were buggered, I suppose? It is de rigueur with those two."

Ibrahim nodded.

"Yes. And I dare say you felt you deserved it. Well, before I tell you why you are here, may I ask you why you left my house so suddenly all that time ago? Without a word? That wasn't very nice, now was it?"

Ibrahim replied, "You gave me alcohol and tried to assault me."

"Is that all? Is that the only reason? Nothing else? Well I am disappointed with you. Such childish behaviour. You only had to say no. I am not, Ibrahim, bestial like the two who arrested you last night. I would have respected your wish. That night I did not pursue you to force my wicked lust on you, did I? No, I let you storm out of the room. 'That's life!' I told myself. But I know you, Ibrahim. I know your people. You came into my house and you learned many things but then, when things got a little complicated, off you went back to your village. You could not stand the conflicts. You hankered after your old simple existence. But it's a small village, Jaheel, isn't it, Ibrahim? And let me guess. When you got home you found that you couldn't settle there either. Am I right?"

Ibrahim nodded.

"Yes, I thought I might be. You couldn't take the pressures of the new life that was being shown you here. You craved your lost little routine at home but when you got home it was painful for you — so painful that you felt you could not do what the village expected of you: marry, settle down and raise a family. All the days of your life endlessly the same without any variety! It was a pain too severe for you to bear, a pain which, to avoid, you were prepared to betray your people. I heard of that betrayal from Hameed Nasr, Ibrahim. He blamed you for your father's death. You know he died of course, don't you? When we spoke I nodded and agreed with him. But to be honest, Ibrahim, I do not blame you. It may sound strange to hear me, your captor, saying this, but I blame myself. I am part of a worldwide army called Progress, Ibrahim. It is my job to push people like you into the twentieth century; to make you dependent on the things we produce; to inflict upon you our production — to make our dependence on things, our lust for gadgetry, our gods of greed — yours also. Let me tell you that we in this worldwide army have an easy task. Our products sell themselves. You haven't travelled, Ibrahim, but if you ever go to the West you will see that we have worked our people into lives completely devoted to the acquisition of goods. It is a vulgar pursuit. It has made them forget that they have souls. They have cars. You can see cars. You can touch them and go from one place to another in cars.

The people in the West have lost their ability to consider the soul. The soul is a subtle thing. Its study and its growth takes effort. We have trained our people to take the easy way out." Nicholson had started pacing the cell. He turned and asked, "Are you with me?"

Ibrahim nodded, though he was not even making an attempt to understand what Nicholson was saying.

"Yes, that is how it is there. And that is how it will be here if we have our way. And, believe me, Ibrahim, we will have our way." He held out a cigarette to Ibrahim who took it gratefully.

Nicholson smiled and lit it for him. "You see? You have learned to smoke. You didn't smoke before you came to Saffina, I'll bet!"

"No, I didn't," replied Ibrahim.

"But you do now and you miss them when you don't have them, am I right?"

"You are right."

"Well it is just the same with everything else. We will make you want what you do not need, crave what you will find out, too late, is not good for you."

The cigarette sent a wave of pleasure through Ibrahim. "Why are you telling me all this? Do you think I don't know it already?"

"Yes, excuse me. Perhaps I am stating the obvious. You should have stopped me earlier. However, the question still remains as to why I have brought you here? It is easily answered, Ibrahim. You are here to do a job for me. You are uniquely placed to do this job because you belong nowhere. You have, forgive me for saying so, no place in the old Arabia. Neither are you a part of the modern Arabia. You're a freak. You can't go back. That's for damned sure. But neither can you go forward."

"I will manage all right! Let me go!"

"So you want to go back to the house of the English teacher, do you? Well, nothing good for you will come out of that little ménage, believe me! Your English friend is a freak too. Not good enough to make it at home in Britain. He is full of silly romantic notions about the Real Arabia. He has got nothing to teach you that will help you, Ibrahim. But if you throw in your lot with me, if you prove yourself by doing this little job for me, I will see to it that you go to the Capital. There you will be taught English and Science. You will be fed and clothed and *trained* to do a well-paid job of work in the modern Arabia. You will be on the side of winners, Ibrahim. At the moment you are a loser and will always be a loser. If you do this little job to prove your loyalty to your king, then you can take your place in society. How does that sound?"

Ibrahim did not like the sound of it at all. He wondered if Nicholson was sane. "What is this job?" he asked.

"A simple job. I want you to kill a woman for me."

"Which woman?"

"A woman of no importance," replied Nicholson. "A foreign woman."

"So is he going to do it?"

Hepworth was waiting for Nicholson when he got back from visiting Ibrahim, a Bloody Mary — his third — in his hand.

"Get me one of those would you?" asked Nicholson. "He says not. Has some scruples about it apparently. I've said I'll give him some time to think it over. Later today I'll let my two bedou loose on him. If that fails then we'll just have to think of something else."

"Well let's hope it doesn't fail. We really need to get on with this and it would be wonderful to be able to pin it on an Arab."

"True enough," replied Nicholson. "Getting Ibrahim to do in Nurse Sissons would be a double for us. We'd be able to quiet the low rumblings in the Saffina bazaars and give a terminal scare to the Central Government at the same time. But I'm not sure he will. He's got a peculiar moral squint that lad."

Hepworth nodded. "Well, Simon, I just want you to know that you can rely on me if the lad remains obstinate."

"That's nice to know, Bob."

They sat down to enjoy their Friday curry.

"What form of persuasion do your bedouin use on prisoners, Simon?"

"Oh," replied Nicholson, cracking a poppadom in two, "friendly persuasion."

"Psychological stuff, eh?"

"Partly psychological, yes. But mainly good old-fashioned physical stuff."

Hepworth nodded and did not pursue the subject further.

"Wonderful curry, Simon! You know, I shall never know why you ever took on a local to do for you. Not when you can get a Hindi so easily."

"No, it was an aberration on my part," conceded Nicholson. "But believe me, I've learnt my lesson, Bob."

"Well that's good. Let's hope friend Ibrahim is quick on the uptake too."

Nicholson shrugged. "Either way, it's the Garden of Allah for him, I'm afraid. Such a silly boy! Such a silly boy!"

Joanna arrived half an hour late at Peter's house. She made excuses, telling Peter about her morning at the hospital as she stepped into the house.

"God, it's hot in here!" she exclaimed. "And what a dreadful smell! Like paraffin."

"Somebody threw my oil lamp against the wall."

"No! Who? Did you have a fight with Ibrahim? Look, Peter. Can we go outside. It's like an oven in here. How do you stand it?"

"With difficulty. I suppose I've got used to it."

"Where's Ibrahim? I was looking forward to meeting him."

They walked outside and sat under the awning that Ibrahim had erected. Peter told Joanna everything that had happened. He finished his account by showing her Ibrahim's scrawled message in the copybook.

"What are you going to do?" Joanna asked.

"I don't know. I keep thinking he might just come back. Anyway I thought I'd wait for you."

"Well, we know where he is. Why don't we go round there and ask Nicholson what's happened to him?"

"Yes, that was my first thought," said Peter. "But, bearing in mind what you said to me yesterday — I mean if you were right and Nicholson and Hepworth are the villains in what's been happening here — what would be the point? He'd probably just say we were mistaken and what could we do then? He's the one with the power. He's the government around here."

"Well it would do no harm to go and pay him a visit."

"I'm not sure."

Joanna brightened. "But look, you said before that they are the government around here. You're right, and that being the case, what could be more natural than for us to go to him and ask his help in finding Ibrahim? We'll go together and see what his reaction is. He could very well have him there in his lounge drinking a Pepsi for all we know."

"After the mess that I found here. I doubt it. Still, you're right. Let's go."

They went in Peter's Landrover to Nicholson's house, having first left Joanna's vehicle in the hospital compound. On the way they passed a party of Westerners who were having a picnic under a palm tree at the side of the road. They waved but did not stop.

"God, I would love to talk with them!" sighed Peter.

"I know what you mean."

They got into Nicholson's compound without difficulty and parked the Landrover next to Hepworth's vehicle.

Nicholson was standing behind the mosquito netting door as they climbed the steps. He had just said, "Let me do the talking!" to Hepworth and was smiling as the two approached. "An unexpected pleasure! What a pity, you're a little late for lunch." He held the door open and they stepped into his cool room and sat down. "Still, you'll have a drink?"

"This isn't really a social call," began Peter. "It's more business."

"Well, let's mix it a bit. It is the holiday after all. What's yours, Joanna?"

Joanna asked for a sherry and Peter, a gin and tonic.

"How can I be of help?" Nicholson asked.

"Ibrahim's disappeared from my house."

Nicholson leaned back in his chair. "And that bothers you, does it?" he asked.

"Yes it does. You see, I know he has nowhere to go. He did not leave a note or anything and the house was turned upside down when I got back this morning."

"Was it now? So you think he may have been taken away by force and . . ."

"And put up a struggle. Yes."

Nicholson said nothing. He took a sip from his drink and smiled at Joanna.

"We thought, as you are the Law in Saffina, that you would be interested," she said. "I mean it could be part of all the troubles here. Maybe the insurgents have kidnapped him."

"I hardly think so!" Nicholson laughed, "No, I would say that Ibrahim has just left. He does have a habit of leaving. Once one starts one finds it difficult to stop, I'm told. It becomes a habit. I wouldn't be surprised if he has decided to give the Capital a try."

"But the house was wrecked! Everything that could be overturned or broken was!" retorted Peter.

"Maybe it was a 'Goodbye and Thank You' gesture," suggested Nicholson with a wry smile.

Peter stared at Nicholson hard and put the gin and tonic on the table. He would not drink any more.

Hepworth broke in, "Of course, there is another possibility. Perhaps people from his village came and took him. That must have been on the cards."

Peter said, "But nobody from his village knew he was with me. He never went out. He never even ventured into Saffina. The only place he went was fishing on the beach north of here. He was petrified of being seen!"

"But Captain Hepworth does have a point," said Nicholson. "You don't know that nobody had seen him. Lots of Arabs going between Saffina and Jaheel walk straight along the beach to get to the track along the cliffs, past old Jaheel. Also, you are out at work all morning. Who knows what he did? No, there is a good chance that he's been taken back to his village."

"And what will happen to him there?" asked Joanna.

"They'll kill him or castrate him or something like that I shouldn't wonder," said Hepworth happily.

Nicholson gave Hepworth a withering look. "Hard to say what would happen, but it really is none of my business. Ibrahim is quite beyond the pale. I did tell you what I thought you should do, didn't I?"

"Yes, you did," replied Peter, remembering why he disliked Nicholson so much. "But, with respect, you are all we have here in the way of Law and Order and we are reporting a missing person. It seems to me that you should show more concern and put personal feelings aside."

Nicholson's smile froze and then disappeared from his face as Peter spoke. Who did this wet little twerp think he was telling him his duties? But he refrained from saying what was on his mind and in an even flat tone replied, "The concept of Law and Order is rather different in Saffina and environs to what you may have grown used to in Watford or Wallasey or wherever. If the wretched boy has been taken away by the village or by the girl's family then I am quite content that they mete out the appropriate punishment. It is no part of my brief to interfere in such matters. If you venture to Zarut you will see a mad woman chained to a stake in the centre of the courtyard of an old sheikh's house. She may just be a shade on the neurotic side for all I know. I feel that to be unusual punishment but I do not go bleating to the sheikh imposing namby-pamby Western values on him. I am here to keep the status quo intact. If the status quo demands the stoning of adulterers then so be it. As long as they aren't plotting against the king they can stone all the adulterers, tie up all the insane, kidnap all the reluctant bridegrooms they want."

"I see," said Peter.

"I wonder if you do. Still, I'm afraid that is how it is."

"So you can't do anything to help us?" asked Joanna stonily.

"Not really. I will make some enquiries. If it will put your mind at rest to know one way or the other, next time I see Hameed Nasr, my contact in Jaheel, I'll ask him about Ibrahim in a by-the-way way. But that's all I can do. You must realise that we have our work cut out at present."

Peter glanced at Joanna, who nodded.

"Well, I think we'd better be going, Mr Nicholson," said Peter.

"Won't you stay for another drink?"

"No, thank you."

Nicholson watched their Landrover leave the compound. When the gate had closed behind them he called out for Murad and Zayn, who came running to him on the verandah.

"Feeling hungry?" he asked them.

The pair nodded.

"Your meal's waiting."

Smiling, he returned to the sitting room and beckoned to Hepworth. "You asked me earlier about bedouin ways of persuasion, Bob. Come with me. I'll show you some of their methods."

Hepworth stood up and obediently followed Nicholson out of the bungalow.

The two men walked across the compound to the cell-block. Nicholson unlocked the door and put a finger to his lips. They tip-toed towards the door of Ibrahim's cell, from which they could hear muffled cries.

Nicholson put his eye to the peep-hole in the door. He did not say anything but Hepworth saw a smile suffuse his features. The smile held steady, as he stared into the cell for a minute or more.

"Come on, Simon," whispered Hepworth. "Give us a look!"

Reluctantly, Nicholson pulled his eye away and looked at Hepworth, his face still wearing its ghastly smile.

Hepworth took his place in front of the peep-hole and looked into the cell, still thinking of Nicholson's gleeful expression.

What he saw there in the cell did not make Hepworth want to smile, however. Rather he wondered what he was doing here like some perverted schoolboy. Nicholson was pushing him, trying to get him to relinquish his place so that he could have another peep. But Hepworth held his ground. The sight in front of his right eye, coupled with the pokes and frantic whisperings from Nicholson, were changing him, showing him a ghastly light. Suddenly, he longed to be in Dorothy's arms and surrounded by Dorothy's things. The right eye, still taking in the torture being inflicted on Ibrahim by his fellow countrymen, torture instigated by foreigners, started to water.

He gave up his place to Nicholson. He reeled away and crept into a corner, still fully aware of Nicholson's muffled giggling behind him.

Peter drove Joanna back to the hospital. On the way they did not speak. Both had been thrown into further confusion by their meeting with Nicholson. He was, or seemed to be, a nasty piece of work, as Joanna put it. He was, or seemed to be, peculiar in the extreme. But both of them, while wanting desperately to point the finger at him and his silly sidekick, could not really believe that the whole thing was happening — that evil had come to reside on their doorsteps.

"This sort of thing always happens to other people," Peter said to Joanna, as he dropped her outside her bungalow in the hospital compound. "I just keep telling myself that there must be some perfectly harmless explanation for it all."

Joanna nodded. "Are you coming in?" she asked.

"Don't think so. I need to think."

He headed back along the track to Bilad Saffina and the prefab. The sun blazed down and it did not seem possible that he had spent such a pleasant morning down at the sea. The land had been bled of colour and reflected the glare of the sun. His sunglasses did no more than render tolerable the light. He still had to squint through the windscreen in order to see the road ahead.

He reached the prefab and sat in the cab of the Landrover looking at it. He could not gather up the energy to walk out of the vehicle across the five yards of sand and open the front door. He knew what was inside and did not want to face it. He wondered if he would ever be able to face the place again. The first few weeks alone had been spiced with novelty; then, when that had started to fade, good luck had produced Ibrahim. There had been times when he would have preferred to be alone but those times had not been many. Now, with Ibrahim vanished as suddenly as he had made his appearance, Peter realised how much his presence had meant to him.

He honked on the Landrover's horn. He was tentative at first, something in him fearing that people would peep through their windows and tell him to be quiet. But he was alone in the desert contemplating an impossibly lonely late afternoon in a lonely oven. He lay his palm on the horn and let the sound go on for half a minute, stopping only when the thought edged around him that he would be flattening his battery. The memory of the sound buzzed about him for a while and then it too disappeared and the silence of the anvil desert once again purred in his ears and told him that he was a stranger in a strange land and that he should not be here.

"Ibrahim!" he called to the front door, knowing as he shouted his friend's name that it was yet another act of foolishness. If he was inside and had not heard the horn he would not hear his call. He was not inside. He had gone — gone back to his village to accept his punishment, been taken away by Nicholson, left to wander away alone, the weight of guilt oppressing him so much that he could no longer stay. The thoughts whirred through his mind making no sense at all. Sweat was trickling down his body and had settled in a lake on the seat of the vehicle. Pushing confusion from his mind by restarting the Landrover and revving the engine until it screamed, he headed off back towards the sea.

On the beach he saw a solitary vehicle and, his curiosity aroused, he made for it. Then, as he got closer, he remembered that he had seen the car before. It belonged to the Europeans who had waved to him earlier in the day.

He drove over to them and stopped the Landrover. Two youngish couples were sheltering from the sun under the lean shadow of the vehicle. A large beach umbrella completed their shade. He saw that they were drinking beer from a huge Colman's chest that one of the men was leaning against.

He greeted them and they seemed happy to see him.

"Where are you from?" he asked them.

The man leaning against the coldbox replied, "Down from the Capital for the day."

"For the day!"

"That's what I've been saying!" exclaimed one of the women. "But we only have Friday off. We don't relish the trip back I can tell you."

Peter shook his head. "I can't believe you have managed to get here so fast."

"Well the new road is two-thirds here. It's very fast. The only problem is that last third. We'll have to start back soon if we are going to make it to the road before nightfall. I wouldn't like to be stuck on the track in the dark."

"Why don't you stay the night with me?"

The four looked at one another and Peter felt suddenly foolish. They did not even know who he was. He did not know their names. He had not thought to ask. "My name's Peter Drury. I work for the Education office here."

Belatedly they introduced themselves. Then they refused his invitation.

"We all have to be at work in the morning and . . ." said one of the women.

"Yes?"

"Well, we want to get back. This place gives us the creeps. No offence meant."

"None taken. At this precise moment it's giving me the creeps too."

"I suppose we're just your normal pampered expats," continued the woman, wearing a kind expression which made Peter want to weep. "Ever since we arrived I've been thinking of my fridge and my A.C."

"Have you seen the fort?" Peter asked them.

"We started to explore it but some kids threw stones at us!"

Peter nodded.

"You've got yourself into a real time warp down here," said the other woman, shaking her head.

"Yes. But it is the last corner of Arabia," replied Peter defensively.

"All the dirt gets stuck in the corners in my experience," remarked the other woman.

Then abruptly the four stood up and started to gather their things together.

"You're not going, are you?" Peter asked, hearing the desperation in his voice.

"Have to if we're going to make the road by nightfall," replied the man who had given his name as Jeff.

Peter stood and watched helplessly as they loaded the coldbox, the umbrella, the Li-Lo, the towels, the bottles of sun-tan lotion, the cans of Off, the thick good read novels, the flip-flops, the Thermos flasks, the promise of companionship, into their cars. He felt like the village idiot in the villages he called at, who always seemed to preside at his leavetaking. They looked on dumbly while he made his getaway. He could tell that he was coming through to these four people as peculiar. He saw himself described pityingly or scathingly at their next Capital Area get together. Yet he wanted to stop them and tell them everything, to hold them back, to make them stay the night. They seemed sane but they were running away.

They sat in the vehicle, then Jeff reached into the coldbox and produced a beer, reached out of the window and offered it to Peter. "Here you are, mate! You look like you could use it!"

Peter took the beer dumbly and nodded. He tried to smile but his face would not work. He was sweating profusely in the still-cruel light of the sun. The people in the car waved. The car started and was gone.

He stood where he was and ran the cold beer can across his face and down his chest. And he thought of those same village idiots who gawked through his Landrover window as he was starting the engine — and how he would reach into the dashboard niche and offer them a toffee or a can of some sweet liquid.

He ran towards the mill-pond sea and as he ran he hurled the can of beer ahead of him and saw it splash a few yards out. Into the myriad of confused thoughts that knotted his brain intruded the thought that, if the beer can broke open, the sea would contain alcohol. The fish would drink it. The fishermen would catch the fish. The fish would be sold to the devout in the market place. The devout would eat the fish and be polluted by tiny residues of forbidden alcohol.

He laughed mirthlessly and plunged himself, fully clothed, into the tepid ocean.

Before this moment, Hepworth reckoned he had seen everything and had long passed the sign on the freeway of life which announced: "Last exit for Shock."

But in that he was wrong, for he had failed to take into account the way that Nicholson had of springing shock upon him.

He had heard of the rough acts which he had so recently witnessed. In the desert during the civil war he had known that such things were happening just out of range. Like Nelson, he had turned a blind eye to these things. They disgusted him because they were not his particular temptation. But then he had reasoned that one could not impose the morality of Surbiton on to rough bedouin troops. He also recalled that buggery had had a part to play in regimental initiation rites back in Blighty. But in the deserts of both Arabia and Colchester he had averted his gaze and consoled himself with pictures of Dorothy in revealing poses.

But now, here with Nicholson, he felt he had witnessed perversity personified. Nicholson had giggled, licked his lips, made ribald comments to Hepworth and assumed — assumed! — that his companion was enjoying the scenes as much as he was.

God, what was he doing here with this man! How had he allowed himself to get involved? Who was this stranger, the body of whom he inhabited, who had allowed himself to go along with Nicholson's madness? Rather than be here it would have been so much more comfortable to join some dole queue. He could have made do at home with his honour intact. Now it was too late. Nicholson had swept across the empty plain of his life like a twister and tossed him up into its eddying, chaotic centre.

Hepworth had watched Ibrahim weep and scream through the peephole. He had watched as Murad and Zayn used him and silently, eloquently, heaped contempt upon him. It was wicked, but more wicked to observe what they had caused to happen. People screwed one another in one way or another the whole world over. There was nothing unusual in that. That, for a Man of the World, could be coped with. But to watch? To gloat at the misery one had brought about? It seemed to Hepworth to multiply the crime and cry to heaven for vengeance.

Nicholson had, he reckoned, done to him what the two bedouin were now doing to Ibrahim. He had been a pawn in a madman's bent game of chess. But everyone in that game was a pawn and could only plod around getting screwed while Nicholson giggled and kept all the best moves for himself.

Hepworth did not think he had ever felt so lonely. Before, the feeling had been one that settled upon him like a fly. And, like a fly, it could be easily dispensed with. A trip to the whorehouse, to the messroom, soon put him back into a good mood, a mood of camaraderie. For it had been comrades that had made him the man he was. Comrades were the mirror that told him he was fine — a ladykiller, a hero, a villain, a man's man, a lady's man, a patriot, a winner, an Arabist, a bit of a lad, a true Brit with true grit . . . But now he was sitting with a stranger. He had let this mad stranger hold a mirror up to him like any other comrade. The image had been a little peculiar, perhaps. Not the usual Hepworth, but not so strange as to make him push the mirror aside and shout, "No! That's not me!"

But now, remembering, he saw a monster gazing back at him. What Nicholson had persuaded him to do was not a mere extension of their exploits during the civil war. Now he, Hepworth, was disturbing the peace with this madman. And, worse, he was the madman's slave.

What to do? There was nothing to be done. He was as much a captive as Ibrahim.

"Well! What did you think of that?" Nicholson asked Hepworth, back in his sitting-room.

"Strong stuff, Simon! If that doesn't make him change his mind I don't know what will."

"Yes. I can always rely on those two to put on a good show. You know, Hepworth, if it weren't for types like Murad and Zayn I'd never be able to achieve anything here. God, it's so lucky that Ras Al Surra is divided. Tribes hating one another is what keeps us in clover, keeps the whole show on the road. The Arab Nation . . ." he continued theatrically. "The very words make me want to laugh — but they could be such a force if they could only get themselves together. But of course they never will. Their various unhappy situations are as intractable as Northern Ireland. Every other Arab's an Ian Paisley. Each little nation is convinced of its rectitude and of its special status with the Almighty. And that's just the start. Within each nation there are tribes and groups within tribes and then down to the family. And each family is convinced that it is not only the best thing since sliced bread but the sliced bread itself. Of course I am not saying that this is an exclusively Arab vice. It's *the* worldwide vice. It's just that the Arabs have it bad . . . So Arab Brother screws Arab Brother screws Arab Brother and we are there to supply them with the very best screwdrivers that money can buy."

Nicholson got up and poured drinks. "Here's to the screwdrivers!"

Hepworth had not been listening. He had heard it all before and he knew that it was true. Beneath the applause at treaty signings, trade agreements, student exchanges, aid packages, could be heard the sound of devout screwing.

He felt empty. When he had replied to Nicholson's banter: "Strong stuff Simon! If that doesn't make him change his mind I don't know what will," he had felt the words rattle in his head like peas in a tin.

He lifted his hands to his face in order to wipe his eyes but found that, instead, he was sniffing his fingers.

He stayed on and drank away the afternoon and early evening. Nicholson was in a talkative mood, but Hepworth hardly listened and Nicholson hardly seemed to notice. Hepworth accepted drink after drink as it was offered, determined that, upon arrival back at the Desert Regiment quarters, he would collapse and sleep at once. Perhaps things would look better in the morning.

An hour after sunset, drunk into depressed sobriety, in despair and near to tears, he downed the last drink Nicholson had placed in front of him in one gulp, and, grabbing his beret, said goodbye. He refused Nicholson's invitation to stay and was behind the wheel of his Landrover unable to remember how he had got there from Nicholson's living room.

He drove back towards the Desert Regiment camp very slowly. As he drove he looked up at the stars and felt tears coming to his eyes.

"Forgive me!" he whispered to the Lord behind the stars, a God he pictured to be like a retired Field Marshal away from it all but still interested in the conduct of His men.

But Hepworth's straight-backed, smartly dressed God looked down disapprovingly from his place in heaven, a heaven imagined by Hepworth to be an Officers Mess on an eternal Queen's Official Birthday party. Hepworth was unconsoled, felt no forgiveness forthcoming. He concentrated on the road and was alert enough to see in the light from his headlights what looked like a neat parcel on the road ahead. It could have been something sent out to him by Dorothy and the girls to console him at Christmas.

But he was not quick enough to react and a hundred yards away a dark finger pressed a button and detonated the powerful bomb in the innocent parcel. Its force transferred the sturdy Landrover into something that more resembled an exploding light bulb.

And among the flying debris, the divided and dividing self of Captain Bob Hepworth, a separated head complete with a red Desert Regiment beret shouted "Oww!" as it rose into the air like a football. "Oww!" repeated the head. Then "No! Not me!" — before the sharp fragments of debris that followed it heavenwards, clipped, sliced, gouged, ripped and hammered the conscious cranium into hard-and-sharp, soft-and-wet, fragments. These, as the sound of the explosion receded, fell back to the desert like a strange and unnatural rain, plopping, clicking and thudding on to the indifferent earth.

When Nicholson and his men shone their flashlights on the scene some minutes later they found it hard to tell where Hepworth met Landrover met dust.

The explosion which killed Hepworth took place about half a mile from Peter's prefab in the direction of Saffina and the sea.

Peter had been writing a letter to a friend at home by the light of his flashlight. The letter recounted his time in Saffina and tried to communicate both to his friend and to himself what had been happening. It was proving to be no easy task. Peter kept gasping and chewing the end of his pen as he read what he had written and imagined his friend reading it in his kitchen, the window of which looked out over the Menai Straits with Telford's bridge in the distance. How could he, he wondered, take in the implications of the letter in that situation? Peter was not able to make any sense of it either and he was in the middle of everything.

Writing usually helped him sort out his own thoughts and feelings but with this letter it was not working. It only served to make him more confused. He had written several times "Joanna says . . ." and given her opinion on what had been happening because she at least had an opinion. He was less sure about it all. The events were incredible to him and enough in themselves to absorb without attempting to tease out an explanation for them. Joanna had pronounced herself "sure" that Nicholson and Hepworth were responsible for everything that was happening. But that was like saying that the police make the crimes they are supposed to be solving. It was too incredible. He kept hoping that Ibrahim had returned to Jaheel, even though the scrawled message told him otherwise. Reading his account to his friend, a friend he desperately wanted to have there in the room with him now to help him out, made him feel weak and indecisive and stupid.

He had been about to write: "And what do I think about it all?" when he heard the explosion. He sat frozen for a while, then saw the glow of flames in the sky and his mouth went dry. Shaking he wrote: "As I write there has just been another explosion over the hill from where I live." He felt as if he were a reporter in the Falklands, counting planes out and counting them back. And again he felt stupid, a non-doer.

He did not get up to investigate the explosion. He was not in the least tempted to. He read what he had just written and was appalled at his own cowardice. He pushed that feeling aside and finished the letter quickly, asking for a fast reply. He sealed the envelope, addressed it and lay back on the bed.

Loneliness enveloped him. He put out the flashlight, and, in the dark, thought of Ibrahim. He prayed for him and wondered if he would be able to bring himself to journey to Jaheel the following day to see what had happened. Then a thought grew in his mind. He tried to dismiss it but it returned again and again. "You're a coward. A complete coward," the thought told him. "Your best friend in Saffina has been taken away and you lie in bed and do nothing!" And, once allowed expression, the thought accused him brazenly. "You *lie* there! You must *do* something!"

"But what?"

"Go and see what has happened!"

"But maybe the insurgents will capture me!"

"What a coward!"

"It's not my business!"

"Well, whose business is it? They've burnt your children's books; they've taken away your friend and your best English student. What more do they have to do before you act?"

"Yes, but I don't know if it was the same people who were responsible for the burning of the bookstore and the kidnapping."

"Of course you do! It's all one and the same thing. Get up, you coward! Go and find out what's happened."

Then the voice asked him why he did not believe in Joanna's intuitions; why he didn't share them. He had no answer to make other than that Englishmen didn't do such things. The voice laughed at that. Of course they did! All the time.

Peter, shaking violently, got up and pulled on his clothes. He searched around for his keys and opened the door of his prefab. On the threshold he stood, once more indecisive, until the voice exclaimed, "Bloody well find out!"

He silenced his thoughts by running over to his Landrover, starting the engine and making off in the direction of the explosion.

He saw the lights of other vehicles before he saw the crater and the debris. He whistled when the scene of devastation came into view. Then he stopped the vehicle, leaving the headlights to blaze on the gore-mottled wreckage. He went over to where some Arabs were standing in a group, silently watching.

"What's happened?" he asked them.

"A bomb has killed the Englishman," said one of the Arabs.

"Which Englishman?" Peter asked, half wishing he had not ventured out.

"Mr Hepworth," replied the Arab.

Peter approached closer to the man. It was Nasser the postmaster.

"Is that you, Nasser?" he asked, dazed, relieved to find someone there he knew.

"Yes. It's Nasser. Was Mr Hepworth your friend?"

"No. But who has done this, Nasser?"

Nasser shrugged.

"Where is Mr Hepworth's body?"

Nasser gestured to the wreckage. "Everywhere," he said.

And Peter looked at the tangled wreckage closely and saw that it was blood-coloured and that unidentifiable pieces of flesh and offal were embedded in it, caught like tinned strawberries in jelly. He felt sick.

Nasser stepped up to him. "Mr Nicholson was here, Peter. He has gone now. He was very angry. I have never seen him so angry!"

"Yes."

He sat down on the ground then keeled over on to his side

and was violently sick. He retched repeatedly, though there was nothing in his stomach to bring up. And in the bitterness and wretchedness of the situation it occurred to him that Joanna's theory was wrong after all. He managed a prayer for Hepworth between spasms.

Nasser crouched down on the ground next to him, tutting solicitously. "You live near here, don't you, Peter?" he asked him as he recovered himself.

"Yes, I do."

"Well maybe it would be a good thing for you to come and stay with me in my house tonight. I think you will not be easy on your own. Am I right?"

"You are right."

"Yes. Come with me. You live alone, don't you?"

"Yes, I do," replied Peter and he began to cry.

Nasser stood Peter up and wiped his soiled face with his headcloth. "You English! Always alone! How do you do it?"

"I don't know, Nasser. But look, I'll be all right. Maybe I should go back to my own place. It will be a lot of trouble for you . . ."

"I insist."

"Thank you, Nasser." Peter smiled. "You're a real gentleman. Lead and I'll follow."

"I just want to render what help I can to you in this crisis," replied Mr Nasser.

16

Ibrahim dreamed that everything was all right. He had married Moona Al Alawi, had taken his place in the life of Jaheel, was consulted by the elders whenever a decision needed taking, accompanied his father to Friday prayers. And he had watched his father's face break into a wonderful wrinkled smile when he had told him that Moona was expecting their first child.

And in his dream Moona had been almost perfect, though at first she had needed a little taming. She had, for instance, complained that Ibrahim could not give her gold and jewels to wear. It was a common complaint among the new wives brought to Jaheel, almost a ritual for women to complain at being brought to a poor place. It was not their fault. All the way through childhood they had been taught to expect that their future husbands would bedeck them with gold and jewels. Their songs were full of promises. Jewellery represented love and security and status. But Ibrahim had not let Moona down. He took her to the sea one night during the full moon. Commanding her to shut her eyes, he had borne her out into the water. Then, upon opening her eyes, the jewels of phosphorescence cascaded down her body. "There you are!" he had exclaimed. "There are the jewels that a fisherman can give you."

Moona had laughed happily and said that it was enough . . .

. . . Then the door of his cell was opened by Nicholson. Ibrahim was at once awake. He was naked, and, not having been allowed out of the cell since being first incarcerated, his body and the cell were covered in filth.

"What a mess!" Nicholson exclaimed. He disappeared and came back with a bucket of water which he threw over the still-prone, naked body of Ibrahim.

"Come out of that!" he commanded. "It's time for you to clean yourself up."

He led Ibrahim down the corridor of the cell block and into a tiny room. The room had a floor level latrine in it and a shower. He turned on the shower and pushed Ibrahim under it, telling him to wash thoroughly.

He watched as Ibrahim cleaned his body and spoke to him in English, though he was really speaking to himself.

"Plans changed a little I'm afraid. Strange thing, eh? You tell people a tale . . . weave a myth. You illustrate the truth of the lie with concrete examples designed to penetrate the densest of grey matter . . . and what happens? Half the people go on as if nothing had bloody happened, while the other half make the myth reality! The mythical monster turned into a true one. I go around and I ask, 'You know what I'm saying, don't you?' And they shake their heads. 'No, we don't know,' they reply. But they know. They know all right! I was a fool to take them for such fools. I didn't think this would happen. I never dreamed. . . ."

Nicholson stopped and gazed at Ibrahim, his head on one side. Then, still gazing intently, not missing a detail of the brown, wet body before him, he spoke again. "Now what?" But this time his words were not loud enough to reach Ibrahim over the noise of the shower. "They got Hepworth and they'll be after me. What do you think of that, eh, Ibrahim? You don't need to kill Nurse Sissons now even if you want to. Do you want to? Don't answer that. It would be too sad. Silly bugger, Hepworth. Probably didn't vary his route. Was too pissed to give it a thought. Still it's solved the problem. Don't need you any more, my lad. So, what to do with you? I don't know. Must think. It would be such a waste to turn that body over to the houris of the Garden of Allah." He sighed and swayed. "I'll miss old Hepworth. Who could have done it? You ask that! I ask that. Anyway it's taken the heat off me. The insurgents are back. I'm back in business. I made the bonfire and they supplied the match. What now?"

Ibrahim had tried to understand what Nicholson was saying but it made little sense to him. This was really not very surprising because Nicholson was both drunk and in a state of shock at what had happened.

He had returned from viewing the wreckage of Hepworth and his Landrover, and had made straight for his drinks cabinet. It was only after drinking three stiff whiskies that Ibrahim had come back into his mind. He would have to go and see the prisoner. But what to do with him?

"I am finished," said Ibrahim.

"Yes, you are finished. How are you, Ibrahim?"

Ibrahim did not reply. There was nothing that he could say. He watched his captor and remembered what the swaying man had caused to be done to him.

"How are you?" repeated Nicholson.

"You know," replied Ibrahim.

"Yes. I know. I'm sorry."

He's sorry, thought Ibrahim. What does that mean? What place can sorrow have for this man? Will his sorrow allow him to give back to me what he has taken away, to take away from me what he has given?

Ibrahim said flatly, "If you are sorry, prove it."

Nicholson swayed from side to side. "How can I prove it?"

"Kill me."

"Is that what you want?"

"That is what I want."

"I no longer want you to kill the foreign woman," countered Nicholson.

"It makes no difference. I would not kill her. You can send your men to me every night for a year and I would not do it. What they do soon ceases to hurt the body. My spirit is past hurt."

"I could still hurt you though."

"Why do you want to? Be merciful and kill me now. You know how to kill."

"Yes, I know how to kill. However, I do not think I will kill you. There has been enough killing for one night. Anyway, that would be too easy. If you wanted to live, then maybe I would kill you. But no, I think I shall surprise you."

"How will you surprise me?"

"I shall let you go."

"Don't do that! Kill me, Mr Nicholson! Kill me!"

Nicholson smiled and swayed. "No, I don't think so. I don't think so. Go back to Mr Drury. Tell him what I've done to you, if you like. I really don't care. I can always justify my actions. I have nothing to fear from you."

He pushed Ibrahim back down the corridor.

"Put on your clothes and I'll take you out."

Sullenly Ibrahim put on his soiled dish-dash feeling once again dirty and full of self-disgust. Then he jumped on Nicholson and beat him with his fists.

Nicholson was taken by surprise and fell heavily on to his back while Ibrahim continued to lay into him with all his strength. But then he recovered from his shock and turned the tables on Ibrahim, pinioning him beneath him.

"You must kill me, Mr Nicholson! If you don't I shall kill you!"

Nicholson laughed, breathing whisky fumes into Ibrahim's face. "I cannot tell you how many times I have been told that, young man."

He seized Ibrahim by the hair and pulled him out of the cell block and across the compound to the main gate. The guard came forwards. "Throw him out!" commanded Nicholson.

The guard pinioned Ibrahim's arm behind him, and giving him a final kick in the rump, pushed him through the gate and slammed it shut.

"You are lucky!" the guard shouted after Ibrahim.

Ibrahim did not feel lucky as he ran wailing towards the dark beyond the range of the compound's arc lights.

Nasser unlocked the heavy wooden door of his house and stood aside to let Peter enter ahead of him. The house lay at the end of a narrow alley close to the main market. It was unexceptional from the outside, somewhat unprepossessing in fact. But Peter loved it as soon as he crossed the threshold. He flicked off his sandals, walking through a vestibule that went the whole width of the house and finished in a glassless window over which decorative bars had been fixed. This gave an uninterrupted view of beach and sea. The walls of the vestibule were high and the ceiling was made of rush matting behind beams of halved palm trunks.

Nasser showed Peter into the majlis at the back of the house. Cushions were arranged around the room and a large window also gave a view of the sea. While Nasser lit oil lamps Peter sat down and exclaimed, "What a lovely house! You are very lucky, Nasser."

Nasser shrugged and disappeared. Peter could hear him talking softly to someone in another room. He lay still and let the sound of the sea calm him. He felt a million miles away from his own house. The peace of this house belied what he had just seen on the road to Saffina.

Nasser returned with a tray on which stood a teapot and cups. Peter sighed and drank a cup of the sweet, mint tea gratefully. They talked about old Saffina before the coming of the king and oil wealth, and Peter detected in Nasser a yearning for the old days. But soon they were back to what was on top of their minds.

Nasser said: "We are living through difficult and dangerous times here Peter. It is hard to know how it will all end. In the old days I seldom used to sit in this house in the evening. I always wandered around with friends, drinking tea in the market place or on the shore. Now, as soon as my work is finished, I return here and stay at home all the time. Saffina became dangerous during the civil war. We got into the habit of being circumspect then. Now it seems that those bad times have returned. I am lucky to have a nice house to run away to, I think."

"Yes, you are lucky," replied Peter.

"I do not understand how you could live alone out there in that little place. Haven't you been afraid?"

"Not really. Anyway, I haven't been alone for most of the time."

Nasser cocked his head and Peter, after an initial reticence, told him about Ibrahim.

"And where is he now? Is he back at your house?"

"No. He disappeared yesterday. I am very worried about him," and he told Nasser everything.

"One thing puzzles me," said Nasser when Peter had finished. "I have heard of this boy and how he ran away from his village. I know Hameed Nasr from Jaheel. He told me all about it. But you say Mr Nicholson said that Ibrahim's father is dead. I had not heard that. I know he was extremely upset about what Ibrahim did but I do not think he died as a result of it."

"Well that's what Nicholson told me."

Nasser shook his head. "Mr Nicholson is a friend of yours?"

"No. Not at all!" replied Peter vehemently.

"It is quite possible that Nicholson did take Ibrahim away. In his time here he has taken many young men away for questioning. Either they come back and are silent about their experiences or they disappear up to the Capital and are not heard of again."

"And you stand for it?"

"What else can we do? He is the government here."

Peter wondered if he should confide his suspicions to Nasser. He hesitated to do so, but then Nasser asked, "And who do you think blew up the power station?"

And before he knew it Peter was telling Nasser everything he knew.

It felt good to unburden himself and he did not care about whether or not it was the wise thing to do. Nasser nodded but said little as Peter told him about what Othman had said to Mary-Anne and Joanna's intuitions.

"You could be right," replied Nasser when Peter had finished.

"Could I? But what about tonight? If Nicholson and Hepworth were involved then who could have killed Hepworth?"

"Perhaps Nicholson did it himself! Anything is possible for such a man. Do not think, Peter, that what you have been thinking has not been thought by the people here. We do not dare to tell one another our fears and suspicions because we fear spies among us. But look at our situation. The king sends us two foreigners who can do what they like and rule over us. We are independent people, Peter. Perhaps that is our downfall. If we were easier to rule, perhaps we would now be ruling ourselves. Anyway to us this is the strangest thing, to be ruled over by foreigners. It is not so difficult after that to believe something much less strange. We can believe without any problem at all that the usurpers would behave in such an evil manner — for have they not already worked evil among us?"

"So what is to be done about it?"

Nasser shrugged as he poured Peter another cup of tea. "That is the problem. It seems as if nothing can be done. Every act of terror makes Nicholson more powerful because it makes the king more fearful. People here say that the king never leaves his palace in the Capital. There he listens to foreign music and leaves his henchmen to do his work for him."

"So you think he may be doing all these things himself ! I have been trying not to believe that!"

"Yes, I think it is very possible. It doesn't strike me as strange at all."

"So what can we do?"

Nasser laughed. "You've already asked me that! I repeat: there is nothing we can do. When God wills all will be made right."

Peter gave Nasser a sideways glance and raised his eyebrows. "You believe that?" he asked.

Nasser smiled but said nothing. Some minutes later he went out and brought Peter some pillows and sheets. "You sleep here. The sound of the sea will help you to sleep," he said. Then he added, "And what about you, Peter? Do you think you ought to stay on?"

"I don't know. I'm scared, but Ibrahim is my friend. I want to find out what has happened. I would also like to make a success of my job here. But I don't know. I'll have to think. I am worried about being alone in that house."

"Well I admire your courage. You are very welcome to stay here as long as you want to. Perhaps tonight will spell the end of the troubles. Who knows?"

"I hope so, Nasser."

Nasser left Peter to sleep. Then he left the house and walked along the alley to the market place. Everything was quiet. He turned left into another alley and knocked at the door of a house.

A man answered the door and let Nasser in at once.

"What is the news?" the man asked Nasser when he had sat him down in the majilis.

Nasser told him the news and the man smiled. "The Englishman has released the boy."

"Where is he?"

The man gestured to the next room.

"And how is he?"

"He is angry and vows vengeance."

Nasser smiled.

The following day, half way through the morning, Peter left Nasser's house.

Through the night a thought had kept coming to him, and had then turned into a resolution. He would go to Jaheel and see what could be found out about Ibrahim. If, as he suspected, the village could throw no light on to Ibrahim's present whereabouts, he would surely be able to find out whether his father were alive or dead.

Though Nasser had had to leave early in order to open the post office, he had left instructions with his sons that Peter was to be allowed to sleep until he woke. Then he was to be given breakfast.

It was ten before Peter, offering thanks to everybody he met in the house — and there seemed to be a huge number of people in it — left and made his way to the post office to thank Nasser.

"Can I expect you again tonight?" he asked Peter.

"I think I'll be all right. Thank you for everything. I feel much better now."

"Yes, but now it is daylight. See how you feel when night comes."

"All right. I will. Bye Nasser."

Peter drove through the market place, and was surprised to see how normal everything seemed. People appeared to have grown used to the wounded mosque, its one remaining minaret

216

standing stiffly to attention, like a surviving soldier surveying the field of battle. A truck loaded with cement was in front of the entrance, and a group of Indian workmen stood next to it, watching two men in startlingly white dish-dashes as they talked and gestured towards the building. Clearly, the mosque was going to be rebuilt. The people of Saffina were not going to allow its wounds to go untreated.

The market was busy. People carried fish to their homes on their heads, or, holding the fish by the tail, the body swinging as they walked. Veiled women sat impassively behind their produce. As usual, the flies were having a feast.

But then, thinking of what Nasser had told him, Peter wondered why this apparent normality should startle him. Saffina did not wear its heart on its sleeve. It could not afford to. But he was now very aware that that heart was beating strongly. How strange not to realise that the people would be wise to what was happening! But that was part of mankind's tunnel vision. He and Joanna could debate about the causes of wretchedness, the cause of Saffina's distress, but it really had not occurred to him to think that the people were thinking exactly the same thing as they were, weighing the evidence and coming to more or less the same tentative conclusions.

He stopped at the hospital and spoke to Joanna, telling her of his planned trip to Jaheel. She had heard about Bob Hepworth's death and said that she had received a telegram from her boss in the Capital asking whether it might not be a good idea for her to leave. She did not know. She wanted to talk.

But she could not talk. A queue of patients stretched along the hospital corridor to the door. Peter said he would come and see her as soon as he got back from Jaheel.

He stopped at the prefab just long enough to fill up his water container and grab some pressed dates to take with him. Then he headed off north towards the mountains.

Like Nicholson months ago, Peter had to follow a circuitous route to avoid the quicksands that lay between the coastal plain and the ocean. He passed the half-buried wreck of an earth-moving truck which had become hopelessly bogged down in the sand and had just been left there. The machine was slowly rusting away into the sand. In a few years it would disappear completely.

He parked the Landrover and started to walk along the cliff path to Jaheel. By one o'clock he was descending to the flat floor of the Wadi Kabir.

Hameed Nasr was closing his shop when Peter approached him and introduced himself. The man was polite enough until Peter mentioned Ibrahim. Then he became taciturn, saying only that the name was one which Jaheel was trying to erase from its memory. Peter did not feel that there was anything to be gained by telling Hameed Nasr the whole story and apologised for taking his time.

He wandered away from the centre of Jaheel and soon came to the seashore where two young men were mending their nets. He introduced himself and talked to them for a while about fishing, thinking how, had things turned out differently, he might, perhaps, have come to Jaheel just for something to do, and be talking to Ibrahim here, mending his nets. He would have seemed as whole and intact as these young men now seemed as they talked proudly of their catches, the way to spot shoals, the best brand of Korean fishing net.

Then he asked them if they had known Ibrahim.

"You know Ibrahim!" exclaimed one of the youths, who had given his name as Rabiah. "How is he? What happened to him?"

Peter told the two that Ibrahim had gone to Saffina and had been working for him, but had disappeared.

"So why have you come here? He would never come back here!" Rabiah's companion, Salem, observed. "To most of the people of Jaheel Ibrahim is no better than an infidel . . . if you'll excuse me for saying so."

"But you don't think that, do you?"

"Well, what he did was very wrong but if I had a chance to leave Jaheel I'd take it and not worry about what the people thought. Who cares about what Jaheel thinks!" replied Rabiah.

Peter did not say anything to that. It was not an answer that surprised him at all. He had scratched the surface and the same blood that had infected Ibrahim had leaked out. "What about his father?" he asked.

Rabiah shook his head sadly. "Ah, his father . . ."

"Is he alive or dead?"

"He's alive, but he is seldom seen. He keeps to himself. He is never seen at the mosque. Never comes down to help with his boats."

"Where does he live?" asked Peter.

"Near here."

"Do you think you could take me to his house?"

"He won't see you."

"Will you just show me where the house is?"

Rabiah nodded. The two got up and Peter followed them back through the village until they came to a small house.

"He is there," said Salem, "but we can go no further. It's up to you now."

"Thank you."

"Mister," asked Salem, "where do you live in Saffina? Now that Ibrahim has gone you will need another servant?"

Peter shook his head slowly and smiled. "I do not need another servant. I'm sorry."

Salem looked disappointed but Rabiah hit his arm and pulled him away.

"Goodbye Mister!"

Peter knocked at the door. There was no answer. He knocked again. At last the door opened a chink.

"What do you want?"

"Are you Ibrahim's father?" Peter asked.

There was no reply. He was suddenly aware of the complete futility of his mission. It was obvious that Ibrahim was not in the village, had not been heard of since he had left. He was about to apologise for intruding when the door was opened.

Peter held his hand out to the old man, Ibrahim's father. The man stared at the proffered hand for a long moment, then reached for it and shook it limply. He mumbled a greeting and gestured Peter to enter.

"I am sorry to disturb you, sir," began Peter.

The old man nodded.

"Your son, Ibrahim, is a friend of mine." And Peter told the old man the whole story, hoping that it would become obvious why he was disturbing his peace.

When he had finished Peter saw that the old man was weeping. They sat in silence until Ibrahim's father said, "When Ibrahim ran off I vowed that I would never forgive him. I let it be known that as far as I was concerned I did not have a son any more. The shame he brought on us was very great. I think you can understand that. However, as time has passed, I have felt myself changing. Now my loneliness is greater than my anger. I am a hermit surrounded by my own people; not because I am ashamed but because I am in mourning. I think I know what was happening in Ibrahim's mind. It is happening in the minds of thousands of young men up and down our land. Ibrahim, God help him, is a product of his times. My mistake was to let him go away that first time. I did not know then that he would never be able to come home again. My time alone has given me a chance to reflect. Our God forgives erring men every second of every day. If I cannot forgive I am not worthy to be called a Muslim."

"Sir, I wish your son were here to hear you. He cannot believe that he will ever be forgiven."

"Well he is not here, is he? In truth I fear for my son. Will you return and tell me when you have news?"

"Yes, of course I will. Perhaps I will be able to bring a friend with me."

"Thank you. However," continued Ibrahim's father, "I have told you that I can forgive him. I do not think the same can be said for Jaheel. I do not think he could ever return here to live."

Peter nodded.

"I am sorry I cannot offer you any hospitality. I am ashamed of myself. What Ibrahim's mother would have said I don't know."

Peter left the old man shortly afterwards. The sun was heading down the sky as he stumbled along the rough track towards Saffina. Jaheel could provide no news of Ibrahim, that was true, but he felt buoyed up by the reaction of Ibrahim's father to news of his son. He examined himself and felt it would have been his reaction too. How would he react if a prodigal son appeared at his own door? He would probably forget everything that had happened and fall on his neck. He hoped that Ibrahim would one day make the difficult journey back and be so received. He hoped so. He hoped that he was right; that people were not so different after all. The thought was being reinforced day in and day out. He prayed that he would always be able to hold on to the notion.

So what was the matter with Nicholson? He had lied to him about Ibrahim's father and he had smiled as he lied. If he could lie about that he could lie about everything else. Peter now knew who the villain was.

It was dusk when he arrived at Joanna's bungalow.

"I wish I had a gun," observed Peter as he sat, drunk and replete, in Joanna's sitting room much later that same night.

"And what would you do with a gun?" Joanna asked.

"I'd get the truth out of Nicholson with it, that's what."

"Too much wine, my dear!"

"So you don't think I could use a gun?"

"Frankly, no. I don't think you're hard enough. You'd have a crisis of conscience, lay it aside and apologise for being so silly."

"Oh, would I now?"

"Yes, I think so."

Peter thought for a moment. "So what *should* I do? I must do something."

"You could go to the Embassy."

"And if I did they'd ask for proof. Where's our proof?"

"We've been through this already, Peter. We don't have any. Oh, let's not talk about it any more tonight. I'm all tied up in knots from thinking about it."

"But what about Hepworth's death?"

"Stop! We can't sort it out now. We're too tired. Just relax and have some more of this disgusting wine."

And, as Peter strove to forget him for a while, Nicholson awoke from a long nightmare of sleep and lay sweating on his bed in his

221

clothes. He had lost a whole day, a day during which he should have been writing reports to the Capital and seeing to affairs connected with Hepworth's death. During that day he was to have made a sweep of the town to pick up possible suspects or anyone who gave him a sideways glance. He should have been showing his teeth and instilling fear.

But instead he had let the day pass and achieved precisely nothing. And sleep had somehow made him fearful. He could not remember any of his dreams but they had left him weak and afraid. He did not know what he was fearful of. Was it Hepworth's spirit calling down vengeance upon him? No, it couldn't be that. He did not believe in such things. He did not believe in anything, did he? Well, not quite nothing, he reckoned. He believed in Nicholson and the power of enlightened selfishness, his vision of wisdom. But just now, just at this precise moment, he wondered if that was enough, wondered if somehow he could have missed something along the way. But what? No, it was foolishness. The feeling would fade as wakefulness ached over him and restored his right perspective.

But, ah, he had been unwary. He had released the silly lad. What had come over him to do that? Too much booze. He had broken one of his own cardinal rules. Never shit on your own doorstep without clearing up afterwards. It would have been so easy to have done away with him, so easy to have dumped his body where no one would think to look — assuming anyone would think about thinking to look. But he had been soft. Why? Was it the well-turned buttocks, the doe eyes? What? Whatever it was he should have resisted, kicked those buttocks until they drooped, fired at those eyes with both barrels until they were dead bloody sockets.

He did not approve of his softness. He did not like himself. Cursing his softness he went out on to the verandah and called loudly for Murad and Zayn.

When they came to him he led them into the bedroom:
"Hurt me!" he told them.

Murad and Zayn happily obliged.

★

That night Nasser took Ibrahim to his house and put him in the very room Peter Drury had left that morning. Then he gave him a powerful sleeping draft, for the lad seemed to have developed a fever that shook him and caused him to sweat, locked the door and left him.

Nasser and his companions had kept Ibrahim up most of the previous night, trying to extract the whole story from him. It had not been easy at first, but, when Ibrahim understood that Nasser was Peter's friend, when Nasser had told him that they were on his side and would help him extract vengeance from Nicholson, he told them everything.

The following morning Ibrahim still slept. Nasser left instructions that on no account was the door to be opened while he was out. Taking his truck, he drove over to the hospital to visit his old friend, Mary-Anne Sissons.

"Come and visit me! You never come these days!" he told Mary-Anne who was busy at the reception desk processing patients and sending them off in different directions with their records in their hands.

"Is this to be a social call or do you want me to bring my little black bag?" asked Mary-Anne.

Nasser smiled and gestured semitically. "My dear Mary-Anne! With you I always want a social call! However, if you could bring your bag too . . ."

"OK, Nasser. When shall I come?"

"As soon as you can."

"It's an urgent social call, is it?"

"Well — yes." He came closer to Mary-Anne, looking anxiously to left and right in the crowded reception area. "We have a sick boy in the house. He cannot be brought to the hospital for a number of reasons."

"I see," said Mary-Anne, "Am I to assume that this has something to do with what happened to poor Mr Hepworth?"

Nasser winked: "You know me of old, I know, my sister. Well it does, yes. But only a very faint connection."

"What are his injuries?" asked Mary-Anne matter-of-factly. It was true, she did remember Nasser of old. During the civil war she had often helped him with the injured. Then she had not asked questions either. She treated government troops, mercenaries and civilians caught in the crossfire of the war. It was also her duty, she had felt, to treat wounded rebels when called upon to do so. It might have cost her dear with the government. At the very least she would have been sent away from Saffina. But, she had reasoned then that she was not a government employee. She was here to serve all the people and show them what God's love meant. Also, had she refused, she would have lost the respect of a large section of Saffina's population.

"He is cut about in a very private place."

"I see," said Mary-Anne. "I hope it is not too serious. I might not be able to deal with it myself. I'm not a doctor you know."

"You are a doctor," asserted Nasser. "The very best barefoot doctor."

"Thank you for that. All right Nasser, I will come later this afternoon."

"And you will stay for dinner?"

"Yes, I will. Thank you." Now it was Mary-Anne's turn to look to left and right. She added, "You're not in any trouble are you, Nasser? Things are bad enough without having one of my best friends involved."

"No, I don't think I'm in any trouble. But you are right. There is much trouble. I and some friends are trying to end it once and for all."

He smiled at Mary-Anne broadly and arranged to pick her up at the hospital later in the day.

Nasser left Mary-Anne to her patients.

She felt uneasy but strangely elated too. "Well," she thought, "it looks like I am going to be brought into the centre of things for a while. That will be nice."

Nicholson felt much better by the following day. He had got up early, showered briskly not sparing himself the loss of a layer or two of skin through brisk use of his loofah. His sufferings of the last thirty-six hours had been assuaged by his physical sufferings during the night. Nothing like real pain to stifle neurotic pain. He surveyed the weals on his back as lesser men might survey their suntans — with satisfaction and a feeling of achievement. They had been hard won, those scars. Murad and Zayn, at first somewhat bemused, had been unstinting once they had entered into the spirit of the thing. Good chaps. Nicholson smiled at himself in the mirror. Then he told his image, "Time to research!"

For the last two days, he had detailed two of his men to follow the movements of Peter Drury. One of these had come to him while he was dressing, and said that he had seen Peter and Joanna get into a vehicle and head along the track which led out of Saffina towards the Interior. Nicholson called the guardroom and ordered Murad to follow them and report to him on their destination. Vaguely he wondered if the two were going to Jaheel to check on Ibrahim. Clearly the boy had not gone back to Peter's house, otherwise Peter would not be spending time with Joanna. No, he'd have been pouring TCP up the lad's arse or have bolted round to his, Nicholson's, house to threaten him with a bad end-of-term report. But Nicholson would never have expected Ibrahim to return to Peter. Not yet anyway. He would spend a day or two in the desert licking his wounds. Perhaps, even after that, he would be unable to return.

His servant served him a light meal and Nicholson ate it with relish. He felt that today he would get a lot of work done. There were reports to write and send, an investigation to be started. Who would he round up for interrogation? Well, there were lots to choose from — the Bu Ali brothers in Zarut, Hameed, the muezzin of the mosque, and, of course, Nasser the postmaster. Then, if there was time, he would have to write a charming letter to Dorothy Hepworth in which he would praise her dead hubby to the heavens and wish her a happy widowhood. It would be a satisfactory day. The livid weals on Nicholson's flesh tingled.

He had been working in his office for an hour when Murad knocked at the door and entered.

"What do you have to report?" Nicholson asked.

"The man and the girl went to a pool in the wadi, the one

near the old watchtower. There they are swimming. They have food. Also . . ."

"Yes?" asked Nicholson.

"They are wearing no clothes, sir!" added Murad in shocked tones.

"The animals!" exclaimed Nicholson to appease Murad's bedouin sensibilities.

"Is that all, sir?" asked Murad.

"Yes, that is all. Thank you."

Murad left the room.

Nicholson returned to his work for a few minutes but he kept thinking of the two cavorting in the pool. That pool had always been a favourite place of his. Before all this there had been nothing he liked better than to go off to the pool with a hamper and an Ayn Rand novel. Now two damned silly troublemakers were cavorting in the nude.

Nicholson smiled and thought that if the insurgents found them, they'd probably take a very dim view of Peter and Joanna for swimming in the nude. They might even . . .

A voice told him to get on with his work and leave it alone, but another voice, the voice of his own pragmatic prudery, kept tutting "in the nude" like some appalled Ayatollah.

Peter had come to the pool in the wadi with Joanna feeling guilty. He had not been to work the previous day and was reluctant to miss two days on the run. It was not so much that his work could not wait, more that he knew Mr Siddiqui, Mr Ahmed and Mr Nasawi would be worried about him. But Joanna had a day off and reckoned that Peter needed to relax for a while. Eventually he had allowed himself to be persuaded.

Joanna had packed a cold box with wine, Pepsi, pistachio nuts, bread, tinned Cheddar cheese from Australia, and half a tin of Quality Street.

Arriving at the place Peter swung the Landrover off the track and up the side of the wadi. Heavy cumulus clouds lurked beyond the mountains needing only a push from the wind to make it over them and inundate Saffina and its environs. But the sun shone strongly.

"Where are we going?" asked Joanna.

"Not very far now. Just round the next bend."

Then, the pool came into sight. Peter stopped the Landrover and hand in hand they walked down to the water.

"This is beautiful! How did you find it?" asked Joanna.

Peter told her how the pool had greeted him the day he had first come down to Saffina. Then he returned to the Landrover to fetch the towels and the cold box. "Here we are," he said.

"I want to swim . . . but I haven't got a swimsuit," sighed Joanna.

"Don't worry about that. Nobody ever comes here."

Joanna stopped to imbibe the sight before her. Across the deep pool some green bushes had somehow taken root and formed a straight line, a border to the backdrop of distant mountains. Upstream the river lost itself in the steep ravine again. Only here, it seemed, had the river made any concession to accessibility. Joanna found herself planning future trips to the place alone. She had already made it her own, a secret garden away from the hospital and Saffina.

There was something moving about the tiny river surrounded by the barren desert. No doubt it was trying to make it to the sea. Perhaps it would after the rains but now it would fade away in the attempt. And that was good too. The river's attempt was everything. It spoke of an attempt at fecundity in a barren, godforsaken place.

Joanna and Peter stripped and swam naked in the pool. The coldness of the water surprised them both. It was a shock. The ocean was always so tepid and it did not seem possible that water in Ras Al Surra could ever be this cold.

Swimming around the small pool, quietly, almost reverently, like visitors in a church during a service, they tried not to disturb the calm of the water or the place. They looked down their noses at the surface and their bodies below it, swaying just enough to keep them afloat and prevent the small starving fish from nipping their legs. How had the near-transparent fish found their way here? Another miracle.

They did not speak. Occasionally the quiet of the place became almost too much to bear and they splashed about a little with their hands, but just a little, just enough to cause a slight change in the tiny swells and retreats of the water, to watch drops gather and flow from their waterproof arms, reflecting the pool and their happy faces. The place made them meditative.

Peter had not forgotten Ibrahim but he had consigned him to the back of his mind. Now, perversely, his mind went back to the silly staffroom at his school in Bangor. What would they be doing now? The PT master marking tests in his track suit while he chain-smoked; the Head of Chemistry snoozing over the New Scientist, turning chalky, drying out in the overstuffed armchair he had made his own . . . leather patched sports jackets, sensible skirts . . . clothes on impoverished teachers which had seen better days and expected worse. And he thought of himself there. The miracle was that he wasn't there! He was here! Here, watching a group of peculiar fish plucking up courage to attack his waving thigh. He let his body go limp and watched them come in for the kill. But their bites merely tickled him sensuously.

He exhaled and the water took him to itself. His feet touched rocky bottom and he allowed his joints to become limp and he keeled over on to the bottom of the pool . . .

"Come, my children, let us away . . . down and away below . . suffer a seachange into something rich and strange . . . ding-dong-bell."

He ran out of quotations and air at more or less the same time and pushed back to the surface of the pool, thinking that in an ideal world drowning would have been like the feeling he had just had down there. But he was not drowning! He was living! Slowly and easily he emerged into the kind sunshine.

"You were trying to make me worried," said Joanna who was performing a very correct version of the breast-stroke, exhaling breath as if she were blowing on a plate of hot soup.

Peter laughed. "Happy?" he asked her.

"Yes. Very happy," replied Joanna.

"Fancy a spot of lunch?"

"That would be nice."

They ate a leisurely meal. Peter talked about Ibrahim; told Joanna how much he missed him; missed the classes he was giving him. Those classes, he told her, had made him feel like a real teacher again. She nodded, lying there on her side, her breasts puckered together by her forward-pushed upper arms. She thought how strange it was that there was not a hint of tension between them now. He could lie there naked and talk of Ibrahim and she could listen. She no longer felt the least desire for him and was flattered that this thin, neurotic fellow should be so comfortable with her as to be able to drop his trousers and his reticence. Joanna felt that though she had not yet found herself a lover in Saffina, she had at least found someone with whom she could be the best of friends. It seemed no mean achievement.

After lunch they lay back to sunbathe and soon, the wine taking effect, fell asleep. Peter dreamed of the Sudan. He had brought his children to a bathing place he had discovered in the middle of nowhere and was watching them delight in the miracle.

"Can we come back tomorrow, sir?" they asked him.

"Of course, you can! Now we have found it, we will come every day. This pool is yours now as long as you . . ."

He was awoken by the shot that killed Joanna. He sat bolt upright and saw her, a neat hole in the middle of her forehead, her eyes closed in sleep, her neat mouth slightly open. He stood up and turned around in a flash. Nicholson fired at Peter, hitting him in the arm.

Peter saw him smiling and aiming the gun again. He turned to run but he ran into the water. He exhaled in a paroxysm of shock and felt an immense pain in his left thigh, a pain the like of which he had never before been able to imagine. The pain spread and he wondered where the bullet had penetrated. He touched bottom. For a split second he was aware of the sun percolating down through the water. He heard the thud of another shot and another. His empty lungs made him gag. He spluttered and inhaled water. He kicked himself along the bottom and there was the hole. He had forgotten the hole.

Could he pull himself through? What about Joanna? He heard another shot but did not feel any more pain. Then he was swimming frantically with his head against the side of the pool, seeking the hole. He wanted to give up and drown but swam against the side of the pool, edging along it. He was not even sure he was on the right side of it. Then he arrived at the hole and pulled himself through it and back to the surface on the other side of the rock. There he sat, coughing quietly, desperately trying not to and watching the water around him turning crimson. He could not see where the blood was coming from but the sight of it revolted him. He vomited into the water and waited for the face of Nicholson to appear above him and calmly, with a smile, snuff out what remained of his life.

He listened but could hear nothing. He felt calmer as time passed but cold too and the cold brought him back towards panic. Where had the pain gone? Where had Nicholson gone? Had he gone? What about the children? He had left them there alone with their dream of cold water becoming a nightmare of violent death! He had left them there at the mercy of wickedness. He had let them down. He was just like all the rest.

Then Peter fainted.

17

Ibrahim cried out and was suddenly sitting bolt upright in his bed in Nasser's majilis. An Islamic text hung from the wall opposite. "In the name of Allah, the Compassionate, the Merciful . . ." Ibrahim read the words again and again. They were the opening of every act in a Muslim's life, the tag uttered before eating or reciting from the Koran or embarking on a journey. But Ibrahim felt he was at the end of everything and the text had no relevance for him.

Nasser had placed a heavy black cloth, a woman's veil, over the window and on the far side Ibrahim could hear the waves breaking. He lay back against the pillows again and listened to them. The sound was not so different from the one he had been able to hear in his own room at home, but here the sea was much closer and almost drowned out any other sounds. Some children were playing quite close to his window. Shards of their chatter reached him when the waves retreated. "Give me your ball!" "I can't. My brother said only I could play with it," and a sound of fighting before the next wave drowned that out. Then he heard the high drone of a child crying.

Nasser and his friends had been kind to him. A friend of theirs who worked for Nicholson had told them what had happened and they had waited near the gate of Nicholson's compound to bring him to them if he were released. When he had stumbled out into the desert he had fought his new captors for as long as he could. Then he had only wanted to die. The world had become like a sandbar going out into the ocean. Each step he took narrowed the road until, kicked out of the Englishman's compound, it had completely disappeared and there was nothing to walk on any more — nothing to do but walk into the steep-shelving-away sea and surrender himself to oblivion.

Before Nasser had arrived at the other house and talked to him quietly, Ibrahim had only been able to speak of his despair and his desire for vengeance. They asked him why Nicholson had done to him what had been done, but Ibrahim would not, could not, answer them.

Not until he was alone with Nasser did he tell the whole story. No point of the story seemed to shock Nasser. When Ibrahim had finished Nasser said, "I cannot tell you how many times what has happened to you has happened to other young men. That is the reason why some of us are fighting. Nicholson is merely a carrier of the disease. Your sins are as nothing when compared with those of others. Believe me, Ibrahim, it is not too late for you. You must pray to God."

"But there can be no forgiveness for me!" wailed Ibrahim. "My father is dead. I have killed him."

"Your father is not dead. Nicholson told your friend, Peter, that he was dead, but he did not speak the truth. Your father is still alive. He is sad, but he is not dead."

Ibrahim had wept with relief to hear that. Part of his load had been removed but the load was still, he felt, too heavy for him to bear.

"But I can never go back," he told Nasser.

"Perhaps that is true. Perhaps not. Time will tell."

And Nasser had given him a bitter drink. Soon after that Ibrahim had slept.

He dozed and was woken by the sound of the door being unlocked. He sat up and saw Nasser enter the room accompanied by Mary-Anne.

"I have brought a friend of mine, a doctor, to look at your wounds," he said.

Mary-Anne greeted him in Arabic and asked him to show her where it hurt. Ibrahim refused at first, but Nasser chided him and at last he lifted his clothing and let Mary-Anne see.

"Goodness! What happened to you?" asked Mary-Anne.

Nasser answered for him. "It is the way that Mr Nicholson uses to torture people. He is not the first so to suffer."

"He is a devil then," murmured Mary-Anne, half to herself, though Nasser overheard.

"Assuredly," he agreed.

"I'll need plenty of hot water. I think I have everything else."

Nasser went to fetch the water.

"Does it hurt very badly?" Mary-Anne asked Ibrahim.

"Not very badly."

Nasser returned and Mary-Anne set about cleaning and treating Ibrahim's bloody wounds. She tutted and shook her head she did so. Ibrahim cried out into his pillow and she tried to soothe him with cooing words.

"You see what the government has come to?" Nasser asked her.

Mary-Anne nodded. Then she looked up at Nasser and asked him in English, thinking that Ibrahim would not understand, "Nasser, who killed Captain Hepworth? Was it your people?"

Nasser did not say anything. He only nodded.

"And all the other things that have happened. Your people too?"

"How could you believe that we would kill Othman? No, we have done nothing until we took our revenge on the Englishman. You see, we had thought that if everything was peaceful here the king would replace the foreigners with somebody we could work with, who wanted our good, who wanted to lead us with justice and understanding."

"But this did not happen?"

"Until the explosions started I think it was on the verge of happening. And that, I believe, was the reason why Nicholson and Hepworth decided it was time to manufacture insurgency. So we decided to get rid of them. What else could we do?"

Mary-Anne said nothing but she thought that Nasser was right enough. She did not say to him that he should forgive his enemies and seek reconciliation. Her training brought this sentiment straight to the top of her mind. It lay just under her tongue but she could not bring it out. Rather she felt that her strange God just had nothing to say on this subject. In the Old Testament He would have had a lot to say. In the New

233

Testament He went strangely quiet. Islam had missed out on that New Testament. An eye for an eye was still the rule. Saffina's people had to take eyes before they lost their own.

She took some ointment and gave it to Nasser. "Tell Ibrahim to use this three times a day. I think he should heal all right." She was still using English.

To her surprise Ibrahim said, "Madam, you can give it to me. I shall use it. Thank you very much for your help. I feel better."

"Where did you learn your English, Ibrahim?"

"Peter taught me. I stayed with him."

"Ah, so you are Peter's friend!"

"Yes, do you know how he is?"

"I haven't seen him recently but I think he is well."

"I am afraid about Peter. Mr Nicholson does not like him. I think he took me from his house to frighten him."

Mary-Anne nodded and turned to Nasser. "So what now?" she asked.

"We must kill Nicholson. The problem is that he is well protected. It will not be so easy."

Mary-Anne knew that she should say, "Don't! Be patient! Try to forgive!" But she thought of Othman dying in the hospital, of all the meek she had treated in her life who had not inherited the earth, of the ideals which always curled up and died before the cruel realities of an Old Testament earth.

She nodded.

Mary-Anne arrived back at the hospital. As she drove through the gate she noted that Mahmoud the guard was staring wild-eyed at her. Then, on entering the building, the Indian nurse at Reception, tears coursing down her cheeks, let out a little cry and covered her face with her hands.

"What's the matter?" asked Mary-Anne. "What's happened?"

But the Indian nurse could not reply and merely pointed along the corridor to the Emergency Room, the same room that Othman had been brought to.

Mary-Anne ran along the corridor and entered the room.

She stopped and let out a cry when she saw a nurse washing the naked white body on a stretcher table. She knew to whom the body belonged even though a cloth had been placed over the face.

"Joanna!" gasped Mary-Anne, hoping against hope that the covered face would reply.

The nurse stepped between Mary-Anne and Joanna's body. "She is dead, Matron," said the nurse.

"Get out of my way!" and she pushed the nurse aside and took off the cloth from Joanna's face.

Someone had placed a bandage around the face to close the jaw. The mark of the bullet in Joanna's forehead reminded Mary-Anne of the beauty spots Indian women wear.

Tears sprang from her eyes. She replaced the cloth and sank down on to her knees next to the body.

The nurse approached and tried to comfort her but she shook off the girl's hands. She knelt in an attitude of prayer but she was not praying. She was thinking: "This is the moment I have come to Ras Al Surra for. This is the moment that I grow up! This is the moment I lose my faith."

Then she stood up and surveyed the pale, cold body of her nurse. "Get me a Kleenex, nurse. Then tell me what happened."

The nurse said that she did not know the circumstances of Joanna's death.

"Then find me someone who does," commanded Mary-Anne.

Mary-Anne was driving back to Nasser's house half an hour later.

Joanna's body had been found by a man on his way to Saffina from the Capital. He had stopped at the pool to rest. It had been his intention to clean the dust from his vehicle. He had been surprised, he said, to see the Landrover there, thinking that he was the only one who knew the spot. He had recognised the naked body that lay by the pool. Joanna had treated his wife only a week before. She had been kind. He had lifted the sad burden into the back of his vehicle, covered its nakedness with his headcloth, and brought it to the hospital.

"And there was no sign of anybody else? Joanna would not have gone to the place alone."

"Nobody else."

"And the Landrover?"

"It is still there," the man had replied.

Mary-Anne hammered at Nasser's door. It was answered by one of his sons. She swept past him into the majilis and told Nasser what had happened. Then she remembered that she had seen Joanna's Landrover parked outside the hospital. She was right. Joanna had not gone out there alone. She had gone with Peter. But where was Peter?

"Nasser we must go back there and see what has happened to Peter Drury. I am sure he must have gone too."

Ibrahim at once got up from his bed and pleaded to be allowed to go with them.

The sun was setting when, with Ibrahim's help, they arrived at the pool. Peter's Landrover still stood where he had left it.

Nasser, Ibrahim and Mary-Anne searched up and down the course of the river but found nothing.

The light was ebbing away. They were near to giving up the search when Ibrahim remembered. He stripped off his dish-dash and, without a word, dived into the pool. He found the hole and pulled himself through it. When he emerged on the other side of the wall of rock into the tiny pool he collided with Peter's prone body.

The water was like blood. Ibrahim pulled Peter's body out of the pool and lay it gently down, then he climbed the rock and called for help.

It took them half an hour to get Peter back to the vehicle. Mary-Anne checked for signs of life and said that he was still alive but that it would be touch and go at best.

They drove back to Saffina and Peter was at once taken to the operating room where the Indian doctor set about removing the bullets from his thigh and arm.

Mary-Anne, Nasser and Ibrahim sat in Mary-Anne's office, waiting for news. They did not speak. The time for words was past.

At last the doctor came in and said that he thought Peter would pull through.

The three smiled. But only for a moment.

Nicholson had returned to his compound in Saffina well satisfied with his afternoon's work. True, he had not seen for himself the dead body of the English inspector, but he had stayed around the pool long enough to be certain that he had died. Before leaving he had wandered the whole length of the pool, and, seeing no sign of Peter's body, had concluded that he had drowned and his body become caught in one of the overhanging rocks below the surface. He admired the work he had done on Joanna. That had been clean and perfect. Hepworth would have praised him for that, he thought. Yes, Joanna's death would have chuffed old Hepworth no end.

Back in the office he completed the writing of his reports and a letter of condolence to Dorothy Hepworth. Then he returned to his house, told his servant that he was not to be disturbed and sat down to listen to music.

He chose *Peter Grimes* and lay, half dozing, half listening to the opera. A bottle of port, a good bottle from a new consignment, stood on the floor by his elbow. He was soon lulled into a state of complete relaxation.

He felt that he was rather like Grimes. A man misunderstood, a hard man in a hard place, surrounded by gossip and enemies. When, in the last scene Balstrode said to Grimes, "Take the boat out and sink her," it struck a chord in him too.

For Nicholson knew that he had gone too far. The killing of Hepworth, he was sure, had been performed by people that knew who was behind the explosions in Saffina. How did they know? Well, presumably they knew that they were not responsible, and then searched around to see who else might have reason. But that had not then been part of his thinking. Then, before it had all started, he had thought that the peace-disturbers had been permanently pacified; peace restored — through a combination of his efforts and King Fadl's offerings of expensive, bribing baubles.

He could imagine the shadowy faces of the insurgents around a fire or a lamp, sipping tea and talking in low tones. And he knew that they would be talking about him and Hepworth. It was clear that an attempt on his life could only be a matter of time.

He was intrigued about its exact manner. Would a rabble of Saffina people, egged on by the insurgents, lay siege to his compound demanding retribution? Would Ibrahim wait patiently until he could catch him off-guard and then push a knife between his ribs, perhaps in the market place? Would someone go to the Capital and get a hearing? At what point did iniquities start exacting retribution? How far could one go? Amin and Bokassa had gone pretty damned far before their number was up. And Amin was living quite happily in Jeddah at this very moment. "One always get one's just deserts." Another sugar-coated half-truth. True for those who believed it.

The opera finished. He was drunk again. He got up and walked out on to the verandah and sat down on his wicker lounger. The moon was full over the water. Saffina, dark except for dots of oil lamp light, looked as it had looked on the day he had arrived. Appearances were deceptive, however. The road continued to edge forward from the Capital. Nothing that he and Hepworth had done had been able to stop it. In a few months, with much ceremony, it would arrive and disappear into the tracks of Saffina. Then everyone could come and see his last corner of Arabia. A new power station would be built, a better-guarded power station. He had heard that a police station was planned, and with it a civilian police force.

So what had he and Hepworth managed to do after all? Not much. He saw that now. Whatever they did, power would have passed out of their hands anyway. Perhaps they had managed to hold on to it a little longer — and have some fun in so doing — but it was fate that it must pass into other hands. Other hands. Perhaps the people of Saffina would one day look back on his time as their king and regret his passing. Compared with the future, perhaps they would look back on his rule in Saffina as a Golden Age.

"My passing. How will it come?" he thought. "Gosh, how morbid! I'm not finished yet!"

And, indeed, looking out from his verandah, it did not seem likely that anything would change. Saffina seemed to be snoozing on.

Then Nicholson saw the lights of a vehicle emerge from the streets of Saffina. It approached along the coast road and came to the gate of his compound. The guard opened the gate, though he was under orders not to. He would have to see about punishing him.

Bemused, Nicholson sat down on his verandah as Mary-Anne approached the house, stopped her car and got out.

"Mr Nicholson," she began, "I'm sorry to call on you at this late hour but there are some things I think you ought to know."

"Oh, yes?"

"Yes, the insurgents have struck again. Joanna Marchant, my assistant, has been killed."

"No!"

"I'm afraid it's true."

"Where did this happen?"

Mary-Anne told him.

"It's getting worse and worse," said Nicholson.

Mary-Anne nodded.

"I can't tell you how sorry I am."

"We are all devastated. Also, Mr Nicholson, we are worried about Peter Drury. Joanna and Peter went together to the place. We haven't been able to find any sign of him."

Mary-Anne watched Nicholson, who seemed genuinely deflated by the news. Her doubts returned. She had trained herself to see the best in everybody; to spot faint silver linings of decency behind dark clouds of clear and incorrigible vice. It took a great effort of will — it came as downright unnatural to her — to step on her nature and cling to thinking the worst.

"Is it possible that the insurgents kidnapped him, I wonder?" asked Nicholson in a low, almost-defeated, voice.

"Anything is possible."

Nicholson was silent for a long time. Then he straightened

up in his chair. "Do you remember the night they turned on the electricity, Matron?" he asked.

She nodded.

"Things went bad that night," Nicholson said. "I date everything that has happened from the night they threw the switch. I remember we stood together just over there. Both of us were wretched, I remember. I wonder, did we intimate all the dreadful things that were going to happen?"

Mary-Anne smiled at Nicholson, but thought to herself, "He is wicked! He is wicked!" and no little voice of soft conscience came back to tell her otherwise.

Nicholson talked on about his time in Ras Al Surra, his love for the country and its people; and she felt as clear as a bell, as if some God-inspired perception was helping her see through his soft, manipulative talk. She sat across from him, smiling and nodding and thinking her own thoughts.

Nicholson told her that they were unique in Saffina, Mary-Anne and he; they were the only ones who really knew Saffina's people and who genuinely held their good close to their hearts. And as he spoke he thought how good it would be to put an end to this smiling, nodding do-gooder across from him. Why not, he thought, go the whole way and kill them all? If they would get him in the end — and he would do his damnedest to make sure they didn't get him — why not be the last foreigner left? Why leave this chirpy little bible thumper around to biff her tambourine and bawl out his requiem?

"Matron," he concluded, "I think it is time you and I did something together to rid Saffina of this scourge."

"I do so agree," replied Mary-Anne, completely ready for Nicholson. "But what?"

"Well, first you can show me the place where all these dreadful things happened. That would be a start. After that, who knows?"

Mary-Anne gave Nicholson a slight smile. "I'll be glad to show you the place," she said. "I guess there's no point going there tonight. Why don't you call at the hospital around ten?"

Nicholson nodded. "That would be fine, matron. It may be the start of our own little crusade."

"Who knows?" said Mary-Anne.

She walked back to her car and Nicholson saw that she was wearing the same washed out, worn out, dress she had worn at his party on the night the power station had been opened. He shook his head sadly. "No idea! The poor thing has absolutely no idea!"

Then he went inside and fixed himself a drink.

As Mary-Anne made her way back to the hospital, clouds covered the full moon.

For the last few days she had watched the great cumulus clouds banking up around Saffina, knowing that it was only a matter of time before the town was inundated by the tail end of the Indian monsoons. It always amazed her how ill-prepared everyone in Saffina was for the coming of the rains. No shopkeeper had ever thought to stock umbrellas and every year it had been a joke with Mary-Anne to remind them. No, the people went around holding pieces of cardboard over their heads, lifting their long skirts. Sandals would be spattered with mud, roads would become impassable. The desert sand, which so thirstily drank up small amounts of liquids thrown on to it, rejected the rains. Puddles would form immediately and as time passed grow into lakes. All but the best four-wheel-drive vehicles would come to grief. The town of Saffina would enter into a wet period of mourning. The children became chesty and morose. The hospital queues lengthened. The mud-brick houses slowly dissolved towards the earth.

As she entered the hospital, heading for the back room in which Peter Drury had been taken to recover, a large drop of rain fell on her right spectacle lens. Then another fell just in front of her and rolled itself in the dust like a tiny truffle in cocoa. She removed her glasses and rubbed the lens on her sleeve, and as she did so she stared angrily up into the empty sky.

Ibrahim sat by Peter's bed, keeping guard over his friend.

"Has he woken up yet?" Mary-Anne asked him.

"Not yet, madam. He has moved a little from side to side but he has not opened his eyes or said anything."

Mary-Anne adjusted the flow of blood from the drip at the side of the bed. Then she took his pulse.

"He is going to be all right, isn't he?" Ibrahim asked in a quiet voice.

"Yes, he is. He's a young man. But it's going to take time." And she looked at Ibrahim. She had heard from Nasser about the boy's despair. "However, Ibrahim, he is going to need good friends around him to help him recover. You are his friend, aren't you?"

"Yes, I am his friend."

Mary-Anne smiled. "That's good."

They sat by Peter's bed for a few minutes, saying nothing.

Mary-Anne was considering tactics. For her whole working life she had tried to be of use. She had done her best to heal Saffina's sick, to lessen its people's pain. She had also hoped against hope that she might also be able to save souls. But now she wondered how she could ever have been so misguided. Saffina's people were as well as could be expected and she wondered how she could have ever had the arrogance to think that her view of God was in any way superior to theirs. Her mistake was the mistake now being made by the newcomers: the salesmen with their Walkmen and fridges and air conditioners and, yes, umbrellas. Why interfere when people were managing quite well without you? Why mess them up?

But she knew she had one last service to perform for the people of Saffina. She had a devil to cast out. But before she performed this action she needed to be one hundred per cent certain. She needed Peter Drury to wake up and tell her. He would only have to answer one question and she would set about the exorcism.

Mary-Anne locked the door of Peter's room and pulled up a chair beside the bed. There, with Ibrahim she began her vigil.

Soon she nodded off and Ibrahim was left to keep watch.

Ibrahim felt a peace growing inside him which he had not felt for a long time. Indeed, he wondered if he had ever felt so calm. The feeling had started to germinate when Nasser had told him that his father was still alive. It had been watered by the promises of Nasser that there might be forgiveness for him. Not even the news of the death of Joanna, whom he had never met, had been able to snuff out the feeling. He felt that he had come through a dark tunnel, a tunnel that had started when he left Jaheel walking behind Hameed Nasr. He was still in the tunnel but there was a chink of light. Even were he to die now, that chink of light, embodied now in the prone figure of his friend and teacher to whom he knew he would in both time and eternity be tied to with bonds of blood and sinew, would shine out strong and do to death all the sorrow he had caused and suffered.

Ibrahim started to cry. The tears were full of sorrow but they gave him a peculiar pleasure too. He made no attempt to stifle them as he had always done in the past. Now was the time for tears. He let them fall down his face and on to the white sheet on the bed.

"Why are you crying?" Peter asked him.

Ibrahim pulled his arm across his face, which, when it emerged, wore a broad grin that Peter had never before seen on his face.

"I'm not crying!" he replied in English.

"Where am I, Ibrahim?" Peter asked.

Mary-Anne had woken up. "You're in hospital, Peter. Do you remember what happened to you?"

Peter did not answer for a long moment. Mary-Anne could hear a torrent of rain falling outside the window. Then a single tear sprang from Peter's eye and fell diagonally across his cheek. "Yes," he said.

"Who did it?" asked Mary-Anne.

"Nicholson," answered Peter and closed his eyes.

"Don't worry, Peter. I'm here. Everything's going to be all right," whispered Ibrahim.

Peter slept again but Mary-Anne and Ibrahim did not. She told him of her plan. He marvelled at the woman's certainty. She was something totally outside his experience. She was magnificent.

"I have a gun, Ibrahim. Nicholson will come to the hospital in the morning. He will come to see me. He wants me to drive out with him to the pool. He thinks we are going to look for Peter's body. I want you to go to Peter's house and stay there. I will get him to come either on the way to or from the pool. When we come you will hold him up with the gun."

"And then?"

"Then we shall shoot him."

Ibrahim thought for a while. Then he said, "No, we won't shoot him. I have another way."

And he told Mary-Anne his plan.

Just before dawn Mary-Anne called a nurse to Peter's room. She gave the nurse a key and told her to lock herself in and answer the door to nobody. Then she led Ibrahim down the corridor and out, across the now-sodden ground, to her bungalow. Inside she found her gun, a gun she had been given during the civil war, dusted it down, loaded it and handed it over to Ibrahim.

Then she had a thought. "It's raining out there, Ibrahim," she said, and went searching in the kitchen for a plastic bag. She found an old Saks Fifth Avenue bag which she had kept as a souvenir after her last trip home and told Ibrahim to put the gun into it. Then, giving him a wink, she sent him off to walk the three miles to Peter's house. "You're going to get wet," she warned him.

"Don't worry about me. Just make sure you get Nicholson to Peter's house. I'll take care of the rest."

And Mary-Anne, feeling a calm that amazed her, watched Ibrahim walking across the wet ground. He lifted his dish-dash with one hand and swung the Saks bag in the other. Mary-Anne found herself wishing she had a camera.

She stayed with the nurse at Peter's bedside until half past nine, then left the room, making sure she heard the key turned in the lock before striding away purposefully down the corridor. Then she stayed around the reception area waiting for Nicholson to arrive.

The hospital clock said ten-fifteen but he had still not arrived. She felt slightly agitated but reasoned that Nicholson might have had trouble with the mud which the overnight rains had spawned. Then at ten-twenty-five she saw his white Rangerover enter the gate and park in front of the hospital in the place reserved for the ambulance.

Nicholson got out and came into reception. Mary-Anne noticed that he had a gun in a holster at his waist. Nicholson noticed that she was wearing that same old dress, and smiled to himself.

"Why Mr Nicholson!" she exclaimed. "I had almost given you up for lost. Did you have trouble getting here in all that mud?"

"No, none at all. I've got the best vehicle in Saffina for dealing with the mud. I got held up in the office, that's all," replied Nicholson.

"Would you like a cup of coffee or would you prefer to get going straight away?"

"Oh, I think we should head out at once, don't you? I've got to be back as soon as possible. I'm rushed off my feet as you can imagine."

She walked out of the hospital door with Nicholson. He opened the passenger door for her. She thanked him demurely and got in.

They drove at speed along the waterlogged track leading out of Saffina towards the wadi. The Rangerover's tyres sprayed water and mud against the windscreen and Nicholson had to keep the vehicle engaged in four-wheel-drive, the wipers working at their fastest speed.

"My, this Landrover certainly makes light work of this weather!" Mary-Anne exclaimed.

"It's a Rangerover, actually, matron. Top of the range as you Yanks say."

She looked across at him. He seemed such a regular guy there behind his steering wheel. She had to pinch herself to recall who she was with and what her aim was.

They were approaching Peter's prefab and Mary-Anne said: "That's Mr Drury's house, isn't it?"

"Yes."

"You don't think it might be a good idea to check it out? Who knows, there may be some sort of clue."

But Nicholson pouted and replied that he didn't think it

very likely. Mary-Anne thought he would not stop. Her heart sank. She did not fancy a trip out to the wadi with him. But then, he shrugged and turned the Rangerover off the road, aiming it across the desert.

"It's worth a try, I suppose," he said.

They stopped the vehicle outside Peter's front door. The door was ajar.

"That's strange, leaving the door open like that," said Nicholson, and he reached for the gun in his holster.

A bolt of fear went through Mary-Anne. Nicholson pushed the front door open slowly and walked into the house. There was no one there. Mary-Anne followed him inside, keeping very close to him, her eyes glued to the gun. Nicholson walked stealthily to the small hall between Peter's bedroom, the bathroom and the kitchen. All three doors were closed.

He eased open the door of Peter's bedroom. The room was empty. Some of Peter's work for the school newspaper lay on the floor. Nicholson picked up a piece and smirked at what he read. Then he tiptoed out of the room.

Mary-Anne knew that Ibrahim would be in one of the other two rooms. She devoutly hoped so, for she had decided what she was going to do. If she were wrong there was no telling what would happen.

Nicholson went to open the bathroom door and was amazed to find Mary-Anne grasp the hand that held his gun and hang on tenaciously. She pulled at the hand and screamed. And as she screamed she reached down and bit his arm. He yelped and tugged his gun hand out of Mary-Anne's grip. "You cow! What do you . . .?"

The kitchen door opened and Ibrahim rushed through and hit him on the head with one of Peter's Chinese enamel saucepans. Nicholson crumpled but seemed to recover almost immediately, so Ibrahim hit him again and again. At last he rolled over on to the floor of the prefab, unconscious.

"Good work, Ibrahim!"

Ibrahim said nothing. He set about tying Nicholson's hands behind his back with washing line. Mary-Anne saw blood oozing through Nicholson's hair and felt momentarily urged to fetch a basin and clean lint to start healing him. But she restrained herself by thinking of Joanna's body on the bed. Ibrahim was winding the line tightly round Nicholson's chest, pinioning his arms at his side. Finally he wound more rope around his ankles, and tied the knots.

They dragged the still-unconscious Nicholson out to his Rangerover and placed him in the front passenger seat, securing him with the safety belt.

Mary-Anne was about to get into the back seat when Ibrahim said, "Please madam, I cannot drive."

She came round and sat in the driving seat and Ibrahim got into the back seat. "You'll have to show me the way, Ibrahim. I hope it isn't too far. I don't feel too happy having him near me."

"It isn't far," Ibrahim promised, "and I have a gun."

Following Ibrahim's directions Mary-Anne drove the Rangerover along the track that wound its way through the coastal plain and its quicksand towards Jaheel. The rain beat down on them again and the Rangerover slid about on the greasy surface.

Ibrahim kept a look out for the stranded earth-mover. He knew that nearby the ground turned suddenly into quicksand. He had often explored when left alone in the house, had dropped Peter's rubbish into the quicksand and sat on its brink, watching it sink.

At last they came to the place. "Be careful, madam," he cautioned.

Mary-Anne stopped the Rangerover at once but it was almost too late. The vehicle tipped forward, its front axle already deeply enmeshed on the edge of the quicksand.

With difficulty Mary-Anne got out, and, helped by Ibrahim, edged her way down the length of the vehicle towards solid ground.

"Now what?" asked Mary-Anne.

"We push it in."

"But . . ." began Mary-Anne. They pushed with all their might but the Rangerover did not budge.

"That's no use, Ibrahim. We need to drive it into the

quicksand at speed. If we can get it out again that is. It's pretty well stuck I'd say."

"Can you try to reverse it?" Ibrahim asked.

"I can try!"

And Mary-Anne manoeuvred herself back into the driving seat. She engaged reverse gear and revved the engine. At last the front wheels engaged solid earth and with a jolt the Rangerover rolled backwards.

She took it about a hundred yards back from the edge of the quicksand. As she put it into neutral another problem occurred to her.

"Ibrahim, we've got a problem. If we're going to drive it into the quicksand, somebody's got to be in the damned thing."

"You're right there!" It was Nicholson. "Whose idea was this? Friend Ibrahim's I suppose."

Mary-Anne ignored him. Nicholson pulled at his bindings but could not move.

Ibrahim opened the door. He said, "I will drive it in if you show me."

Mary-Anne sat Ibrahim down in the driving seat and showed him what to do. Then she showed him again. Nicholson looked on, a slight smile on his face.

"But how will you get out?" asked Mary-Anne.

"Through a window."

"No, there's a sunroof. Open that."

Ibrahim did so.

He revved the engine as Mary-Anne had showed him. She reached over and put the Rangerover into first gear, then watched, on tenterhooks, as he lifted his foot from the clutch.

The engine died. Nicholson said in Arabic: "You can't do anything right, Ibrahim! You're just a donkey! A vacuum cleaner is all you'll ever be able to manage. That's what your friend, Peter Drury, said. You don't think he was really your friend, do you? He was just like the rest of us. He is in Ras Al Surra to take, to take you in . . ."

Ibrahim tried to engage first gear again but again the engine died. "Give it more juice!" commanded Mary-Anne.

Nicholson continued. "I'm surprised to find you involved with that old witch, Ibrahim. You really have no idea, have you? None at all. Think you'll solve anything by killing me? You won't solve anything. There's an endless supply of people like me with their bags packed just waiting to fly in and take my place. And what'll you do then? There just isn't enough room in this quicksand to bury the lot of us. Our name is legion."

Ibrahim, his face set hard, gave the Rangerover more juice, engaged first gear and aimed it at speed towards the quicksand. The engine screamed. When it reached the edge, the Rangerover continued skimming across the surface of the quicksand. A ruffle of mud built up in front of the bonnet. The momentum caused it to drift out like a ship. Then it slowed and slowly turned, as if mounted on a turntable, until its windscreen faced back to the distant edge. It stopped, and Ibrahim could see Mary-Anne running towards the brink. She ran too far and was suddenly immersed in mud up to her knees, only extricating herself with difficulty. Then she looked anxiously out at the stranded Rangerover.

Ibrahim pulled himself out through the sunroof and across the bonnet. But the edge of the quicksand seemed an impossible distance away. He could hear Nicholson laughing at him from inside.

"I can't get back!" he shouted to Mary-Anne, who stood on the brink wringing her hands. Then she started ripping off her clothes.

A loud farting sound could be heard as the Rangerover settled itself down into the mud. The back sank two feet, half covering the rear window, as Mary-Anne frantically tore up her dress. She hesitated momentarily but then took off her bra. Then she set about turning her discarded clothes into a rope. Ibrahim could see what she was trying to do. He took off his dish-dash, weighted it with a handful of mud and threw it to her on the bank. This she ripped up too, adding it to the length.

She was naked now except for her pants and Nicholson shouted obscenities at her. "All off . . . gerrit all off !" He was like a football hooligan. He foamed at the mouth.

Ibrahim felt muddy water covering his feet. The whole front of the vehicle was now slowly sinking. He stepped back on to the roof, shut the sunroof, and took a run, diving off the vehicle — a belly-flop designed to keep him in the horizontal. He skimmed across the mud and Mary-Anne, knowing that there would only be one chance, and that a slim chance, picked up a stone and tied it to the rope of clothing. Then, praying, she threw it out towards Ibrahim.

He caught it and pulled himself towards the shore. But as he pulled, Mary-Anne, weeping with frustration, was being pulled in her turn towards the brink. He gave up on the rope and tried to paddle through the mud, but it took hold of him and pulled him down. He was buried up to his chest now and could only watch as Mary-Anne gazed at him helplessly, her lips moving in prayers that were orders to the Almighty, aware all the time of Nicholson behind shouting abuse.

Ibrahim did not panic, however. If it was time to die, he would disappear placidly. Had he not, just two days ago, desired nothing but death?

"*Bis M'illah, Al Rahman, Al Rahim* . . . In the name of God, the Compassionate, the Merciful . . ." And as he said the words his feet touched solid earth. Slowly and tortuously he pulled himself towards Mary-Anne. She watched fascinated as Ibrahim's body miraculously emerged from the mud like some primeval creature from the deep, his underpants sagging, heavy with mud.

Ibrahim and Mary-Anne stood, filthy, near-naked and shaking on the edge of the quicksand, staring at the slowly sinking Rangerover.

"Are you sure it's going to sink?" asked Mary-Anne.

Before Ibrahim could reply, the whole Rangerover shifted forward and let out another loud fart. The bonnet arched downwards and half disappeared.

Nicholson heard the sound and felt the shift of the vehicle. The realisation that he was going to die stopped his laughter but he continued to stare steadily through the windscreen at the macabre couple watching him. Never in his wildest dreams could he have imagined the sight of the naked couple, a wizened hag and a muddy young Arab, which now confronted him. Daylight ebbed out of the cab. He could no longer see anything. He had an impression of movement and was nauseated by the feeling that the vehicle was travelling down and down into the depths.

"This is it!" he told himself out loud, and his voice echoed flatly. It had become suddenly stiflingly hot. He began to hum the tune of *Sailing*. It had not been a bad life.

He completed a verse of *Sailing* and then started into *Land of Hope and Glory*, but was suddenly aware again of the hollow echo of it in the cab. He started struggling. "It's getting hot! It's unbearable! And I can't breathe!" With all his might he pulled at his bonds but could do nothing to shift them. He started to scream and panicked when he heard his screams and screamed because someone was screaming.

Then the windshield broke and a great weight of mud crashed into his face like a custard pie. "I'll hold my breath!" he thought but he realised too late that he was still screaming into the mud, and on completion of the exhalation he knew that he had no further options open to him other than to take another breath. He sucked in mud hungrily. The mud clogged his lungs and he coughed mud and then clots of blood into the mud and he opened his eyes to the black embrace of the mud. Through the foul-smelling blackness he had a vision of his fridge at home and the bottles of excellent sherry on top of it and the French cheeses inside it. Now his whole being became engaged in fighting a war with the mud inside him. The mud won and in agony Simon Nicholson rendered up his spirit to the God of Battles.

Ibrahim and Mary-Anne watched the quicksand return to tranquillity. Then they walked slowly back to Peter's prefab, keeping alert for any sign of people. But the rain was falling so heavily now that it hid them from view behind a million harp strings. The rain washed their bodies as they walked.

"We can find some clothes at Peter's house," said Ibrahim.

Mary-Anne nodded. She felt satisfied at having performed one last great service for Saffina.

"What will you do now, Ibrahim?" she asked him.

"I will stay with Peter until he is better. Then I will return to Jaheel — at least to say goodbye," Ibrahim replied.

Inside the house, as Ibrahim was sorting out some clothes for them to wear on their way back to Saffina on foot, and Mary-Anne was concocting a story to answer any questions that might be asked, she saw several house-lizards snoozing on the wall. "Look, Ibrahim!" she exclaimed. "Isn't it amazing how those creatures can hold themselves so still and peaceful with all the racket that's been going on round here?"

Ibrahim agreed that, indeed, it was amazing, but that Mary-Anne must know that the lizards only waited in stillness so that they could catch and eat any insects that came within range.

Mary-Anne looked disappointed. Ibrahim smiled at her and handed her some of Peter's clothes to wear.

18

Now, try again.

There is no moon tonight. Row your boat out from the shoreline of Saffina. Listen to the water lapping its sides. Hear the sounds of humanity reaching you across the water in the dark. Fish jump. The jewels of phosphorescence, which can bring satisfaction to a fisherman's wife who had hoped for harder jewels, still glisten. The stars gaze down, phosphorescences in the ocean of the sky.

No lights spoil the view. Nicholson's compound is dark. The tiny pin-pricks of light you see from the people's candles and oil-lamps complete the trinity of jewels in the three elements before you.

Dive in! Dance in the waters of the present moment and forget what has occurred and what will occur.

If, as you frolic, thoughts must intrude, observe them merely and do not let them spoil the magic.

It is certain that a new Japanese ship will plough through the ocean where you are now treading water, bringing a crown of piping to once again lighten Saffina's nights; certain too that law and order will return — perhaps better, perhaps worse, than the picture you have just glimpsed. The black ribbon of road will certainly not stand idle once it has arrived. Should any of the expatriates in Saffina leave the town and return in a year or two for a nostalgic visit, they will be hard-pressed to find the houses of friends among the spanking new concrete villas and businesses . . .

Only the myths people weave to cover themselves from the nakedness of a spell on the planet will remain intact. A river that cannot reach the sea, but drains ever into quicksand, will cause conjecture. Lizards will inspire thoughts in people which other people will laugh at — which even lizards, if they could, would laugh at.

The ocean will see it all, and, ever the most forgiving of elements, will settle itself innocently down again — then plunge its eroding, sculpting edge towards the temporary upheavals caused by Japanese ships, expatriate litter and fishermen's tears.